MAGICAL HISTORY TOUR

~

Murder, Mystery, Buried History

PETER BRONSON

~ CONTENTS ~

✧ INTRODUCTION ✧

AS British explorer Howard Carter squeezed through a dark, claustrophobic tunnel and shined a feeble light into King Tut's tomb in Egypt a hundred years ago, he was dazzled by reflections from gleaming gold and sparkling jewels. But what probably thrilled him as much as the fabulous riches were the ancient artifacts: painted canopic jars of human organs, chariots, ornate furniture, statues of strange gods such as the dog-deity Anubis, royal sandals, board games, daggers, armor and mummified remains that were Tupperwared in airtight coffins, preserved like forgotten leftovers after almost 4,000 years.

Who has not dreamed of discovering buried treasure?

But we don't have to travel to Egypt to find the riches of history. They are right here in Cincinnati's backyard, without any scorpions and cobras. We don't even have to pick up a shovel. These treasures can be uncovered by simply turning a page.

Studying, researching and writing about history is "armchair archeology." And Magical History Tour is like opening a pyramid tomb to discover our exciting, surprising, inspiring, forgotten past.

This archeological excavation digs into buried treasures hidden away in libraries, museums and on the internet. With a few mouse clicks, it's possible to find original documents written by early settlers, presidents, generals, adventurers and ordinary citizens. They tell us as much about how people lived and what they believed as all the creepy canopic jars, mummies and clay god-idols in Tut's tomb.

Court records and newspaper accounts help unravel old mysteries and murders. Local museums are pirates' chests of history. And books written by and about the people who came long before us are like treasure maps.

The stories in this book are artifacts from antiquity: They speak to us now with uncanny wisdom. By telling us where we have been, they tell us where we are—and where we are headed. There are five stops on this tour.

In 1878, Cincinnati was shocked and revolted by a ghoulish crime: The son of a former president had been dragged from his fresh grave in North Bend by body-snatchers and delivered downtown at 3:00 a.m. to the Ohio Medical College, to be dissected like a frog. Surely, we are too civilized to tolerate such cruel desecration of the dead today. Or are we?

In 1850, a young man from Wilmington, Ohio set off on the grueling, hazardous Oregon Trail to join the Gold Rush in California. It was the beginning of a lifelong journey of adventure. Along the way, a great Western city was named after him. He chose the name of a state. He tamed "Bleeding Kansas" during a dress rehearsal for the Civil War, and fought at the Battle of Corinth with General William T. Sherman. Yet few today even know about him.

Two young women died in a Cincinnati hotel room in 1877 after they were banished from the Whitewater Shaker Village north of Harrison. What happened to them? Was it suicide? Or murder? What happened to the Shakers? How did they live? Why did their thriving, prosperous Society vanish? What can we learn from them?

Cincinnati's first convicted serial killer also became the first woman in Ohio to be executed in the electric chair. The story of the Black Widow's murders of lonely, elderly victims and the detectives who stopped her spree is one of the first cases solved with the help of doctors and chemists at the University of Cincinnati. It is one of the most chilling stories of heartless cruelty in local history.

In 2008, Cincinnati was dragged into a national diet-pill scandal when a group of Kentucky lawyers went on trial in the Covington federal courthouse. Cincinnati's own "Master of Disaster" also got stuck in the litigation tarpit, and that was the downfall of one of the most famous tort lawyers in the nation. The case still has lessons for us today.

For those who want to do their own armchair archeology, this book includes Ten Places to Discover Cincinnati History. Most sites are local. Many are places I found while researching my previous books: *Forbidden Fruit, Not in Our Town, The Man Who Saved Cincinnati,* and *Promised Land.* Only one requires a drive of more than an hour. They are places I wish I had known about when I was new to Cincinnati in 1992, raising my children—places to soak up and understand the history of our city the way we would learn the life story of a good friend.

Unfortunately, schoolbooks often make history as dry and bloodless as an Egyptian mummy. It doesn't have to be that way. Behind all those boring names and dates are amazing adventures of courageous men and women.

A lot of Cincinnati's fascinating history and the people who made it are mostly forgotten. On these pages, they live again.

A NOTE ABOUT THE BOOK

These stories are real history, with occasional fictional characters and conversations added to shine a brighter light into the past. For example: Tom Farrel, the fictional reporter in *"Snake in the Garden,"* is named after a handsome, hard-drinking Irishman in my family tree. But the stories he writes are lifted from the pages of the local newspapers at the time. The fictional reporter "Jim" in *Resurrection Men* and *Feeding Frenzy*, is borrowed from my book, *Not in our Town*, where he was City Editor Jim Gardner. Detective Bill Reany was real. He was also in *The Man Who Saved Cincinnati*. There is no record that he investigated the suicides of two Shaker women, but he could have, and the investigation is accurate.

Any mistakes are mine alone. All these stories are faithful to the people and their times. Primary sources are used, and footnotes are provided to amplify, explain, cite sources and follow occasional detours that would otherwise interrupt the journey. Those who skip the footnotes will miss "Aha!" information and occasional "Ha!" entertainment. Maybe even "Ha-ha" amusement.

As always, I hope you enjoy reading these stories as much as I enjoyed discovering and telling them.

———————————— ✧ ————————————

ONE

RESURRECTION MEN

*The night body snatchers
took the president's son.*

Congress Green Cemetery

1878

1852 · 1877 · 1937 · 2008

Dr. Amos Woods had quite a reputation. He was descended from Nehemiah Woods, one of the Squirrel Hunters who volunteered to save Cincinnati from a Confederate attack in 1862. His Christian name, he said, was a tribute to one of his great-great-grandfather's lifelong friends who served at his side during the Siege of Cincinnati, Amos Breyer.[1]

His collection of historic relics included a tattered tricorn hat that looked as if it had been half eaten by a bear, and a razor-sharp tomahawk decorated with Indian beads and hawk feathers. They had been worn and used by his great-great-grandfather at the Battle of Fallen Timbers that won freedom and safety for settlers in the Northwest Territory.

With a family tree so deeply rooted in the compost of Ohio history, he was fated to spend a lifetime studying every branch, leaf and twig.

"Doc Woods," as everyone called him, was stout, tall, imposing, with swept back white-yellow hair like folded wings, left longish more from absent-minded neglect than from any sense of style. Eyebrows as white and feathery as milkweed sat above a pair of Ben Franklin half-glasses with gold rims.

His vest was stretched tight enough to bounce a dime and flashed a gold chain linked to an ancient gold pocket watch nearly as big as a hockey puck. His middle was as blunt and rounded as the bow of an 18th century wooden sailing ship. He gave the impression of being built of oak and floated around a room as if he was propelled by billowing sails.

But on a spring evening in 2008, he was running out the big guns for a broadside.

"Let me begin with a story," he said. "I will do my best to keep it short to spare those of you who are disabled by cellphone separation anxiety."

The crowd chuckled but Jim inwardly groaned. "Keeping it short" and "begin with a story" invariably meant a dazzling presentation that

---

1   Nehemiah Woods and Amos Breyer are fictional characters in *The Man Who Saved Cincinnati and Promised Land*, also by Peter Bronson (www.chilidogpress.com). Dr. Amos Woods is also fictional, but the story he tells is true.

would hold the audience spellbound for at least an hour. It would give him an Anaconda Copper Mine of raw materials for a column in The Cincinnati Enquirer tomorrow, but this was the second evening this week that Jim had been out covering the latest cultural uproar in a city that made chronic uproars a hobby the way hypochondriacs obsess over every cough and sniffle.

It was always the same, Jim thought: *What will everyone think of us?* The answer: *They don't.*

"In my wild youth, a cell phone was something you used to call your lawyer from the county jail," Doc Woods quipped. "Not that I would know. But now we clutch these high-tech pacifiers so we can talk more and say less, or twiddle thumbs over them like a witch doctor's curse." He looked pointedly at a few people who did not get the hint until a gentle elbow nudged them to put their phones away.

"And don't get me started on that logo. Hasn't anyone noticed that a bitten apple is the biblical symbol of forbidden fruit? Could it be that *someone*"—he rolled his eyes toward the ceiling—"is warning us that social media is the second biggest mistake by mankind since Eve went shopping in the Good and Evil aisle at the Eden Kroger?"

This time the laughter was hearty from older people, but tepid among those under 30.

"But let's get started. We begin in 1788," he said, shuffling a few notes and scraps of paper on the lectern. The man was a walking World Book Encyclopedia. His capacity for local history was legendary. If every man contains a world, Dr. Amos Woods contained galaxies that would overload an IBM mainframe. Even in his 70s he could still call up ancient dates and names like pulling a stuffed Sponge Bob from the claw machine at the county fair. Every time.

He wore a navy-blue poplin suit over an un-ironed white shirt and a sagging red bow tie—one of the few men who could pull off a bowtie without looking fey or pompous. It was easy to mistake him for a professor-PhD "doctor," but he was in fact an actual doctor, a retired pediatrician. And historian. And amateur anthropologist. Author, theologian, philosopher, gourmet chef, fly fisherman, skilled bluegrass banjo picker, expert on Dostoevsky and throwback renaissance man with a scalpel wit.

And now he was sailing off on another voyage through local history. When the *USS Woods* finally returned to shore almost 90 minutes later, Jim realized he had become so wrapped up in the adventure he forgot to take notes or look at his watch.

It started with a funeral.

"On May 4, 1878, John Scott Harrison went to bed," Doc Woods began. "As far as we know, he is still sound asleep 130 years later, awaiting the wake-up call of Gabriel's Trumpet. If the name Harrison sounds familiar, it should. He was the son of our ninth president, William Henry Harrison, and the father of our 23rd president, Benjamin Harrison. He was and remains the only American who could claim to have been both son and father to presidents—which is a good thing to know for trivia night at the Stumble Inn, but it's not why we're interested in him tonight."

The ninth president of the United States, William Henry Harrison. He was the commander of Fort Washington and aide de camp to "Mad" Anthony Wayne during the Battle of Fallen Timbers.

Dr. Woods paused and looked at the crowd, meeting eyes, taking their pulse. They laughed politely, then went quiet like kids waiting for a magic show.

"No," he continued, "this gentleman farmer, former Congressman, beloved family man and respected statesman of our region is remarkable for refusing to stay buried. His funeral ignited a scandal that brought disgrace on science, shamed the medical profession and raised our moral standards for treatment of the dead."

Ah, Jim thought. *There's the connection.* The topic for the public forum at the historic Queen City Club was the most recent culture clash in Cincinnati, *Bodies: The Exhibition*. It was a traveling circus of Chinese corpses, skinned like rabbits, frozen in lifelike poses—conducting an orchestra, serving a tennis ball, running, shooting baskets... The zombies were brought to macabre "life" through a process called "plastination." Chemicals injected immediately after death preserved the body indefinitely, like gas station beef sticks or holiday fruitcake. Or so they claimed. But there were troubling reports of unwelcome odors and leaking fluids at some shows.

The ads claimed the Bodies Exhibit was "Amazing!" Billboards shouted, "Educational!" "Inspiring!" "The Experience of a Lifetime for Children and Adults!"

Jim thought taking kids to see human taxidermy was felony child abuse, but local schools apparently disagreed. They brought children by busloads.

Dr. Woods cleared his throat with a sound like gravel in a dishwasher and continued. "Have you ever wondered why we are buried in vaults?" he asked. "Have you asked yourself why wealthy families seal up their loved ones in mausoleums that look like miniature banks or hobbit temples with iron bars? If Mr. Harrison could speak from his grave, he would tell you why."

The story continued, and it was spellbinding.

Harrison had died suddenly overnight at age 74. Three weeks later, on May 29, hundreds attended his funeral at Congress Green Cemetery, overlooking the Ohio River in North Bend.[2] As men and women draped in black like a conclave of priests and nuns made their way up a sloping hill through the new spring grass and spongy graveyard soil, a few of the mourners peeled off to visit the recent grave of their friend Augustus Devin, whose family was close to the Harrisons and related through marriage. Devin, only 29, had wasted away and died just a few weeks earlier of tuberculosis.

Before his death, he was visited by John Scott Harrison, who seemed healthy until he failed to wake up one morning.

---

2   Originally known as the Pasture Graveyard, it was owned by the William Henry Harrison family. Revolutionary War veteran and founder of Cincinnati John Cleves Symmes is also buried there. His daughter, Anna Symmes, was married to the Indian fighter and future president, William Henry Harrison.

As they approached, they were shocked to find the mound of bare earth over Devin's grave was torn up. Hogs, they thought. Then as they got closer they thought again. They could see deep into the grave. The coffin was ripped open, empty.

The mourners were shocked and outraged. The funeral for Congressman Harrison continued, but when it was over, his sons organized a team to reinforce and protect his body, to make sure it would not be stolen like Devin's. The grave was dug even deeper, and stones were placed over the coffin, including one immense slab so heavy it required 16 men to carry and place it. The Harrison family also hired a night watchman to guard the grave for 30 nights.

The youngest son, John Harrison, and a grandson, George Eaton, left for Cincinnati that afternoon to look for the body of their friend Devin. It was no mystery. Everyone knew the Ohio Medical College[3] hired graverobbers called "resurrection men," "body snatchers," "stiff raisers" and "bag stuffers." Fresh corpses were in big demand for the students to dissect.[4]

Medical schools were opening all over the Midwest and demand for stolen cadavers was booming.[5] Without modern embalming chemicals, bodies had to be dug up as soon as they were buried so they would not be too rank and decayed for the medical students to practice on. The students and their professors didn't care and did not want to know where they came from, as long as they were fresh from the grave.

But dead bodies for dissection were usually taken from cemeteries for the poor and blacks, who were helpless to do anything about it.[6] Robbing a grave just a few feet away from the tomb of a former president was an outrage. This time the grave robbers had chosen the

---

3   Later moved and became the University of Cincinnati Medical School in 1896.

4   The practice of voluntarily donating or willing bodies to medical schools for anatomy dissection was 100 years in the future.

5   In 1800 there were only four medical schools in the young country. By 1876, there were 73 and the number was growing fast. "A True Tale of Grave-Robbing Horror," The History Blog, October 31, 2016.

6   Many states allowed medical schools to use the bodies of men killed in duels, as an additional way to discourage dueling.

wrong grave. The Harrisons were a powerful family, and John Harrison immediately got a warrant to search the Ohio Medical College with the help of Cincinnati Police detectives.

The Ohio Medical College.

The morning after the funeral, as they set out for the medical school, they read a report in The Cincinnati Enquirer about the "mystery" of a white-draped "stiff" that was dumped at the medical college at 3:00 a.m. overnight. The searchers were sure it would be Devin's body.

When they got to the college, they were greeted by the janitor, E.Q. Marshall, who stalled and acted "squirrely." The Ohio Medical College was in a massive five-story building that stretched between Race and Vine streets along Sixth Street. It was described as a gloomy, "dreary old building," a brooding wall of bricks with dark, narrow windows and medieval spires topped by crosses along the roof.[7] The search team started in the cellar, where they found a huge chute that connected to an opening in an alley behind the school.[8]

Nearby in the dank cellar was a big furnace with wide doors that was used to cremate body parts, and a curious shaft, about three-feet

---

7   The Ohio Medical College building, later known as the McMicken Building, was torn down in 1935. The only reminder is College Street, which runs north from Sixth Street in the middle of the block between Race and Vine at the east end of the Cincinnatian Hotel.

8   Probably Morand Alley.

square, that extended upward into soot-black darkness. In a corner, they found large sacks with dark stains and a two-piece shovel often used by graverobbers, because it was easy to unscrew the handle for concealment.

And all about them there was the smell of offal, decay, blood and putrefying corpses. It was described as something like a sewer, but much worse.

The men moved on, floor-by floor, checking rooms, barrels, closets, any place that might hide a body. The dark stairs, hallways and rooms were hot and reeked with a stench some of the detectives recognized from their service in the Civil War. As they looked, the janitor, Marshall, said he wanted to go summon the dean of the school. Cincinnati Police Detective Thomas Snelbaker,[9] noting Marshal's jittery, darting eyes, sent a man to shadow him.

Marshall did not go to the dean's office. He went to the fifth floor—the dissection room. He was about to enter when he realized he was being followed and quickly turned around. The search party had their target.

As they approached the dissection room, the searchers found a box of arms and legs in the hallway. Tossed in with the limbs was "the body of a beautiful baby, six to eight months old…as white as

---

9   Colonel Snelbaker, son of Cincinnati Mayor David T. Snelbaker, was Cincinnati Police Chief from 1875-77. Police detectives often worked also as private detectives. He had been removed as chief for corruption but was still a detective during the medical college investigation. Later, he retired to manage a burlesque theater he owned on Vine Street. In 1880, he shot a policeman to death and was acquitted on grounds of self-defense. The shooting of Policeman Armstrong Chumley began with an "affray" on a streetcar that drew hundreds of onlookers who blocked Vine Street to watch. Snelbaker's former mistress and Vine Street Opera House treasurer, Ella Chumley, who had once tried to kill him, attacked his latest mistress, Virgie Jackson, who was a star at his Opera House. As the women were "pawing and clawing at ten-tomcat rate," Policeman Armstrong Chumley boarded the car and began beating Snelbaker, the former police chief. Snelbaker fought back and hit Chumley with a "loaded cane." Snelbaker was arrested for disorderly conduct. At the station, Chumley confronted Snelbaker, who warned, "Keep away from me or there will be trouble." When Chumley ignored the warning and rushed him, Snelbaker pulled a .44 caliber Pacific Bulldog pocket revolver and shot Chumley three times, in the hand, chest and groin. Chumley died of internal bleeding two days later. Snelbaker died in 1888 of a brain infection caused by syphilis. "Women's War: Much to do With Love, But More With Hate," *The Cincinnati Enquirer*, August 8, 1880. Also: Kramer, Stephen, Cincinnati Police Museum

alabaster."[10]

Inside, standing over a dissection table was a student in bloody overalls, cheerfully cutting away at the upper half of a black woman's corpse as if he was slicing a Thanksgiving turkey. Around the room were jars filled with pickled organs and body parts like something from a mummy's tomb—hands, feet and other pieces of men and women.

There were sinks that contained more body parts, and a large tank shaped like a coffin that was full of festering, fermenting, brined bodies. The stench was so strong when they lifted the lid that it nearly knocked them to their knees.

"At one side of the room was an open trap door, revealing the square top of the shaft they had seen in the cellar," Dr. Woods said. "A hoist with a hand crank was braced on stout timbers above the shaft, with a rope dropping into the darkness below. Snelbaker tested the rope. 'It's taut,' he said. 'Somebody is down there.' So he cranked the winch and gradually, a corpse rose up like Lazarus from the grave—without the wrappings."

There was nervous laughter.

A drawing of the dissection room and the winch that brought bodies up through a trapdoor (left) at the Ohio Medical College. From *The Cincinnati Enquirer*, May 31, 1878.

He described the scene: It was the body of a man, naked except for a tattered, torn shirt draped over the head and shoulders. The rope had been looped under one armpit and around the neck. An incision

---

10   "Human Hyenas," *The Cincinnati Enquirer*, May 31, 1878.

in the neck was oozing blood, but had been stitched up, probably after it was used to inject some primitive embalming fluid containing arsenic, mercury, turpentine and zinc.[11]

John Harrison looked at the pathetic corpse hanging like a hog in a slaughterhouse. He was disgusted, nauseated and horrified. He shook his head and said, "That's not the man. Devin was emaciated. Much younger."

As John Harrison turned to leave and escape the hellish scene, Snelbaker said, "You had better take a look. What if you are mistaken? You will never forgive yourself if you are wrong."

"Well, if you insist," Harrison said.

They lowered the body to the floor and Harrison reluctantly bent down to gingerly uncover the head and face. As he looked, he gasped and turned as white as the bloodless corpse.

"What's the matter?" Snelbaker asked.

"It's father!" Harrison replied, almost unable to stand on his shaking legs.

The flowing beard and mane of white hair had been cut away. All of his carefully chosen burial clothing was gone.[12] But there was no mistake. This was the body of husband, father and grandfather John Scott Harrison, buried just yesterday afternoon under almost a ton of stones, guarded by a watchman.

Family members checked the grave and found the body snatchers had broken into the foot of the coffin and dragged their father out by his feet to avoid moving the massive stones. The watchman finally confessed that he was too spooked to stay in the cemetery and had gone home. He said he was passed by a carriage as he left—undoubtedly the graverobbers.

---

11 The concoction was sold by the Victorian Durfee Embalming Fluid Co. The mixture was highly toxic and dangerous. It was developed during the Civil War to preserve bodies for shipment home. Bodies were also placed on ice if relatives needed time to travel to the funeral. Brenner, Eric, "Human body preservation—old and new techniques," *Journal of Anatomy*, January 18, 2014.

12 Fingers and ears were often cut off to recover jewelry. Graverobbers stripped the corpses and sold their burial clothing to unwitting customers.

'TORN FROM HIS GRAVE'

Future President Benjamin Harrison, second oldest son among ten children, called Alan Pinkerton in Chicago, whose famous detective agency had started as Abraham Lincoln's spy network during the Civil War. Pinkerton dispatched his best detectives to Cincinnati.

"Let me read from the headlines the next day," Dr. Woods said as the crowd sat as silent as a tomb. "Human Hyenas… torn from his grave… dangling in the 'dead shaft'… naked and mutilated… foremost medical college… most horrible episode in the history of the city… thieving human ghouls."

"I guess you get the picture—a scene that could be painted by Hieronymus Bosch." He paused, noted some blank looks and added, "You can Google that later, if you can spell it."

A man with a gray ponytail and John Lennon glasses raised his hand. Jim guessed he was faculty at the University of Cincinnati. Woods nodded in his direction and the man asked, "What did the medical school have to say? Couldn't they explain that having cadavers was an imperative for science?"

"Good question," Doc Woods said graciously. "The dean of the medical school made things worse. When Benjamin Harrison, the future president, came from Indianapolis to investigate, Dr. Bartholow told him it would be unfair to punish doctors for killing their patients if they could not have corpses to practice on. His associate Dr. Seely said, I quote, 'It will be all the same on the day of resurrection.' As you can guess, that did not go over well with the son of the man they had chosen for surgical practice.

"This is the same Dr. Bartholow who, assisted by Dr. Seely, had killed a young woman by pushing electrode needles into her brain to study her involuntary nerve reactions[13] the same way many of you made the legs of a dead frog jump in biology class. As you may recall, Dr. Mengele also defended his work by claiming the *imperative of science*." Dr. Woods used his fingers to make air quotes around the last three words, leaving no doubt where he stood.

"But let me continue," he said. "The city was shocked and sickened. The use of these resurrection men to rob graves was an open secret, especially to those who came near enough to smell the cremation, death and decay at the medical college. As long as it was restricted to the poor, it could be ignored. But not when it was done to the family of Cincinnati's first president."

Doctor Woods picked up one of the papers on the lectern and adjusted his Ben Franklin cheaters. "The newspaper said, 'Our civilization, patriotism and culture have been violated and shamed.'[14] And of course, Cincinnati was most worried about what the rest of the world might think about the Queen City."

Jim nodded and chuckled, but not many joined him.

"A few days after the discovery of former Congressman John Scott Harrison hanging like a fish on a hook, a reporter tracked down a genuine body snatcher and interviewed him. The graverobber said he would never rob the tombs of wealthy stiffs. I'll read you his comments. He said, 'When we'd come to where we knew it was the poor lot where the people without any friends are buried, then we'd dig down to the coffin, break it open and put a rope around the neck and pull the body out. Then we slip the head into a sack. Press the knees up against the chest and stuff the body in and tie the sack.'

"Asked if he enjoyed his work, he said, 'It wasn't very pleasant at first, but one gets used to it. It is for the good of science, and I think it is just as right and honorable as for the man what does the dissection.'"[15]

---

13   Dr. Roberts Bartholow, on the faculty of the Medical College of Ohio in Cincinnati, conducted the experiments on Mary Rafferty, a "feeble-minded" Irish maid, age 30, by inserting electrodes through a hole in her skull caused by a terminal cancer. His report in 1874, "Experimental investigations into the functions of the human brain," in the *American Journal of Medical Sciences*, caused an uproar and is still cited in histories and research articles about the neurosciences. Dr. Bartholow was accused by a colleague of being "cruel in his professional duties, when it came to physiological investigations." Bartholow was censured by fellow doctors for causing "pain, convulsions, and probably hastening death." The medical council said, "these experiments are so in conflict with the spirit of the profession, and opposed to our feelings of humanity, that we cannot allow them to pass unnoticed. Resolved, That in our opinion, no member of the medical profession is justified in experimenting upon his patient, except for the purpose and with the hope of saving said patient's life, or the life of a child in utero." (*Cincinnati Medical News*, 1874, p. 385). Harris, Lauren Julius, Michigan State University, "Probing the human brain with stimulating electrodes: The story of Roberts Bartholow's (1874) experiment on Mary Rafferty, *Brain and Cognition*, April 2009.

14   "Human Hyenas," *The Cincinnati Enquirer*, May 31, 1878.

15   "The College Horror: Graphic Chat With An Old Grave Robber," *The Cincinnati Enquirer*, June 4, 1878.

He looked up at the audience with angry eyebrows and sparking blue eyes, as if there were graverobbers hiding among them. And judging by the body language and frowns, Jim guessed there were a fair number who were eager to see the Chinese Bodies Exhibition, or already had.

"Is any of this starting to sound familiar to you?" Doc Woods asked like a dad scolding misbehaving children. He began using the air finger quotes again. "For the good of science? We don't know where they came from? Only the poor who have no friends? Distinguished doctors approve?

"Should I show you pictures of medical students in the 1870s who propped up dissected cadavers as if they were playing poker at a card table? Does any of this ring a bell?"

Jim knew exactly what bell was clanging. But the doctor spelled it out in bold capital letters for anyone who missed it.

"The Bodies Exhibition at the Cincinnati Museum Center insists their specimens are unclaimed bodies of the poor. But they cannot provide any paperwork to prove it. Protesters in San Francisco, London, Seattle and Amsterdam say the victims of plastination were political prisoners, executed in Chinese work camps and gulags, then paraded like a freak show."

Most, he said, were Christians or part of the Falun Gong movement in China—a cousin of Buddhism that involves healthy exercises, truthfulness, compassion and forbearance.

After the Chinese Communist government outlawed Falun Gong[16] in 1999, he explained, millions were arrested, tortured, imprisoned, sent to work camps and killed.[17] Dissidents such as Harry Wu[18] escaped to

---

16   Also called Falun Dafa, "An advanced practice of self-cultivation" and "assimilation to the highest qualities of the universe." www.minghui.org.

17   Falun Gong refugees in the US say Chinese Communist Leader Jiang Zemin initiated the oppression in 1999 and declared it was legal to kill anyone caught practicing this "evil cult." That gave China's secret police, called the 610 Office, permission for torture, prison, slave labor, rape, organ harvesting and other atrocities.

18   Wu was imprisoned for 19 years in the Chinese gulag called "laogai," which means "thought reform by hard labor." Laogai camps make many of the common products sold in America. Wu escaped to the US with $40. He returned to China three times to document human rights abuses and was put on China's most wanted list. He was captured and sent to a Chinese prison on his third return, but a worldwide campaign forced China to release him. In 2008, he founded the Laogai Museum in Washington, DC. He died in 2016.

the US and testified that China was using its inventory of political prisoners to harvest organs for sale. Kidneys: $60,000. Hearts: $200,000. Eyes, lungs, livers—just place an order, then fly to China for a new pair of corneas.[19]

China could easily find a donor prisoner to match any blood type. They were doing 100,000 transplants a year in hospitals that were conveniently located next door to prisons.[20] Plastination labs were also close and handy, giving China two ways to profit from forced organ donations.

"Why would Falun Gong be outlawed and persecuted in China?" a skeptical reporter for the *Cincinnati Post* asked. Jim knew the guy—50-something, still wearing long hair and shabby jeans as if he was back in college protesting the War in Vietnam. It was obvious from the needling tone of his question that he wasn't buying any of it.

Doc Woods looked him over and seemed to dismiss him like a buzzing housefly before answering. "Communism is a jealous god," he replied. "It is atheistic and will not tolerate competition from any religion. More than 100 million practice Falun Gong—and tyranny won't allow what it cannot control."

He told stories from his two-year mission trip to China.

A couple in their 80s, arrested and thrown in prison for doing Falun Gong exercises. When they both died in prison three years later, the secret police went after their children's families to pay for their "crime."[22]

"There's a reason they can honestly say some of these bodies are unclaimed," Doc Woods said. "Family members are persecuted and arrested if they claim the bodies."

---

19   Davis, Charles, "Communist China's Forced Organ Harvesting Practices Garner Global Attention," *Epoch Times*, March 15, 2025.

20   As of September 2025, the practice continues in China. At the 2025 World Transplant Congress in San Francisco on August 2, 2025, surgeons, anesthesiologists, nurses and other medical personal signed petitions condemning forced organ harvesting in China. Ying, Wang, "Doctors at World Transplant Congress Condemn China's Live Organ harvesting," *Minghui*, August 7, 2025.

21   In 2008, Premier Exhibitions, presenter of the Bodies show in Cincinnati, was forced by the New York Attorney General to admit, "The remains of Chinese citizens or residents exhibited in this exhibition come from the Chinese police."

22   www.Minghui.com.

He told about the first-person account of an intern who was ordered by the military to assist in an emergency organ transplant. The donor was still alive and twitching while the surgeons opened his body to cut out his kidneys. The victim was gagged so he couldn't talk or scream. No anesthetic was used. After the Kidneys were taken, the intern was ordered to remove the young man's eyeballs, but he refused because the victim was staring at him in extreme terror, still alive.[23]

There were gasps and moans as Woods described the torture reported by Falun Gong and Christian victims: scalded with boiling water, burned with cattle prods and cigarettes, gang rapes and sexual torture of women, cages, psychotropic drugs, sleep deprivation, beatings…

"What's wrong with harvesting organs from prisoners who are executed?" the reporter asked—more of a belligerent argument than a question.

"Think about it. They *schedule* organ transplants. There is no way to do that ethically. In many cases, the organs are harvested without anesthetic to make sure lungs, kidneys and beating hearts are undamaged and fresh.[24] The world has not seen such malignant evil since the Nazi death camps and Aztec human sacrifice."

He turned back to the reporter: "Does that put flesh on the bones for you?"

Someone in the audience spoke up, "This plastination sounds a lot like the medical college body snatchers."

"Yes, precisely. So who is more barbaric? The ghouls who dug up corpses for the medical college? They at least had the excuse of teaching anatomy. Or are the real barbarians the families who buy tickets for the Bodies Exhibition at the Museum Center to see mutilated corpses playing chess? Men and women who were someone's mother, daughter, son, father—brutally tortured and butchered for profit and entertainment.

---

23   The surgery occurred in the 1990s. Ling, Yi, "Former Chinese Hospital Intern Recounts a Live Organ Harvest," *Epoch Times*, March 9, 2025.

24   *Bloody Harvest: Revised Report into Allegations of Organ Harvesting of Falun Gong Practitioners in China*, David Matas, Esq. and Hon. David Kilgour, Esq., January 31, 2007.

"Just as in 1878, these bodies on display at the Museum Center come from the poor, the friendless, the abandoned. Try to imagine if someone did this to your friends or your family. And like the body snatchers, these exhibits have turned desecrating the dead into a profitable business, making millions of dollars.

"They claim it's for the good of science, but plastic models can teach anatomy as well or better. How would you feel to see someone you loved peeled like an orange and propped up under lights?"

The crowd was quiet, shocked, thinking, taking it in.

A woman near the front wiped her eyes as she raised a hand to ask, "What became of the graverobbers and the medical college? Were they held accountable?"

"Sad to say, they were not," Dr. Woods answered. "Detective Snelbaker was certain the graverobber was a failed medical student named Morton, who had many aliases but went by the clever name Gabriel—the angel of resurrection. Morton was traced back to his professors at the University of Michigan in Ann Arbor, but they denied any knowledge of his whereabouts. They were lying. Probably afraid their supply of fresh bodies would be cut off.

"Morton was finally caught and put in jail, awaiting trial, but he faked smallpox by blistering his skin with toxic croton oil that was smuggled to him by his wife. Quarantined in the Toledo Pest House—yes, there was such a thing—he escaped in the confusion when a vigilante mob came to lynch him. He probably escaped with the help of sympathetic doctors so he could move on to harvest the dead somewhere else.

"The investigation revealed that Cincinnati was the New York Stock Exchange for bodies. They were supplied from all over Southwest Ohio and shipped in barrels as far as Ann Arbor, where police found more than 40 from Cincinnati, including the body of Augustus Devin. Only the janitor at the Ohio Medical College was jailed. The dean of the college urged leniency because Marshall had a wife and five children who lived with him at that ghastly castle of horrors.

"After reading news accounts and putting together the clues, I believe the body of John Scott Harrison was stolen on orders of Dr. Bartholow and Dr. Seely. They visited Marshall in jail—probably to promise support if he kept silent about their involvement. Also, the body snatcher interviewed by the newspaper said doctors at the college were getting more aggressive to get the bodies they wanted. School was not in session and it was getting hot—usually a slow market for bodies. So why John Scott Harrison? Because he died suddenly of unknown causes. Seely and Bartholow were curious. And immoral."

"Were there any changes as a result of the scandal?" Jim asked.

"Yes, the legislature passed a bill providing whippings and prison for grave robbery. And licensing of doctors began in Cincinnati as a result of this scandal. But both were tepidly enforced."

"What about the Harrison family?"

The tomb of President William Henry Harrison, left, towers over Mt. Nebo in North Bend, overlooking the Ohio River, across the road from Congress Green Cemetery. His son, John Scott Harrison, is safely behind bars in the tomb (right), next to the more ornate vault for his father, the president.

"Their father's body was reburied in a secure tomb next to his father, William Henry Harrison. His son Benjamin Harrison, who was elected president 11 years later, had the last word in an open letter to the people of Cincinnati. I will read a few words from it.

"He wrote, 'God keep your precious dead from the barbarous touch of the grave robber and you from the taste of hell which comes with the discovery of a father's grave robbed and the body hanging by the neck like that of a dog, in the pit of a medical college.'

"He blamed the faculty. And he was right. On a follow-up search, detectives found men's and women's clothing from the dead—including Harrison's—stuffed into the rafters of the attic at the medical college. The students and faculty knew very well where the bodies came from. They paid from $15 to $25 for each of the cadavers robbed from graves—which would be $300 to $500 now in 2008."

Dr. Woods gathered his papers and stacked them on the lectern, signaling that his story was coming to an end. "One more thing," he said. "In 1778, a hundred years before the Cincinnati scandal, there was a deadly riot in New York City when a man found his wife being dissected at Columbia Medical School the day after her grave had been robbed. We don't know if they carried pitchforks and torches, but the angry mob that stormed the medical school could have been extras from a scene in the movie *Frankenstein*. Remember, the real monster in that movie was the doctor."

During the following weeks, the Museum Center reported record attendance and long lines for the Bodies Exhibit. It was the same in cities all over the US. The traveling corpses were so successful they were still taking bows in Las Vegas, Mexico City and other places in 2025.

And over the years, the exhibits stretched the boundaries of taste and morality even further. An exhibit called Cycle of Life showed a fleshless, plastinated couple having sex. Another showed a pregnant woman with a plastinated unborn child in her cutaway womb. In 2004, a German magazine reported that some of the plastinated bodies on display had execution-style bullet holes in their skulls.

But it was all packaged in pretentious babble about "confronting mortality," "pushing the frontiers of knowledge" and "blending art, science and emotion." Which was just enough high-minded moonshine to disguise the fleshless face of evil.

Doc Woods looked at his big pocket watch, put it away and said, "As you go home tonight past the billboards for the Bodies Exhibition, ask yourself if that body snatcher in 1878 was right when he said, 'Anyone gets used to it.'"

He paused and looked over the audience. Some were stunned, others were shifting uneasily, eager to leave.

He shook his head sadly and said, "God forgive us if we get used to it."

TWO

RIFLES AT FORTY PACES

*The duel that shaped
American history*

Emigrants Crossing the Plains—Sunset, Albert Biersatadt, 1869.

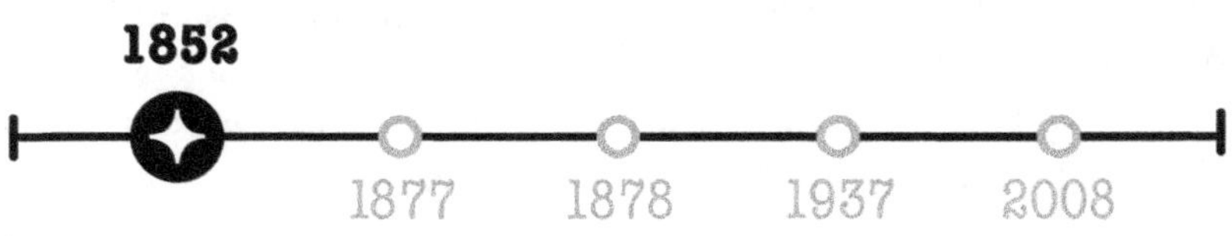

The sun would rise in Sacramento at 6:09, scattering its gold dust through the soft, hazy light of Northern California that could make the most rugged Sierra Nevada Mountains look soft and inviting.

But whatever time it came, sunrise would be too soon for Edward Gilbert.

As he tossed in a sagging bed on a thin mattress that remembered too many unwashed bodies, a thousand thoughts marched through his mind like a brass band, with crashing cymbals and pounding drums that were nearly as loud as his heartbeat. It was impossible to sleep. He might have only hours to live, yet he was wasting the night crossing and recrossing his own trail like a bloodhound trying to pick up the scent of his fatal mistake.

It was all because of words. Just words. Spoken into the air, they would have dissolved and blown away like smoke. Even words as hot as the burning coal of a lit cigar could waft away on the cool breath of a breeze.

But words on paper were his profession and his life. He had written them in thick strokes of angry black pencil. They were handed to his typesetter, who arranged each letter in each sentence, every comma and period, every dotted "i" and semicolon. All were carefully lined up in reverse, like a newspaper held up to a mirror. When the whole page was complete, all those tiny letters cast in lead were baptized in sweet-smelling ink and fed to the big cast-iron Washington Hand Press that waited with its jaws gaping, hungry for scandal, murder, rumors and alarms.

With a clatter of gears, the pressman pulled the fat, ink-blackened wooden handle that levered the press mouth closed, then pushed it back and the jaws opened wide again, belching out another edition of the *Alta California*. And in less time than it took to sharpen his pencil, Edward Gilbert's

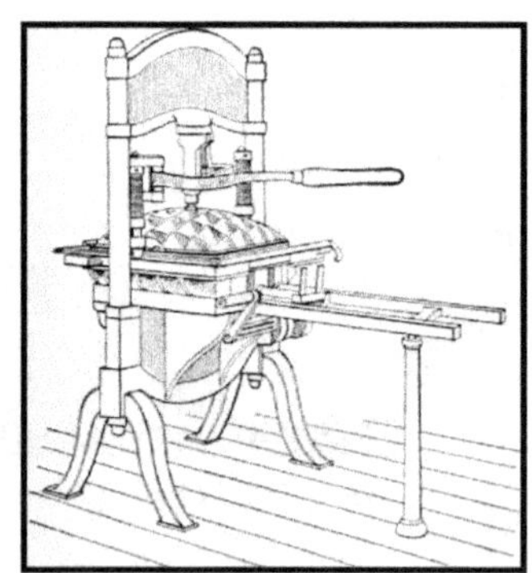

Drawing of a Washington Hand Press, from The New International Encyclopedia, 1905.

fate was sealed.

Once on paper, his editorial became more than spoken words. Printed words were freighted with the power of the press, tattooed in ink as permanent as a tombstone, circulated to thousands of readers.

"Toadies," he had written. He called the governor "silly" and "ridiculous." He compared him and his friends to a traveling circus— suggesting clowns, jugglers and knuckle-walking apes.

It all began with urgent reports that thousands of new Gold Rush emigrants were trapped in the Sierras on their way to California. Governor John Bigler and the state legislature responded with an emergency $25,000 rescue appropriation, to send eight large wagons of supplies, blankets and food. The governor's close friend and leader of the state senate, James W. Denver, was appointed to command the mission of mercy.

With lusty cheers and flags waving, the California Relief Train set out from Sacramento on June 25, 1852. Each wagon was heaped with supplies strapped under canvas and was pulled by two teams of mules or horses. Governor Bigler escorted it through the streets on horseback, waving his hat to the cheering crowd.

Edward Gilbert was outraged. As a fierce partisan opponent of the governor's administration, his political hostility blinded him to the obvious charity of the mission. The next day, he published the fateful editorial in the *Alta California* that scorched the spectacle as a grandstanding political stunt. "Governor Bigler was silly enough to make himself ridiculous by riding at the head of the procession," he wrote. He grudgingly wished the rescue train success, but mocked the "immodest attempts of the governor to manufacture personal popularity out of the affair."

That could have been the end of it. His editorial was typical of the newspaper business in 1852. Editors and their newspapers were rabidly partisan. Party affiliation was even proudly displayed in mastheads: *The Wisconsin Democrat*; *The Boston Emancipator and Republican*; *The Richmond Whig*. Reporting was saturated with slander, rumor and invective. Editors such as Gilbert saw themselves as frontline infantry in the political skirmishes of the day.

But that was not the end of it. Gilbert was the editor and part-owner of the *Alta California,* one of the most successful newspapers in boomtown San Francisco.[25] The words were written under his name, under boldface headlines. And he knew that the targets of his insults would take notice.

In the West, slander and personal insults in print were not answered with lawsuits and strong letters to the editor. The demand for a retraction was personal, delivered man to man at sunrise with lead, not lawyers.

Senator James Denver and the Relief Train were off in the mountains saving lives when the editorial was published, so it took a month for them to see Gilbert's mocking diatribe and send a response. Their reply was published in the *Daily Democratic State Journal* in Sacramento on July 24.

Gilbert read it with a creeping sense of dread.

"None but a personal enemy could imagine any such thing, and that enemy must be of the smallest possible caliber, who could descend so low as to pervert the facts," the letter said. "We can have but one opinion of this attack on the Governor—that it could only have emanated from an envious and malicious heart."[26]

It was signed by 11 men but was written by Denver, Gilbert decided. Denver was a state senator and lawyer,[27] more educated than most men on the frontier, who would not use words such as "emanated" and "malicious." Denver was also a former editor and owner of two newspapers, *The Thomas Jefferson* in his hometown of Wilmington, Ohio, and another one in Platte City, Missouri.

Gilbert had met his match in the editorial fencing ring. The words stung. He realized he should have expected as much, but the personal insults and damage to his reputation as a newspaperman—"pervert the facts"—still caught him by surprise, as if he had fired a gun in the air and somehow managed to hit someone who was now shooting back.

---

25   The population of San Francisco was 800 in 1847. Three years later, the Golf Rush had filled the city with 50,000 residents.

26   *The Daily Democratic State Journal,* July 24, 1852.

27   Graduate of Cincinnati College of Law (University of Cincinnati) in 1847.

He could bandage the wounds with gauzy words that would slow the hot blood and allow time for tempers to cool. But he refused to do that. Not again. And that took his thoughts back to something else he could not leave alone, that kept nagging at him like the jagged edge of a broken tooth.

Five months ago, John Nugent, editor of the *San Francisco Herald*—the arch-rival of Gilbert and his paper—had been awarded an advertising contract with the city of San Francisco in a bidding contest against Gilbert and the *Alta Vista.*

Gilbert was sure he had been cheated. He went to war in print, and the battle steadily escalated until Gilbert accused Nugent in print of lying, and called the contract a crooked backroom deal.

Nugent replied with a clear warning: "We hope our contemporary [Gilbert and the *Alta California*] will not lose its temper, as in such an event we would be apt to lose ours, and that state of things both of us might afterwards regret."

It was not a threat to be taken lightly. Nugent was one of the toughest hombres on the Gold Coast.

But Gilbert would not let it go. He kept pushing and needling until finally, he challenged Nugent to a duel.

Such dramatic, sensational newspaper battles were good for circulation. Readers watched the artillery battle of words with great amusement and excitement. But as the sun rose on the morning of the duel, it dawned on Gilbert with sudden alarm that Nugent was the kind of man who might put a bullet in his heart and stop his own personal circulation, permanently. The *Herald* editor had been in at least three duels and had survived them all, even after taking a bullet in the thigh that broke his femur. When Gilbert thought of Nugent, he saw his own grave.

AN ABJECT APOLOGY

That morning, he met Nugent at the place of honor in front of scores of witnesses—and grabbed for his last chance to back down before shots could be fired, the way a drowning man clutches a floating branch in a flood.

The next day, he had to publish his cringing apology: "The senior editor of the *Alta California* takes pleasure in disavowing all intention of reflection personally on the Editor of the *Herald* in the remarks heretofore made. The difficulty which occurred between the senior editor of this paper and the Editor of the *Herald* has been amicably adjusted to the satisfaction of all the parties concerned."

That rose garden of flowery of words—"takes pleasure in disavowing," "amicably adjusted"—could not hide the thorns of humiliation and the stink of his shame. At the time, he thought that day was his darkest day of disgrace. But every day after got worse. Wherever he went, he thought he saw "craven coward" in the eyes of everyone he met. His own reflection in every mirror and shop window sneered at him. He could hardly stand to go to his office or leave his house. It felt as if all of San Francisco was laughing at him with contempt.

To make it yet worse, he had lynched his own reputation in a noose that was every editor's favorite target: hypocrisy. He had regularly used his editorial platform to ridicule "bloodless duels," in which men go through all the formal dance steps of the dueling code, face off valiantly with firearms—then fire into the air and deliberately miss each other so they can satisfy the demands of honor without risking a crippling wound or sudden death. And now he was the most shameful example of his own editorial mockery.

The Edward Gilbert who wrote those scornful editorials in the *Alta California* was like a stranger to himself—a blustering, gormless tinhorn with a sequoia mouth and acorn courage. He became a recluse who walked the streets alone, shoulders slumped, defeated and disgraced, with no friend but his dog.

No, he could not back down again. This time, he would redeem his reputation and his honor. Honor was everything. Without it, a man was nothing. *Death before dishonor*, he thought, dramatically picturing himself striking a heroic pose on the dueling ground with a smoking pistol in his hand—noble, victorious and fearsome. He would vindicate himself or die trying.

There would be no words of conciliation this time, no apology, no retraction. After reading Denver's letter in the State Journal, he sat down at his desk and brandished his pencil like a sword, determined to escalate the skirmish with an even more scathing editorial. It was splashed on the front page of the *Alta California* on July 26, under the headline, "Governor Bigler's Attempt to Manufacture Political Capital Out of California Relief Train."

He sneered at the governor's friends and supporters who "aid and abet that notorious individual in his paltry attempt to manufacture political capital out of the expedition… Such barefaced electioneering and such palpable want of dignity must result in disgusting all right-thinking men." He called Denver's letter defending the governor an attempt to "make a whistle out of a pig's ear."

The editorial sizzled and spit like fat in the fire. He closed it with a challenge: "If any of the gentlemen attached to the train, or any other friend of the governor, desire to make an issue upon the matter, they know where to find us."[28]

There it was: In the stilted language of Gold Rush California, behind the editorial "we," Edward Gilbert had personally called out James Denver. It was as crude as a slap in the face with a leather glove.

Denver replied in the *State Journal* that it was what he would expect from a dishonorable and contemptible "blackguard"—one of the most incendiary fighting words of the West. He told Gilbert, "You know where to find me," and promised he would get all the "satisfaction" he asked for—and more.

Gilbert had issued the challenge. Denver accepted. After that, it was left to their appointed "seconds" to negotiate the details.

Now, as Gilbert stared at the ceiling in the Oak Grove Hotel, the minutes dragged like hours and hours sped by like minutes as he waited for dawn, when he would meet Denver face-to-face to settle their dispute on the field of honor.

✷

A few rooms away, in the same hotel near the place chosen by Gilbert, eight miles south of Sacramento, James Denver was also awake. He checked his pocket watch again in the moonlight that streamed through a window: 4:45 a.m. He shrugged and decided he would make good use of the time he had left before his "appointment" at dawn.

---

28 Barns, George C. *Denver, the Man.* 1949.

"Wake?" he said softly.

"Yes, I am a Wake," said his friend Dr. Wakeman Bryarly.[29] They both chuckled at the play on words, not for the first time.

"The name fits," Denver said. "I am lighting a candle, Wake."

Bryarly heard the scratch of the match, the short snake-hiss flare of the flame, and then watched as the room they shared partially emerged from dark shadows. It was a typical hotel in the newborn state[30] of California—nailed together in a hurry to accommodate the thousands of "49ers" who flooded in after gold was discovered at John Sutter's Mill in the Sierra Nevadas, northeast of Sacramento, not far from where they were tonight. They were almost at the bubbling source of the Amazon River of dreams that had engulfed the whole nation with Gold Fever.

The hotel's doors and floors were uneven, crooked, as if the whole building had been built by a drunk and then knocked cattywampus by the backhand blow of an earthquake—both, probably. The walls were washed in thin white paint that had turned gray from grime. Heavy, drooping, blood-red curtains, sad and tired as a saloon girl's last good dress, modestly covered gaps around the windows where dust and wind came and went as they pleased.

Bryarly thought the hotel was a lot like California: a crooked frame covered in a thin coat of whitewash—the whole thing cockeyed, tilting, lunging drunkenly for riches like a man running downhill on a wooden leg.

Nobody cared if the whole red-curtained shoddyocracy collapsed. They would just nail together a new one. California had an incurable epidemic of gilded greed—a delusional optimism that everyone who could get there in time would get the chance to shout "Eureka!" and pull buckets of gold from the ground. Multitudes of emigrants with eyes like glittering coins were hell-bent to risk their lives—literally dying to get there.

---

29   Dr, Wakeman Bryarly co-authored a book about his adventures on his journey to California during the Gold Rush, *Trial to California: The Overland Journal of Vincent Geirger and Wakeman Bryarly*. He was a respected surgeon who served in the Mexican-American War.

30   California became the 31st state on September 9, 1850.

Denver interrupted Wake's thoughts with a question: "What do you know about Mr. Gilbert?"

Wake Bryarly sat up. He was fully dressed, had no real intention of sleeping. His job was to be there at Denver's side, ready with whatever was needed. He was the surgeon who would be standing by to bandage wounds or declare death on either side. He had carried messages to Gilbert's seconds, who were likewise entrusted with negotiations for the duel.

He and Denver had gone over the Irish Code Duello together: 25 explicitly worded rules to govern maiming and death like some kind of military marching orders on the road to hell.

"Rule 1: The first offense requires the first apology." Gilbert had initiated the confrontation and challenged James Denver. So Gilbert had the burden to make amends to avoid bloodshed. But Gilbert had stubbornly refused.

"Rule 7: No apology can be received after the parties have actually taken their ground, without exchange of fire." Until they toed their marks on the dueling ground, with weapons in their hands, there was still a chance to resolve the dispute without shooting. But after that, there was no back door, no way out. After they exchanged shots, the negotiations could be reopened, and an apology could be made with honor. But only after the first shots were fired.

"Rule 16: The challenged has the right to choose his own weapon." Denver had that privilege and chose Wesson Rifles at 40 paces. The new Wesson Rifles were the latest advance in firearms. They had a self-contained cartridge—a hollow lead bullet filled with gunpowder. A primer was attached to the back, and the cartridge was inserted in the breach, which opened and closed with a lever mechanism.[31] Each shot had to be loaded by hand. The bullet was not especially powerful but it was not small: .41 caliber.

"Rule 17: The challenger chooses his ground." Gilbert had selected this place, which gave him time to prepare. Denver was notified only the day before, to be there at dawn.

---

31   Invented by Walter Hunt, the early Wesson Rifle pioneered a design that was adopted by Winchester to make the famous lever-action rifle that tamed the West. The first Wesson was called the Volcanic. Later, D.B. Wesson partnered with Horace Smith to form Smith & Wesson.

"Rule 21: Seconds are bound to attempt a reconciliation before the meeting takes place, or after sufficient firing or hits are specified." Dr. Bryarly had tried. But Gilbert and his seconds were unmovable.

Bryarly thought about what he knew of Gilbert.

"He is not a good shot," he said, choosing the best news he could think of to raise Denver's spirits. "He served in the Mexican-American War, like you and me, but he saw no combat the way we did. He was a collector of taxes and duties at the Port of San Francisco. He spent the war sitting at a desk. Nothing like our experience. Where were you again?"

"I arrived at the port of Vera Cruz. Then served at the National Bridge and the Battle of Churubusco in '47. I cannot claim much glory. Just before Churubusco,[32] I had a severe attack of yellow fever and was so weak I could not even roll out of my cot. I could not stand up if you lit a fire under me."

"I heard about the attack at the National Bridge. It must have been quite thrilling."

"It was," Denver said, thinking back to his service. "As you know, I was a captain of the infantry. We arrived at the bridge on July 21st.

It was extremely hot. The bridge was considered one of the strongest positions on the road to Mexico City. I was there as a scout."

"I was very grateful for the work of our own scouts at Buena Vista,"[33] Bryarly said.

Denver nodded. "Our job was to stay on either side and ahead of the army. We were often compelled to scale mountains thousands of feet above sea level and above the road the army was traveling. We could see the clouds far beneath us. It was cooler up there. Quite a sight. I will never forget it. We went into valleys so deep and dark I could easily believe the foot of man had never touched them."[34]

---

32   US Grant, who served as a second lieutenant in the Mexican-American War, called the Battle of Churubusco "about the severest battle fought in the valley of Mexico."

33   The Battle of Buena Vista was one of the biggest of the Mexican-American War. It took place on February 22-23, 1847. The US victory was led by Major General Zachary Taylor, a future US President. The Mexican army was led by Generalissimo Santa Anna.

34   Barns, George C. *Denver, the Man.* 1949.

THE MARCH TO MEXICO CITY

"Tell me about the battle at the National Bridge."

"More of a skirmish," Denver said, shaking his head. "When we arrived, the Mexicans had occupied the highest points on the other side of the bridge, and the bridge was blockaded with obstructions. When our company got to the barricades, the whole opposite side of the bridge erupted in firing and was covered in a cloud of gun smoke, with the sharp rattle of small arms. We immediately fired back and with a shout, our men overran every barrier, scaled the heights and carried everything before them with ease. The Mexicans had all run away before our men got to the top. It was strange. Our men were crowded on that narrow bridge in point-blank range, and the enemy poured shot on them like hail, but not one of our men was killed. Only a half dozen were wounded."[35]

Bryarly said, "I have seen that. Yet at other times, such as Buena Vista, I saw the Mexicans fight valiantly to defend their homeland."

"They were deadly guerrillas," Denver agreed. "Any man who fell behind our rear guard was sure to be murdered. On just a single day, four men were killed that way. We marched 84 miles in four days. Our victories were sweet revenge. El Presidente and Generalissimo Santa Anna was bold enough when he was butchering the wounded prisoners at the Alamo and Goliad in 1836. But when we got to Mexico City, he begged for peace on any terms."

"Did you see John Riley at the Battle of Churubusco?" Bryarly asked. "I heard he was captured there."

"Yes, he and his St. Patrick's Battalion of American deserters. They fought well and accounted for our heaviest losses. Riley said he had worn out his sword on the Mexicans trying to keep them from running, and if they had only stood their ground, he and his artillery would have destroyed our whole army. That rascal had run his race. Fifty of his men were hanged after the battle. He escaped hanging because he deserted before the war was declared.[36] The luck of the Irish, I guess."

––––––––––––––––––––

35   From James Denver's letter to his sisters, written on September 1, 1847, near Mexico City.

James Denver was the oldest of 11 children born to immigrants who had fled oppression in Northern Ireland, but he spared no sympathy for the Irish deserters led by Riley. And he knew all his words about the war were just the skin on the apple. There was no way to describe the way his heart swelled in his chest until he could hardly swallow as he watched the Battle of Molino Del Rey from a housetop on September 8, 1847.

He was part of the rearguard, keeping watch over more than 2,500 corralled prisoners with fewer than 200 guards and two cannons loaded with grapeshot. He was almost unable to stand and walk that day, ravaged by yellow fever chills, headaches, muscle pain, fatigue and nausea. But every man was needed and he answered the call.

As he watched from his flat rooftop at daybreak, the first cannons were fired at the Mexican lines. Then the whole line fired at once, lighting up the landscape for more than a mile, flashing bright as a bursting star in the dim, gray dawn. That triggered return fire by the Mexicans, who outnumbered the US Army by three to one.[37] It was one of the most terrible battles of the war as they fought their way up the bloody road to nearby Mexico City.

The fighting was house to house, room to room, hand to hand. Nearly every house in the little village was filled with bleeding, moaning, suffering and dying wounded men. "Some of the bravest officers of the army died in the house where I had my quarters," Denver wrote to his wife.[38] "It was a dearly bought victory, and the only good resulting from it was that it convinced our men that they could whip the Mexicans, no matter how great the odds against us in numbers."

He had many memories of the war. But he seldom talked about them to anyone. "I don't like to bore people with my experiences in

---

36   Riley and his St. Patrick's Battalion were celebrated by the Mexicans. His bronze bust still decorates a plaza in Mexico City. After his capture, he was court martialed and branded with a "D" on his cheek, for "deserter." At his court martial, he testified that he had deserted because of anti-Irish and anti-Catholic bigotry and mistreatment in the US Army.

37   Modern sources disagree. But Denver was there. His report on the odds was three-to-one in favor of the Mexicans.

38   Written from Washington, DC on September 8, 1867, on the 20th anniversary of the battle. Cook, Edward Magruder. *Justified by Honor*. 1988.

life," he wrote to Louise, who must have ached to learn more about his experiences as she waited in sleepy Wilmington, Ohio afraid he would never return.

After Churubusco and Molino Del Rey came the terrible battle of Chapultepec followed the battle and fall of Mexico City. After that, the war was winding down, but it was over for ailing James Denver. He was finally discharged along with other sick and wounded officers and soldiers on October 26, 1847. There were 25,000 Mexicans killed in the war and 13,000 Americans. Most of the American deaths were from illness.[39]

The war still dragged on until March 1848 when a truce was declared. The Treaty of Guadalupe Hidalgo made the Mexican defeat official. President Polk was half inclined to take the whole country of Mexico for new United States territory, but support in Congress for the war was dwindling, so he settled for a little more than half of Mexico. Mexico was paid $15 million for 525,000 square miles of land that would expand US territory by adding what became the states of California, Nevada, Utah, Colorado, New Mexico and Arizona, plus parts of Colorado, Wyoming, Oklahoma and Kansas. Mexico also agreed to forfeit any claims to Texas.[40]

Denver remembered how his law partner in Platte City, Missouri, Bela Hughes,[41] called him a fool for going off to war. "You will lose all the business you have—lose all the time you are out and come back poorer than when you started," Hughes had said. "A man situated as you are must be a damned fool to quit his business and go to cutting throats."

---

39   There were more than 18,000 casualties among 75,000 Americans who served. More than 11,000 were caused by diseases such as yellow fever, cholera and dysentery.

40   Mexicans living in the territories surrendered by Mexico were granted US citizenship if they chose to stay. For more about how Cincinnati saved Texas in its war for independence, see *Promised Land* by Peter Bronson, www.chilidogpres.com.

41   Hughes later became a US Senator from Missouri and was president of the Central Overland California and Pikes Peak Express Company, one of the first major stagecoach lines in the West. He also operated the Pony Express. He was one of the early pioneers in Colorado. He is one of 16 men in the Colorado Hall of Fame display of portraits in stained glass at the state capitol. Also in the display are Ute Nation Chief Ouray, Christopher "Kit" Carson and James William Denver.

Hughes was mostly right. Denver limped home to Wilmington, Ohio to slowly recover for nearly a year before he was ready for another adventure. He had lost a lot. But his destiny was already being steered by one of those new states that were won in the war, California. He didn't know it yet, but two more states, Kansas and Colorado, would forever change his life and make him wealthy and famous. And he would personally give the name for another state, Montana, while he gave his own name to the capital of Colorado.

Denver realized he did not have to describe anything about the Mexican War to his friend Bryarly, who had seen horrors of his own, especially as a battlefield surgeon. He came back to the present. "What else do you know about Gilbert?" he asked as he sat on the edge of his bed to pull on his boots.

"I asked my friends in San Francisco," Wake Bryarly said. "They told me he was an orphan. He was apprenticed to a printing shop in a town called Cherry Valley, in upstate New York. He worked his way to a job as an editor at the Albany Argus. He raised a company of volunteers for the Mexican War. And the army in its inscrutable wisdom sent him to San Francisco, where he returned to the newspaper business after the war."

"And turned to politics," Denver said. "Congressman, briefly?"

"Yes, he was the youngest delegate to California's Constitutional Convention, and that led to his election to one term in Congress. Apparently, that was enough for him."

"I can hardly blame him for that," Denver said. "That's more of a curse than a blessing. Just getting to Washington can kill a man. I've seen all I want of the Oregon Trail crossing. Three thousand miles of Indians, deserts, thirst that makes you want to cut your own throat, starvation so bad you will boil your own boots—or worse. Snows that bury a wagon and a team of oxen, mountains that pierce the clouds, deadly river crossings, terrible sickness, sudden accidents… Did I leave anything out, Wake?"

Bryarly shook his head and went to the wash basin to splash cool water on his face. "I would add the bugs that tormented us and drove our horses mad. But that about covers it. Next time, I will take my chances around the Horn.[42] Twelve thousand miles of gales, waves like mountains, iced decks and months of seasickness are almost paradise compared to the Oregon Trail."

Denver chuckled. Bryarly shook his head and marveled at Denver's ability to laugh with the "appointment" just an hour away.

"You can have the Horn," Denver said. "I hear the Isthmus of Panama is the adventure of a lifetime. Five thousand miles by sea, then 50 miles by rail, mule trains and blistered feet."

"And bandits behind every banana tree, ready to chop you to scrapple with their machetes."

"Who can blame the poor beggars?" Denver laughed. "All that gold carried through their jungle—they only have to reach out and take it. Let the poor miners waste years of their lives coaxing it out of the ground here. The bandits only have to wait for the mule trains loaded with bullion, and trade ounces of lead for pounds of gold."[43]

"You almost make the Oregon Trial sound more inviting," Bryarly said.

"Then you must have been hit in the head," Denver chuckled. "Did you forget ice a half-inch thick on a bucket of water in June? The cholera? Quicksand and broken axles, drowned mules, no water for days, and if water, no grass for the oxen, and if grass, no wood? I started out with 34 in my wagon train and lost a quarter of my party—all good men, good friends."

"It all comes back to me," Bryarly said. "Every time I wake up shivering or dream of the Indian attacks and all those lonely graves along the trail. I can still smell the death. Dead oxen for miles. We saw a thousand littering the trail. And the cast-off possessions—horse-

---

42 Cape Horn, the southern end of Tierra del Fuego on the tip of South America, where the Atlantic and Pacific Oceans meet. It's famous for violent weather, high winds, turbulent seas and shipwrecks.

43 Almost $98 million (about $4 billion today) in gold bullion was moved from California to New York between the annexation of California in 1848 and 1852, according to the *Nevada Journal* of Nevada City, California (August 7, 1852). The highway robbers on the Isthmus of Panama, along the Las Cruces Trail, nearly provoked a US invasion of Panama in the 1850s. Two US Navy warships and a group of Marines were sent to secure a railroad station in Panama City in 1856, to protect gold carried across the Isthmus by California miners.

shoes, furniture, abandoned wagons, clothing, boxes containing who knows what. Pilgrims pay a steep price for the Promised Land."

Denver asked, "How long was your journey?"

"Four months, give or take a day. Faster than most. Yours?"

"We left Fort Leavenworth on May 20 in 1850 and finally arrived at our destination in California on September 5, less than a week before statehood. Altogether, 108 days. We took a cutoff."

Bryarly shook his head. "We were warned, whatever you do, don't take a cutoff. They all lead to disaster."

"They were not far from wrong," Denver said. "Isn't that what happened to the Donner Party?"

"Yes, the Hastings Cutoff. Caught in the mountains by an early snowfall. Got so desperate they ate their Indian guides, among others. Eighty-seven took the cutoff and only 48 came out the next spring. Did I tell you we came upon the very place?"

"No," Denver said. "Tell me."

"The first thing we saw was the mournful monuments of their burned cabins. There were piles of bones around but mostly of cattle, although I did find some half dozen human ones of different parts. Just to the left of these was a few old black, burnt logs, which evidently had been one of those cabins which had been burnt. Here was nearly the whole of a skeleton. Several small stockings were found which still contained the bones of the leg and foot. Remnants of old clothes, with pieces of boxes, stockings and bones in particular, was all that was left to mark that it had once been inhabited. The trees around were cut off ten feet from the ground, showing the immense depth the snow must have been."[44]

They were quiet for a minute as both revisited their vivid memories of death and tragedy. Denver recalled digging graves for his friends. Bryarly remembered "The Elephant"—the daunting steep slopes of the Sierra Nevadas. Each daunting elephant peak only led to one even higher and steeper.

"We were lucky," Denver said. "Nothing like the Donner Party. Just cholera, a man crushed by a tipped wagon, drownings, that sort

---

44   Geiger, Vincent Eply, and Wakeman Bryarly. *Trail to California*. Andesite Press, 1945.

of thing. We chose oxen. Slower than mules, but tougher. Some days we made 50 miles. Some days we struggled to make 12."

They both sat silent again, taken back to the scorching heat of the deserts and the icy blast of mountain winds. Trailside mounds of fresh earth marked by crude crosses. Broken arms and legs. Fatal injuries. Disease. Snakebites. Bears. Indians. All set against the most breathtaking, cruel beauty they had ever seen and hoped never to see again.

"Maybe we should speak of happier things," Denver said. "Tell me more about our friend Gilbert."

Bryarly laughed. "I'm afraid I already emptied the saddle bags, sir. I have little else to say about him. A curious man. Put a pencil in his hand and he is Hercules. Take it away and he is Samson with a haircut. Did you know he was challenged by Bill Nugent and backed down? It seems to have rankled him like a burr in his boot. Maybe enough to make him seek trouble at the next opportunity."

"Nugent is no man to trifle with. I heard about that. And now Gilbert hopes to save his own reputation by attacking mine. He will find I am no man to trifle with, either. I could not stand by while he mocked our rescue effort. Not after all that we went through on the trail, knowing from my own heartbreak how those people were suffering."

Bryarly thought to himself, *I feel more nervous than he is.* He asked Denver, "I wonder about you, James. How do you stay so calm at a time like this?"

"I've been in worse scrapes, I reckon. And the way I see it there is no alternative. He has given me no choice. I must defend my honor. As the challenged party, I have no path but one to follow. That simplifies things. Whatever happens at sunrise is in the hands of the Lord."

Wake Bryarly looked around at the rough plank walls and crude furniture. The false dawn was breaking; he could now see what had been shadowed in darkness when they first began talking, and if anything, the room looked more shabby and derelict. He pulled his pocket watch out of his vest, took a look and said, "James, it is time."

✱

By 1852, dueling was gradually falling out of favor on the frontier, and would soon become as uncouth in polite society as taking scalps. But it was still fairly common. Local sheriffs would look the other way, even warning citizens to avoid the chosen dueling spot to avoid injury from stray bullets. The dueling place had to be a secluded spot. And any man who failed to answer the call would be branded a coward and bring shame to his name and his family.

In Europe, the Code Duello had been crafted in 1777 as a way to formalize hostilities over insults and to defend a lady's honor. It was meant to prevent vendettas that might tangle whole families in spirals of violence that could go on for generations. Dueling was considered more honorable and humane than bushwacking and backshooting. Medical care was required to be available to treat the injured and pronounce death. Witnesses were present to make sure the confrontation was conducted with honor. And all nonviolent means of settling the dispute had to be exhausted before a duel could take place.

In England, dueling had been going on for so long and claimed so many lives, young gentlemen were trained in "fisticuffs" to settle disputes with a safer method: pugilism.[45] It was regulated under the Marquess of Queensbury rules—no eye-gouging, biting, kicking or blows below the belt. The beatings could be savage, but were less deadly than duels with swords or pistols.

Dueling was not unusual or unpopular in America until Vice President Aaron Burr shot and killed his political rival Treasury Secretary Alexander Hamilton in 1804.[46] The young nation was shocked. Burr's political career was ruined by the duel, and dueling became criminal in the North.

During the lawless California Gold Rush, it was still popular. And in the South, it remained a part of the code of honor. After the Civil War, it was spread throughout the West, mainly by Texans who drove cattle to other Western states—where it became part of American legend as the gunfighters' "showdown."

Until the Colt .45 revolver was invented, single-shot duels were often harmless. If both men missed—which was not unlikely with

---

45 The origin of boxing.

46 Future President Andrew Jackson was a notorious duelist and killed a man in 1806 after he was shot first, in the chest. Charles Dickinson had accused Jackson of cheating in a horse race, then insulted Jackson's wife, Rachel. Jackson carried the bullet, lodged near his heart, through the War of 1812 and for the rest of his life. He became president in 1829.

smoothbore dueling pistols—there was a pause to reload and reconsider. But with the six-shot Colt "equalizer," there was no "timeout" to negotiate peace or an apology. With six-guns, both men could keep shooting until their Colts were empty, making Western "showdown" duels almost invariably fatal.

✳

Once they were dressed and ready and had said their prayers, Denver and Bryarly took a carriage to the place chosen by Gilbert, who was waiting there with his seconds. "Look at his clothing," Denver said. "Does he think that suit of green will hide him?"

Gilbert was a small man, slender, with dark hair that met his collar and a full, drooping mustache. He looked mild for someone who could be so vituperative in print. His shirt, trousers and vest were in various shades of green, but the color was too dark to blend in with the background of laurel and scrub oaks.

He was talking to a taller man, Henry B. Livingstone, his chosen second. The sun was just beginning to paint the morning sky in vivid red and pink as it rose behind the distant sawtooth mountains. There was enough light to see a blanket spread on the ground. On it were two new rifles: identical Wessons. Someone had paced off the distance—40 yards—and put small stakes in the ground.

'CHOOSE YOUR WEAPONS'

Denver was drawn to the guns. Beside each rifle was a small box of the new self-contained cartridges he had heard about. Curious, he picked one up to take a look. Someone among the Gilbert party cleared his throat loudly, meant as a warning.

"I don't think they want you to handle the weapons," Bryarly said. Denver nodded and put the cartridge back. He would look later, if able.

A crowd of witnesses and spectators was still gathering. More than 60 had arrived overnight.[47] Some were friends, others had read about the duel in the newspapers.

---

47   Barns, George C. *Denver, the Man.* 1949.

At his end of the clearing, Gilbert was putting on a good show—stoic, straight-backed, his face blank, showing no emotion. But there was something about him—an almost invisible tremor. Darting eyes. Words a bit too loud, too hurried. Livingstone could tell he was afraid. Who wouldn't be?

At the other end of the 40 paces—about the distance of six Conestoga wagons, end to end—Denver looked like a giant. In any kind of fight without firearms, Gilbert would have had no chance. Gilbert reassured himself. "The bigger they are…" he said softly to himself.

"The harder they fall," Livingstone finished. He saw Bryarly approaching and said to Gilbert, "Excuse me, sir. Formalities are about to begin."

The two seconds met in the middle, formal and stiff. Bryarly, stocky and muscular, Livingstone, rangy and taller. They shook hands wordlessly. Both were aware that if things went wrong and a dispute over honor could not be resolved, the seconds could find themselves dueling as well, like Act II in a deadly play.[48]

They looked each other in the eye and Bryarly spoke first. "This is the final chance before they take their places. Has there been any change of heart? Does Mr. Gilbert, the challenger who gave first offense, wish to make an apology?"

Livingstone frowned and leaned back as if he smelled something offensive. "Certainly not. He is adamantly resolved to have his satisfaction. Is your man having second thoughts?"

"None at all," Bryarly said lightly, but with a knife edge. "Shall we proceed?"

Livingstone bowed in answer and the men turned and walked together to the blanket where the rifles waited. Each of the seconds had already handled the rifles and cartridges and loaded them easily. The lever was pushed forward with a mechanical click; one of the cartridges that had been carefully inspected was loaded in the breech, and the lever was retuned with two clicks—one closing the breech and the other pushing the hammer back to the firing position.

---

48   Rule 25 of the Code Duello: Where seconds disagree and resolve to exchange shots themselves, it must be at the same time, and at right angles with their principals…If with swords, side by side, with five paces interval.

Each walked back to his man and handed him a rifle. "Loaded and ready to fire," Bryarly said to Denver.

Denver acted as if he was eager to hold the gun and get a look. He gripped it easily in his big hands, as if he had always owned it.

Gilbert, at the other end, looked awkward. The gun was heavier than he expected. He had very little experience with rifles in the army, and had never fired a shot at a deer or a pheasant, much less another man. He looked at the sky, turning brilliant, magical gold as the sun rose higher. Dust motes that fell between the tree branches looked like beams of light directly from Heaven. Everything around him seemed gilded in the morning light—trees, bushes, grass and rolling hills. Were mornings always so beautiful, he wondered, or was he noticing only because these minutes and seconds might be his last?

A voice barked, "Ready!"

Denver took his position comfortably, making sure that his feet were well behind the stake marking 40 paces, with his body in the shooter's stance, angled, his left side facing his target. He held the rifle tilted at the sky, the way his men had carried rifles into battle in Mexico.

At this distance, he could see Gilbert quite clearly. The man looked harmless. Uncomfortable. Like a boy playing a man's game. Denver, at 34, was only one year older, but Gilbert looked to him like an adolescent, standing proud, acting out a role, but with fidgeting hands that betrayed his nerves.

"Aim!" the voice said clearly.

Edward Gilbert brought the heavy rifle to his shoulder. His left hand was on the fore stock, his right hand on the breech, his finger circling the trigger with his cheek meeting the stock behind the hammer. It felt like a poor fit. He heard a symphony of songbirds greeting the morning—the harsh scrub-jay, a lilting tanager, the shrill, urgent goldfinch. His hands gripped hard. He felt unusually focused, as if every leaf and twig was traced in gold. He lined the notched rear sight up with the post of the foresight at the end of the long barrel, until they were centered on the big man in black across the clearing. The front sight made tiny circles on his target as the rifle was wobbled by his pounding heart. His body refused to still itself, but he was sure he couldn't miss. He moved the sight to Denver's white shirt above his vest. His knuckles were white with tension.

"Fire!" the voice shouted. Gilbert, startled, yanked the trigger and his gun went off with a terrific boom that jolted his shoulder and shrouded him in a cloud of smoke. For a quick second he could not tell if he had hit his target, but he felt a huge swell of elation. He was still standing. It was ecstasy. He was alive. He had survived. It was over.

Then the smoke cleared, and there was Denver. He stood as still as a boulder, looking down the barrel of his Wesson Rifle, right into Gilbert's eyes. It suddenly dawned on Gilbert: Denver had not fired yet. His elation swirled away like smoke in the wind. The ecstasy of survival flew off with beating wings like a startled bird. He was doomed. The rifle drooped in his hands.

The small crowd of witnesses realized it at the same moment and gasped. Then the field of honor fell silent. Even the birds had stopped singing, hushed by Gilbert's shot.

Gilbert felt a trickle of sweat roll down his neck. He had heard stories that James Denver was a dead shot who could hit a hummingbird at 50 paces. Something he probably learned as a boy growing up in Ohio. A natural aptitude with firearms, honed through combat in the Mexican War and Indian raids on the Oregon Trail. But by the time Gilbert had learned about Denver's deadly marksmanship, it was too late to turn back.

All this flashed before Gilbert's mind in the blink of an eye. He imagined he could see the bullet that would take his life, still sitting deep in the black tunnel of the rifle barrel, a cold lump of lead waiting for the merest twitch of a finger to drop the hammer, ignite a primer and set off a tiny explosion that would send it hurtling through space into his heart. His mind screamed "Run!" He wanted to fly away like a bird, curl up on the ground, disappear. But he stiffened his spine, stood straight and refused to flinch. He lowered his gun with shaking hands, lifted his chin and prepared to meet whatever came.

Denver had heard the bullet from Gilbert's gun whistle by his left ear. Missed, but not by much. It was not an unfamiliar sound. He had been shot at before. You never heard the one that killed you.

He looked down his sights at Gilbert as the gun smoke swirled and cleared. A sweet, cool breeze from the north brought him the familiar aroma of spent gunpowder that conjured scenes of dead and dying men on a battlefield, moaning, screaming for mercy, some mangled beyond human shapes.

He watched the man in his sights waver, then stiffen and stand taller. *Just a boy,* he thought. *He did his best to kill me but I will have none of this.* James Denver jerked his rifle upward to the right and squeezed the trigger, sending his bloodthirsty little bullet harmlessly into the distant sky.

He saw Gilbert sway backward at the sound of the shot as if he had been hit with a violent gust of wind, his eyes shut hard. Then Denver turned to Bryarly, his face clouded by anger and full of disgust. He nodded, and Bryarly nodded back, looking relieved. Nothing more needed to be said. The intemperate little editor with the poison pen could now leave the field with his fragile honor intact—even restored. Each man had taken his shot. Gilbert should have learned, finally, that the pen is not mightier than the sword, and it is no match for a well-aimed rifle.

Livingstone, meanwhile, was studying his man Gilbert, whose face was changing faster than colors in the sunrise—first relief and joy. Then confusion. Then dread, followed by heroic resolve. Finally, Livingstone saw the face on Gilbert that he had seen too many times lately: ugly, stubborn, petulant, bitter, angry.

Bryarly approached. "Mr. Livingstone, the requirements of the Code Duello have been fulfilled," he said. Most witnesses were quiet, breathless, waiting eagerly to see if there would be more shooting and bloodshed. A few whispered to explain the circumstances to others who were confused: Any decent apology by Gilbert could end it all.

"I will consult with Mr. Gilbert," Livingstone said, turning. Before he could take a step, Gilbert announced loudly, "No! I will not apologize. I am not satisfied. I demand another shot."

Livingstone's shoulders slumped. He retrieved Gilbert's rifle and began to reload it, thinking, *Oh, you stupid, vain fool.*

Denver froze as he was about to put his jacket back on and stared at Gilbert in disbelief. Could the man be so stupid? Given a second chance at life, only to throw it away? Such prideful idiocy made him furious.

As Bryarly took his rifle to reload it, he heard Denver say in a voice as cold as a Rocky Mountain blizzard, "I am not going to stand around here all day and be shot at. Now I must defend myself."

Bryarly recognized that voice. Denver was a man whose compass registered only in two directions: right and wrong. For James Denver, there were no "cutoffs" or shortcuts to doing what is right. Once decided, he would not waver. Gilbert's stubbornness would be fatal.

The witnesses murmured little moans of disbelief and alarm. The rifles were handed back, loaded and cocked, ready to fire. This time there were no birds singing, no gold dust in the heavens, just a harsh voice in the back of Gilbert's mind, cawing like a raucous crow, "You fool! You fool!"

"Ready!"

"Aim!"

"Fir—"

Before the word was finished, one rifle roared and Edward Gilbert was on the ground, looking at the sky, his rifle laying in the dirt nearby. He wasn't sure if he had fired it or not. He was only sure that something terribly wrong had happened. It was that irreversible mistake that haunts every mortal as the panicked mind says to itself, "Oh, no, no, no!" He felt no pain yet, only wetness down his leg near his hip and a deep, aching pressure in his lower abdomen. The world that had been so sharply focused moments ago began to blur. *I did it*, he told himself. *I did not flinch.* But the crow voice cawed regret, sorrow, sadness. Everything lost. And for what? Just words?

Then Livingstone was there, on his knees in the bloody dirt, lifting Gilbert's head onto his lap. "Edward. Oh, Edward." There it was, that same voice of irreversible catastrophe. The final mistake that can never be corrected. He heard in Livingstone's voice what his mind already knew: death.

Denver watched the scene from his assigned distance. He muttered bitterly, "You stubborn, reckless fool!"

Gilbert was shot clean through his body just above his hip bone on his left side. The ball probably nicked his femoral artery. He bled out in five minutes and died in Livingstone's lap without any valiant last words of wisdom or courage. Just an overwhelming weakness and black grief that circled and cawed like a murder of crows as the golden California morning light dimmed and went dark for Edward Gilbert.

✻

Out of a guilty conscience or ironic professional courtesy, the same newsmen in San Francisco who had ridiculed Gilbert as a craven coward for backing down from a duel with John Nugent, now sang Gilbert's praises as if he was Saint Edward of San Francisco.

"Mr. Gilbert was universally beloved and respected here, and his sun thus setting in blood has caused unmitigated sorrow and regret," one of the local editors wrote. "Thousands followed his remains to the city cemetery, where a soldier's burial was given him."[49]

Another asked in anger, "Upon whose head rests the responsibility for the blood thus recklessly shed?" The answer was obvious: Edward Gilbert. But instead, the newspaper put the blame on everyone and nobody: "Have we no laws? No virtue?"[50]

With the kind of maudlin drama editors love, Edward Gilbert was given posthumously all the respect, honor and reputation he was denied while he lived. And by the strange fecklessness of fate, James Denver's courage and grace that gave Gilbert a second chance and saved his own life became his cross to carry for the rest of his days.

If someone used scissors and glue to paste scraps and sentences from the various partisan newspapers together, it would have been possible to find the true story: Two lives were ruined that morning at Oak Grove—one cut short, the other cursed.

Popular opinion began to condemn dueling at the same time dime store novels glorified it in Western myths of high-noon showdowns and fast-draw shootouts. The men who had once been feared and celebrated for surviving a duel would soon be shamed as outlaws.

But at first, Denver rose to glory in California as the victor of one of the most dramatic duels in the American West. All agreed he had

---

49   Barns, George C. *Denver, the Man.* 1949.

50   Ibid.

been valiant, showing unmatched courage by calmly standing up to Gilbert's first shot, then firing into the air to spare Gilbert's life. Not even Gilbert's friends could deny that James Denver had every right and duty to defend himself with that second shot.

Rombach Place, 149 E. Locust Street, Wilmington, was the home of James W. Denver. It is now home to the Clinton County History Center. Courtesy of the Clinton County History Center.

He was soon elected as California's secretary of state. Then voters sent him to Congress—a long, hazardous journey back to Washington. In 1856 he returned to his hometown of Wilmington, Ohio and married Louise Rombach, whose wealthy family lived in one of the most stately homes in town, a two-story, white stucco mansion with twin square pillars framing a classical entry like a Greek temple.[51]

In 1857, while Denver was serving in Congress, President James Buchanan appointed him as the US Commissioner of Indian Affairs.

That was just the beginning of a spectacular political career and a life full of adventure, courage and honor.

But as the years passed, his political opponents kept picking at the scab of that duel he fought in 1852.

---

51   The Rombach House at 149 East Locust Street in Wilmington, Ohio has been restored and is now the home of the Clinton County Historical Society and its collection of James W. Denver papers, uniforms, portraits, guns and artifacts.

A LIFELONG BITTER ENEMY

An incident in Kansas was typical. When James Denver was appointed Governor of the Kansas Territory, a widely feared militia leader in violent, "bleeding Kansas," Gen. James H. Lane, wrote to the local newspaper and called Denver "a professional duelist with his hands reeking with the untimely shed blood of his fellowman."

The editor responded on behalf of Denver: "This comes from a man [Lane] who has been involved in 10 to 12 such difficulties [duel challenges] but backed out in every case." The paper called Lane "a miserable object" who rode under a "treasonous banner."

There was widespread agreement that Lane was a bully and a scoundrel who had enriched himself with land scams, political schemes, looting and even murder. His insulting letter was only the beginning of the attacks on Denver by Lane. And it was a reminder that wherever he went, James Denver would be haunted by the ghost of Edward Gilbert, the man who had insisted on being shot.

In 1876 and 1884, James Denver was considered for nomination on the Democratic ticket for President of the United States. But each time, the duel came up and his name was crossed off the list.

In 1876, in a letter to a friend, Denver wrote, "I have never heard any honorable man, who was a friend of Mr. Gilbert, blame me. … They all conceded that I had acted, not only honorably, but generously. Mr. G. evidently intended to kill me if he could and I am satisfied now it was from no want of *will* on his part that he did not do so."

"I acted as my judgment and sense of honor prompted me to do."

He never reproached himself with second thoughts, only regrets for Gilbert's death. "It is true, I would much rather Mr. Gilbert had not been killed, but at the last moment he forced the issue of my life or his."

Even Henry Livingstone, who had held his friend Gilbert in his lap as he bled to death at dawn in 1852, sent a telegram to James Denver in 1886, when Denver's political opponents in Ohio were lying about the duel to tarnish his reputation. "I saw the duel, and in justice to you, I declare that your conduct was perfectly fair and honorable."[52]

But in politics, truth has no hope of surviving a duel against scandal.

---

52   Cook, Edward Magruder. *Justified by Honor.* 1988.

DECEMBER 10, 1857

Six years after the fatal duel, James Denver was back where he had started so long ago—only a few miles from Fort Leavenworth, where his long, punishing trek to California had begun in 1850.

He was living in Lecompton, capital of "Kanzas Territory,"[53] serving as Commissioner of Indian Affairs. Only eight months before, he had been in Washington as a member of Congress from California, when President James Buchanan sent him off on another adventure in the West.

Since then, he had been traveling almost constantly to visit the reservations where dozens of tribes were relocated in the new Kansas-Nebraska Territory. He became the first Commissioner of Indian Affairs who made a sincere effort to see the places and conditions of the relocated tribes under his supervision.

But on this day, back in the territorial capital, an early snow dusted the plains outside his windows. He sat near a crackling fire in his study and returned to his reading, with nothing but the moaning wind to keep him company. He was working his way through the most comprehensive and current report of its kind yet written: History of the Indian Tribes of the United States: Their Present Condition and Prospects and A Sketch of Their Ancient Status.

It was addressed to President James Buchanan and James W. Denver, Commissioner of Indian Affairs—more than 900 pages of meticulous research, beautiful lifelike drawings and handmade maps, all by Henry Schoolcraft, a famous American explorer who spent more than two years on the project.[54]

Schoolcraft's cover letter to Denver began by describing the Indians as they existed before relocation: "Roaming over vast areas, cultivating little, and often failing by their exertions to secure the scant means of subsistence, their very existence as tribal communities presents a problem which is somewhat difficult of solution. White men,

---

53   The spelling was common on some government documents in those days. It later became Kansas.

54   Schoolcraft discovered the source of the Mississippi River in 1820, married into the Ojibwa Tribe and became Superintendent of Indian Affairs in Michigan (1836-41).

who possessed industry, care, and foresight in such a limited degree, would certainly perish. Destitute of arts or agriculture, possessing no domestic animals, and nothing at all that deserves the name of a government, it should excite no surprise that public sympathy is frequently appealed to on their behalf, to avert from them the impending horrors of pestilence or starvation."

That was true, Denver thought. Those who lived in the East, where the Indian threat had been crushed and removed, could well afford to shower sympathy on the Indians. All of the states east of his own home in Ohio had finally pushed the fiercest tribes into the empty map beyond the Mississippi River. The fearsome Shawnees who had once terrorized his hometown in Wilmington, Ohio were now nearby on a reservation in the Kansas Territory, tamed and almost civilized, according to Schoolcraft's report.

He paged ahead to a spot he had marked about the Shawnees. It began with an inventory of the Indian tribes relocated to Kansas Territory:

"Delawares, Shawnees, Wyandots, Miamies, Weas, Piankashaws, Ottowas, Chippewas, Pottawattamies, Kickapoos, Sacs and Foxes, Senecas, mixed Senecas and Shawnees, Peorias, Kaskaskias, Iowas, Stockbridges or Mohicans, and Munsees, and portions of the Iroquois, forming together an aggregate population of 30,893."

The Shawnees were doing better than most tribes, Schoolcraft reported. "The Shawnees were in a state of enviable advancement; they were thrifty farmers; possessed good habitations, well-fenced fields, and large stocks of horses, cattle, and domestic animals; and had public roads, ferries, schools, and meeting-houses. They dressed in the English style, most of them speaking English, and their horsemen are provided with superior saddles, and bridles. To the observer, the settlers present every appearance of thrift and contentment."

Denver shook his head, skeptical. The sources for many reports were federal Indian agents. Like the governors sent to rule provinces in the ancient Roman Empire, those agents had enormous opportunity for graft and corruption—and equally numerous motives to report that all was well while they plundered the locals.

He read on: "The country occupied by these tribes is high, rolling, healthy, and finely watered springs in every direction, of the best water, sometimes gushing out of the solid rock in streams large enough to turn a mill. Where it is fit for cultivation at all, the land is fertile; much of it is hilly and barren, worthless except for the timber.

"They all live in comfortable cabins, perhaps half or more of good hewn logs, neatly raised; they have outhouses, stables, and barns."

So this is what happened to the fierce Shawnee who made Southwest Ohio the 'Miami Slaughterhouse' and terrorized the Northwest Territory, he thought. *How much of that civilization did they learn from the Ohio settlers they raided, tortured and murdered?*

Denver got up and put another log on the fire as he heard the cold prairie wind whistle around the windows and groan over the chimney.

He sat down again in his big cowhide-covered wingback chair and flipped again to another page where he had turned down a corner:

"When I first came among them, these people were in a wretched condition, spending most of their time in drinking; sometimes the whole tribe together passing days, and even weeks together, in a state of intoxication. Literally every dollar they could raise went for whiskey. Many of them lived on roots, and they were often on the verge of starvation. In appearance, they were squalid and poverty-stricken, the greater part in rags, the children generally naked."

That description of the Quappas Tribe more accurately described the conditions Denver had seen on many reservations. Poverty. Starvation. Apathy. Defeat. Alcohol abuse. Child neglect. And the reason was hidden between the lines for a sharp reader to see:

"The Indians have been prejudged, misjudged, and subjected to harsh judgments in various ways," Schoolcraft's Preface said. "They loved their hunting-grounds, highly prized their independence, exulted in their freedom from all the restraints of labor, and spurned the maxims of civilization."

And, "Such a people had some noble elements in their character. Fearless of death, brave in war, and eloquent in council, they were exemplifications of the highest perfection of the (wild and natural) state."

Now all that was taken away. They were confined to lines on a map that made no sense to them; nomadic hunters restricted to boundaries they could not imagine. Then unscrupulous traders and Indian agents sold them whiskey to dissolve their last bit of dignity in alcohol.

And yet, without the terrible relocations, their extinction was all but certain, Denver knew. They could still win battles in the West, take scalps, carry away women and children, torture captives and terrorize settlers, then celebrate all of it with bloodthirsty war dances. But in the long run, they were doomed to lose everything, even their very existence, if not protected from the relentless advance of American settlers.

That was certain ever since their defeat at Fallen Timbers in 1794, when General Anthony Wayne crushed the Indian Confederation and broke their alliance with the British. After that, it was all relocation and cleanup. And soon more relocation would be needed. Denver found that his job as Indian Commissioner required him to protect the Indians from settlers as much as he protected settlers from Indians.

He heard the approaching clip-clop of a horse outside. It stopped in front of his house, snorted and stomped a hoof to get warm. He knew it meant a messenger, probably from Fort Leavenworth, and he pitied the man who was forced to be out for a long ride in the cold prairie wind and snow. It was the kind of day that made him feel again the icy fingers of the cruel winds in the Rockies.

As he heard a knock on the door he was already up to answer. It was a young man, bundled in scarves and a heavy cloak, powdered with snow like something fresh from the bakery. The cloak and boots were US Army issue. Underneath there would be a uniform to match the gold-striped blue trousers.

He invited the soldier in to warm up, rang a bell to have the horse fed in the barn, and offered the man a shot of brandy, which was welcomed gratefully.

"So you have a message for me?" Denver finally asked after the young soldier had unpeeled like an onion and they settled near the fire.

The soldier was warming his hands at the fire, fingers splayed, both palms out in a gesture that looked as if he was trying to push the flames away. "Yes, sir," he said. He wiped a wet hand on his knee, reached into his tunic and took out a folded yellow envelope and offered it to Denver. It was a telegram—something still to be marveled at on the frontier. With a few clicks of a key, a message could be sent across the nation at a speed infinitely faster and safer than the previous fastest communication, the Pony Express.

Denver held it in his hands with a mixture of dread and excitement.

As he prepared to read it, he thought of a letter he had sent to his sister, long ago, saying, "I think I must have been born under the influence of some comet which prevents me from remaining long in any one place."

Thousands of miles on the Oregon Trail, back to Washington and Ohio, and now back West again, had still not cured his wanderlust. The words to his sister had become a prophecy of his own destiny. And now he sensed that another sudden change in direction was coming—like Ulyesses tossed about by the fickle Greek gods.

The telegram was from Jacob Thompson, Secretary of the Interior. Denver's instinct was right. It said: "You have been appointed Secretary of State of Kansas, instead of Stanton, and confirmed by the Senate."[55]

President Buchanan had finally dropped the axe on Acting Governor Frederick Stanton. Kansas was about to boil over and Buchanan had just turned up the heat while asking James Denver to throw himself into the fire as the lid on the pot.

"It seems I have been promoted from supervising domesticated Indians to supervising savage Kansas," Denver joked.

"I wish you luck, sir," said the soldier with a smile in his voice.

"Do you have any news of recent troubles?" Denver asked, looking up.

"Some, sir. As you know, Governor Walker is in Washington and told the President that if he continues to support the Lecompton Convention, our territory will erupt in bloodshed and chaos."

Things were happening fast. The Lecompton Convention was a fraud and everyone knew it, even Buchanan, who supported it anyway to appease the Southern Democrats who ruled his party—and because Buchanan was sympathetic to the slave economy that powered the South. The Lecompton Convention—written in the town by the same name—had been hijacked by proslavery delegates, who had seized power through a rigged election. They wrote a state constitution that would make slavery a permanent cornerstone of a new Kansas state and imposed severe penalties, including death, for anyone who dared to question slavery.

---

55   Barns, George C. *Denver, the Man.* 1949.

KANSAS: HINGE OF AMERICAN HISTORY

The future state of Kansas was the door to America's future. It would swing open to free Western expansion—or slam shut to save slavery. Freedom in all the new states won in the Mexican-American War was at stake. Both sides of the violent national fight over slavery rushed to the battle lines with reinforcements. Abolitionists sent thousands to Kansas; Southerners and "Border Ruffians" from slave-state Missouri flooded across the border into the Kansas Territory to protect their way of life that kept men and women in chains.

With the number of slave states and free states precariously balanced, the decision in Kansas would tip the whole nation's future. And President Buchanan stubbornly backed the proslavery Lecompton Constitution. He would pull every greasy string and yank every well-oiled Washington lever to get Congress to approve it.

Congress had already ducked the slavery debate by telling Kansas to decide for itself. The same senators and congressmen who beat their chests in speeches for reelection suddenly lost their nerve to make a decision after May 26, 1856.

That was the day Rep. Preston Brooks of South Carolina walked into the Senate and beat abolitionist Sen. Charles Sumner of Massachusetts nearly to death with a cane. Sumner had cruelly mocked Senator Andrew Butler, the elderly uncle of Brooks, in a marathon, incendiary speech against slavery. The beating made Brooks a hero in the South and a monster in the North, as the press did all it could to incite more violence on both sides.

The destruction of the city of Lawrence, Kansas, and the massacre of its inhabitants by the Rebel guerrillas, August 21, 1863. Quantrill's Raid. *Harper's Weekly*, September 5, 1863. Library of Congress.

Washington did what it has always done best: It threw the smoking, short-fused bundle of dynamite into the lap of Kansas, where the vote was so fraudulent it was no choice at all. Abolitionists knew it was rigged, so they abstained. Only 2,200 of 9,000 registered voters showed up to vote on the Lecompton Constitution.

Like a small-scale working steam-engine model of the looming Civil War locomotive, Kansas was split between proslavery Lecompton, the territorial capital, and abolitionist Lawrence, 14 miles to the southeast, founded by transplants from Massachusetts.

On May 21, 1856, proslavery raiders attacked Lawrence, fired cannons on the Free State Hotel, threw printing presses for local abolitionist newspapers into the river and looted homes and businesses. One of the raiders was the only person killed, but the Eastern newspaper headlines yelled "Slaughter!" and gave it a melodramatic name, "The Sack of Lawrence."

Incited by the false headlines, Free State abolitionists in Kansas retaliated with terrorism, looting, riots, raids… and savage murders.

Three days after the raid on Lawrence, a fanatic abolitionist from Ohio, who claimed he was doing God's work, butchered five innocent men in the name of "justice."

John Brown, who came to Kansas from Akron with a wagonload of guns, led a party of eight men who called themselves "The Pottawatomie Company." The group included five of his sons and his son-in-law.

At 10 p.m. on May 24, they knocked on the door at the cabin of settler James Doyle. When Doyle answered, Brown's vigilantes pushed the door open and dragged Doyle and his two sons into the yard. Brown shot the father in the head with a pistol, while his five sons hacked Doyle's unarmed sons to death with swords.

The next stop for the fanatic abolitionist was the home of Allen Wilkinson. He was dragged out while his sick wife begged Brown for mercy. Brown ignored her and hacked Wilkinson to death.

At the nearby home of James Harris, they confronted several men they suspected of being proslavery, and brutally murdered William Sherman.

It was a barbaric, bloodthirsty, psychopathic murder spree. Whoever Brown was serving, it was not God.

But the Eastern papers, including *The New York Times*, made excuses for John Brown and his sons. Their stories made it sound as if the victims deserved to be murdered, and claimed that Brown was falsely accused, which was a lie.

Any recipe for a civil war should include a dishonest press that incites and excuses violence; weak, cowardly politicians; lawlessness and corruption; fanatics who believe they are justified to do anything in the name of their "righteous" cause; and crooked elections.

Then stir in something new: telegraph lines that could carry sensational headlines immediately, making it possible for New York newspapers to exaggerate and inflame violence in Kansas daily.[56] The new "real time" media allowed no pause for thought or argument—only urgent headlines demanding violent action and reaction.

All these ingredients were poured into the kettle of Kansas. And that was the chaos that James W. Denver was ordered to keep a lid on by the telegram that made him secretary of state.

Buchanan soon fired the acting governor, Frederick Stanton. Then the appointed territorial governor, Robert J. Walker, resigned while he was in Washington attempting to talk sense into President Buchanan, imploring him to abandon the fraudulent Lecompton Constitution.

Just 11 days after the telegram was delivered, Denver was appointed territorial governor to replace Walker and Stanton.

This was all in the future on that cold December day, as Denver sat by his fire watching the soldier's wet wool uniform steam as he thawed by the hearth. But he could see it all coming.

He closed the book by Schoolcraft on the status of the Indian tribes, and asked the young lieutenant, "What do you hear about General Lane?" He spoke the word "General" with obvious sarcasm, but the soldier was taking no chances.

"May I speak plainly, sir?"

"Yes, please do," Denver replied.

"I hope Jim Lane—I will not give him the honor of 'general'—is no friend of yours. Because I know him to be a thief, a scoundrel, a

---

56   Mark Twain was probably thinking of the telegraph when he said, "A lie can travel half way around the world while the truth is putting on its shoes."

liar, a coward and a murderer. He would burn down the territory and the whole nation if he could profit by a dollar."

Denver nodded and took a sip of brandy. "He is no friend of mine. Quite the contrary," he said. Like John Brown, Jim Lane exploited the lawlessness of the territory to recruit gangs of looting mobs he called his "militia." He claimed to be anti-slavery, but he was the kind of dishonorable man who would choose whatever side gave him the best opportunity to steal land and increase his wealth and power.[57]

"We know he means trouble," the lieutenant continued. "His militia was authorized by the Lecompton Legislature, but the rest of Kansas knows they are a fraud. He needs to be stopped. Sir, pardon me if I speak out of order, but it looks like you may soon have the power to do that. You have the only authority backed by this," the soldier said, pointing at his uniform. "Until Kansas becomes a state, the only authority here is federals. The governor has us at his command, but the command must be given."

"I hope that won't be necessary," Denver said. "But you are right. Both sides need to know it can be done."

In early January, James Denver told Kansas what to expect from him as the new governor of the territory.

His speech said he was prepared for the worst: "It would be unreasonable to expect anyone occupying this position to escape misrepresentation and abuse." But he refused to believe there was "no one willing to listen to the voice of reason."

Speaking directly to Jim Lane, John Brown and the Border Ruffians, he said, "There are some violent men who have assumed to speak by authority for the people at large." Following them, he warned, was a path to "bloodshed anarchy and confusion."

Denver offered an open hand and pledged to "protect all citizens in the exercise of their just rights," and "treat every one alike." Those rights included free and fair elections.

And then came the fist: "If civil power is insufficient for this purpose, the troops of the United States should be employed."

---

57   Before he became known as an abolitionist, Lane told friends he was only pretending to be anti-slavery to get support from Free-Staters. He sponsored a bill that was a Kansas version of the pro-slavery Runaway Slave Act—demonstrating his chameleon morals.

He had the authority to use the US Army at Fort Leavenworth, and he was not afraid to use it. His proclamation was a direct attack on Lane, who had been appointed general of the territorial militia formed by the illegitimate proslavery legislature. Denver was daring Lane and his posse of raiders and bushwhackers to challenge the US Army at Fort Leavenworth, Fort Riley and Fort Scott. Lane had to back down. His "army" of looters, thieves and back-shooters would have been crushed.

Denver's goal was simple. He would not take sides on slavery—except on the side of the law. Wherever laws were broken, they would be enforced like a hammer on an anvil. Wherever elections were held, they would be honest and legal—nobody would be intimidated or threatened for voting their conscience. There would be no more ballot-box stuffing by outsiders from Missouri or Massachusetts—no more intimidation by abolitionists or border ruffians.

He would bring peace to Kansas, and he wanted everyone in the territory to know that it would be better to do it "through the ballot box" rather than "by the sword."

He pledged "severe penalties on persons engaged in election fraud." On one occasion, he visited a Kansas town on the violent Missouri border that was one trigger tug away from a war over rigged elections. He ordered everyone to line up on the town square behind the candidate of their choice. The outcome was obvious. The election was free, transparent and clean.

Jim Lane continued to goad Governor Denver with vituperative, insulting letters to Kansas newspapers; they were "full of brimstone," one newspaper said. Lane called Denver "a calumniator, perjurer, tyrant and pet appointee of the oligarchical administration." One paper said Lane challenged Denver to a duel.

But Denver refused to be baited. He was through with dueling and had nothing to prove. He ignored Lane, which infuriated the radical Jayhawker (antislavery raiders) all the more. When General Lane sent one of his commanders to recruit militia members in the capital, Governor Denver publicly warned that only he had the authority to raise and command troops. Anyone joining or supporting Lane would face the wrath of the governor. Lane and his recruiter backed down.

And that was the end of Lane's reign of lawlessness and terror—at least while Denver ran the territory.

Governor Denver was just as quick to punish proslavery outlaws, many of whom were not residents of Kansas.

By refusing to join either side, he earned the respect of both.

President Buchanan tried to bribe Kansas with extravagant promises to give the new state 23 million acres of land if it would ratify the Lecompton Constitution. The bribery failed. Given a second chance to vote on the Lecompton Constitution with free and fair elections, Kansas rejected the slavery-forever farce in a landslide. Buchanan was humiliated.

Denver had prevented a civil war in Kansas, but it was only delayed for the rest of the nation—a cork in a bottle that was doomed to explode. The terrible Civil War that followed would be known as "Buchanan's War"[58] because of his stubborn stupidity. And John Brown would light the fuse by seizing the federal arsenal at Harper's Ferry, Virginia, in his fanatical crusade to incite a slave rebellion.[59]

Newspapers reported that Governor Denver served "faithfully, fearlessly and impartially…. He has brought order, almost, out of chaos, he has inculcated a spirit of loyalty and good feeling among the great body of people."[60]

Denver often was discouraged, and his friends in Washington wrote to offer support. Indiana Senator Thomas Hendricks wrote: "I think you have adopted the right course with Lane. I hope you have no further difficulty, but if you do, give him a thrashing." He said Denver's job was the "most difficult…in America."[61]

Jacob Thompson, secretary of the interior, wrote: "The character you are destined to win for yourself by discharging the duties and

---

58   One more reason Buchanan has earned his rating as one of the worst presidents in American history.

59   Brown was hanged on December 2, 1859—the eve of the Civil War—after he was convicted of treason, murder and inciting a slave insurrection. The man who led US Marines to stop Brown at Harper's Ferry was Col. Robert E. Lee. John Brown, the Charles Manson of his day, became a martyr to the abolitionists and their partisan newspapers.

60   *The Kansas Herald*, March 1858. Barns, George C. *Denver, the Man*. 1949.

61   Kenneth Spencer Research Library Archival Collections, University of Kansas.

bringing order out of confusion in enforcing the law and bringing personal security to an agitated people will be worth far more in the future than any personal sacrifices you make."[62]

But as the hot and violent summer came to an end, Denver had seen enough of Kansas. He wrote to ask President Buchanan for permission to resign so he could go home to Wilmington and see his wife. Buchanan reluctantly agreed. Denver left office on October 10, 1858, after serving nearly 11 months of the most savage chapter of "Bleeding Kansas" history.

As he reunited with his family in Wilmington, Denver's friend and acting governor of the Kansas Territory, Hugh S. Walsh, wrote him letters to describe the quick deterioration of the relative peace that Denver had established.

A month later, after hearing from Walsh, Denver wrote to a Kansas newspaper to warn that violence had returned.[63] This time, it was the Free Stater abolitionist Jayhawkers who were using their new elected power to take revenge on the defeated proslavery Kansans.

DENVER LEAVES, VIOLENCE RETURNS

"In Doniphan County," Denver wrote, "an effort was made to assassinate the gentlemen who were elected to the Legislature… and although they escaped for their lives, they were plundered of their property and their houses burned."

He said Free State officials looked the other way while ballot boxes were stuffed and votes were destroyed. Outrageous acts were committed in two more counties by a band of Free State outlaws, Denver wrote, "which was to drive a farmer from his home on pain of death, then take the ladies of his family, strip off all their clothes and make them walk backwards and forwards for their amusement."

The town of Fort Scott had been set on fire by an outlaw gang of abolitionist Jayhawkers, while volleys of rifle fire were poured into the town to prevent the residents from putting out the flames.

---

62   Ibid.

63   Letter from Hugh Walsh, October 28, 1858. Kenneth Spencer Research Library Archival Collections, University of Kansas.

Denver also blamed the "hired reporters of Eastern newspapers" who were among the most active in the outlaw gangs.

"The Proslavery Party have abandoned the contest. The Free State men have a majority in every county in the Territory, and they have the sheriff and all other local officers in all but two or three counties and there is no county in which the sheriff cannot preserve the peace *if he desires to do so.*"

But local officials did not desire to preserve the peace. And President Buchanan seemed to encourage the chaos by giving public offices to the worst murderers.

From a report in the *White Cloud Kansas Chief* in 1860:

> S.W. Clark murdered Thomas Barbour during the Kansas War by shooting him the back. He was made a Purser in the Navy.
>
> James Gardiner, abettor of murder, was made Postmaster at Lawrence.
>
> Frederick Emery, who murdered Phillips at Leavenworth and headed the band which murdered a poor German laborer and murdered and scalped (another man) was given a post in the Ogden land office.
>
> J.S. Murphy, who murdered and scalped a man was made agent of the Potawatomi Indians.
>
> Rush Elmore, who tried to assassinate a public official, was made a judge of the United States Court in Kansas.[64]

"Licentiousness, profligacy and dishonesty have never prevented any applicant for office from getting the favor he sought of Mr. Buchanan," the paper said.

And so it went. As soon as James Denver left the territory, the fragile peace he had enforced by fair and tough enforcement of the law, was torn apart like a tent in a tornado.

---

64   "The President that Rewards Murder," White Cloud Kansas Chief, August 30, 1860.Letter from Hugh Walsh, October 28, 1858. Kenneth Spencer Research Library Archival Collections, University of Kansas.

*

While James Denver packed his wagon in Lecompton to leave Kansas for Washington and Ohio, he saw a group of men who were passing through town on their way to western Kansas Territory (now Colorado), where it was rumored that gold was discovered at Pike's Peak in Arapaho County. The previous officers in that county had run off, and Denver needed new ones. So, on the spot, he appointed the men as officers of Arapaho County.

When they got to a place called Cherry Creek, they sat down to choose a name for the new city they laid out. It was only a few shacks, shanties, lean-tos and tents, but they had big dreams. Sitting around a campfire that warmed them on the outside while whiskey warmed them from within, they tossed around various names. Eldorado sounded good to profit from the Gold Rush. So did Eureka. No and no. Not enough votes.

They tried Excelsior. Too grandiose. Marshall. Too common. Jefferson, Columbia, Mineral and Mountain City were all suggested. None of them fit.

Finally, Gen. William Larimer, a claim jumper and big talker, suggested: "Why not name our city after the popular, respected territorial governor who finally tamed Bleeding Kansas?" It was part flattery and part strategy. Latimer figured Governor Denver would surely make the new town named after him the seat of Arapaho County in the Kansas Territory.[65]

The vote was unanimous. Denver City was born. By the time Colorado became a state in 1876, it was simply Denver—one of the great cities of the West, named after a man from Wilmington, Ohio.

The city of Denver did better than the founders hoped. It became the capital of the new state. Meanwhile, the man who gave his name to the city was already on his way to Washington, where he would be reappointed as Commissioner of Indian Affairs.

As James Denver told it in his typically sparse, modest way, "They

---

65   There are many versions of the naming of Denver. This one fits with the story told by James W. Denver, and matches the version used by the City of Denver.

laid out a town just below the mouth of Cherry Creek and did me the honor to name it after me. This is about the whole story."

He visited "his" city in 1875 and 1883. He was impressed with its beauty and progress, but underwhelmed by the city's appreciation. "Our reception, on arriving, was as cool as mine had been eight years before," he wrote in 1883. "There was nobody to receive us or to give us information. The city authorities did not put in any appearance, and we received no attention more than any stranger received. ... I thought there were not many people in Denver City who cared much about me."[66]

But back in 1858, as he left Kansas for Washington, Denver had high hopes to see his wife again in Wilmington and leave the chaos of "Bleeding Kansas" behind. But as it turned out, the bush fire that started in Kansas would soon rage across the nation and he would be swept up in it again.

After Denver made Kansas safe and free, it was admitted as the 34th state on January 19, 1861. Only three months later, the first shots were fired in the Civil War. And James Denver was touched once more by his comet "that never lets me stay in one place." He was off to war again.

AUGUST 15, 1861

"I had made up my mind to abandon public life altogether and devote myself to my family, but now it comes up in a new form," Denver wrote to his wife.

He had supported his good friend Stephen Douglas in the 1860 presidential election. In fact, it was Douglas who invited Denver to name a new state.

Denver was visiting Senator Douglas in Washington after leaving Kansas when Douglas asked him to suggest a name for a new Western territory to be included in his bill.

"Montana," Denver suggested.

When Douglas asked him what it meant, the veteran of the Mexican War replied, "It's Spanish for 'mountainous country.'"

---

66   The city of Denver showed its appreciation later by putting a stained-glass portrait of James W. Denver in its capitol.

Douglas agreed that it fit, and the name was written into his bill to create the state of Montana.[67]

Denver was a Democrat. President Lincoln was a Republican. The parties were as far apart as Mississippi and Massachusetts. But in 1861, the first year of the war, Lincoln surprised Denver by making him a brigadier general in the Union Army in spite of his support of Douglas in the 1860 election.

The honor was unsought and unexpected, but Denver welcomed the adventure. His only regret was that it would take him away from Louise and his home in Wilmington—"Rombach Place," the cloud-white mansion on Locust Street, named for his wife's family and built by her father.

In those days, a political leader who had battle experience, such as Denver, was as valuable as a division of infantry. Political leaders were able to use their influence and connections to recruit soldiers and organize volunteer regiments. And veterans who had "seen the elephant" and been to war were scarce. Some of the best commanders in the Mexican War joined the Confederates.[68] The Union Army had only 16,000 men when the war began, with only 1,000 officers—and very few had any formal training.

James W. Denver photo by Mathew Brady, 1861.

The army knew Denver would be most valuable in Kansas, which was erupting with new violence from "Jayhawkers," whom Denver called just "another name for horse-thieves and all sorts of robbers." So he was sent to Leavenworth City, to do again what he had done so

---

67   Barns, George C. *Denver, the Man.* 1949.

68   Confederate General Albert Sidney Johnston, killed at the Battle of Shiloh in April 1862, was acknowledged to be the best commander on both sides. He was crushing the Union Army led by General Ulysses Grant on the first day of battle, until he was shot in the leg and bled to death. Grant rallied on the second day and routed Johnston's second in command, Gen. P. T. Beauregard. After Johnston died, it was said, "The South never smiled again."

well in 1857-58—lay down the law like a thunderbolt.

In Kansas, he found, "The war is carried on here with a fierceness and recklessness heretofore known only to savages. All the worst passions of human nature are brought out. Murder and wholesale robbery are of everyday occurrence on the border."

But just as he got control of the situation he was transferred east, to Wheeling, Virginia (now West Virginia), to serve under Gen. William Rosecrans, who became a good friend.

Behind the scenes, his old nemesis James Lane was urging President Lincoln to keep Denver out of Kansas, so Lane could rule that lawless territory himself.

On September 23, 1861, Lane led a band of cutthroat raiders to the outskirts of Osceola, Missouri. As the townspeople scurried for safety, Lane's Jayhawkers rode through with guns blazing, throwing torches onto the bone-dry wooden stores and houses. They brutally sacked, looted and burned the little border town, and executed at least nine prisoners.

Lane's extreme cruelty, murder and theft drew the attention of his commander, Union Maj. Gen. Henry Halleck, who condemned Lane for causing a backlash that turned pro-Union men in Missouri into Confederates.[69]

Retaliation came in 1863 when William Quantrill and his "Bushwhackers" raided Kansas and burned most of Lawrence—the headquarters of abolitionists—killing 150. Lane narrowly escaped by hiding in a cornfield while his home was burned down.

With blood and fire, Kansas had distilled itself to the most extreme elements that split the nation. Lane won election as the first US senator from Kansas and ingratiated himself with President Lincoln, finagling an appointment as a brigadier general.

A friend warned Denver about Lane in a letter, "He hates you with more intensity than ever."[70]

---

69   The Western novel *Gone to Texas* tells the story of the raid by Jim Lane. It was made into a movie, "The Outlaw Josey Wales," starring Clint Eastwood. In the story, Wales finds his wife and child murdered and his home burned by Lane and his Jayhawker raiders. Carter, Forrest. *The Rebel Outlaw*, Josey Wales. 1973.

70   Barns, George C. *Denver, the Man.* 1949.

Lincoln favored Lane, but the commander of the Western Theater of War, General Halleck, supported Denver. So Denver was bounced back to Kansas to suppress Indian attacks, using his knowledge of the tribes as Commissioner of Indian Affairs. But after just a month, Lane pulled strings again and Denver was sent to the Army of the Tennessee at Pittsburgh Landing. He arrived just three weeks after the Battle of Shiloh in Southern Tennessee, on the Mississippi border.

"It seems that Lane has at last molded the President to his will," Denver wrote to his wife, Louise.

Denver arrived on May 2 and was put in command of the Fifth Division under Major General William T. Sherman. Denver had seen death, bloody battles and scorched earth in Mexico. He had heard the trumpets and drums of war. But Shiloh was something else altogether—an orchestra of destruction. Steamboats lined the banks of Pittsburgh Landing like suckling piglets, unloading men and supplies and taking away wounded soldiers, who seemed endless.

The stench of death was a wet fog that saturated food, clothing and the air he breathed. Horribly mangled men waited forlornly for help. Burial details pushed thousands of decomposing, bloated corpses into huge pits: horses and mules in one pit; sons, brothers, husbands and fathers in another—when it was possible to tell them apart.

He was surprised to see doctors and nurses from the Hamilton County Sanitation Commission of Cincinnati aiding wounded men from both sides of the battle. Those who could be moved were put aboard the riverboats and shipped back up the Tennessee River to Paducah, Kentucky, where the Tennessee joined the Ohio River. From there, the riverboats made the long journey northeast past Louisville to Cincinnati, where the Little Miami Railroad took them to a hospital hastily set up at Camp Dennison, near Indian Hill.

Denver found the haze of confusion nearly as thick as the stink of death. General Ulysses S. Grant, who had finally won the battle and driven the Confederates back to Corinth, Mississippi, had been relieved of command by Halleck. The Confederate attack had caught Grant by surprise as he sipped coffee over breakfast in a comfortable mansion seven miles from Pittsburgh Landing, across the flooding Tennessee River from his camped army. Grant's dereliction of duty had nearly lost the battle. And now he was demoralized, given nothing to do, but not allowed to transfer. He was left to wander around like a ghost. His good friend General Sherman may have saved the Union by talking General Grant out of resigning from the military.[71]

General Halleck, who was so quick to replace Grant, took every opportunity to hesitate. Steeped in book battles as an instructor known as "Old Brains" at West Point, he was unfit for battlefield command, where theory is blown to pieces by the shrapnel of reality. He dithered, finally moving out toward Corinth a month after the battle, as if the Union, not the Confederates, had been beaten.

It took him three more weeks to travel the same road the Confederates had covered in three days. The goal was Corinth, "The Crossroads of the Confederacy." It was the place where railroad lines met—the supply arteries of the Confederate Army.

General Grant wrote in his memoirs, "If we obtained possession of Corinth, the enemy would have no railroad for the transportation of armies or supplies…. It was the great strategic position in the West between the Tennessee and the Mississippi rivers and between Nashville and Vicksburg."

Grant saw the urgency. Halleck saw only risk. Each day's march inched a few miles closer to Corinth, 20 miles south. He stopped every afternoon and put his army to work building an elaborate defensive perimeter, as if the whipped Confederates would rise out of the ground at any moment. The army moved like a glacier, pushing a wall of logs and earth in front of itself to guard against attacks that never came.

THE SIEGE OF CORINTH

Denver caught up to his new commander, General Sherman, less than five miles north of Corinth on May 14 and saw his first action the same day. As he rode out on his new horse to inspect pickets (sentries) a mile ahead of the camp on the main Corinth Road, he

---

71   Would the Union have won the war without Grant? Perhaps. But there was a reason Lincoln valued him so highly. "I can't spare that man," he said. "He fights." When Halleck and others who were jealous of Grant's success accused him of drunkenness, Lincoln asked his staff to find out what kind of whiskey he was drinking so he could send a barrel of it to every general in the army.

came to a bridge, where the Confederates kept up a steady fire at the Union scouts. The crackling music of war was in his ears again.

"General Sherman got tired of this, and we went forward with two field pieces to drive them away," Denver wrote to his wife. "My horse behaved splendidly, although not more than forty or fifty yards from the guns, and the first time he had been tried."

It was typical of Denver to write about his horse while leaving out his own "boresome" brush with death.

The fighting around Corinth surged and ebbed for a week, sometimes intense. Hundreds were killed and wounded in a skirmish on May 9. The heavy rain that had turned the Shiloh battlefield into a churned porridge of mud and blood returned that week. Roads were slippery and treacherous. The infantry sank over their boots and wagons got mired to the hubs. Bridges were washed out.

But the Union Army of about 120,000 slowly constricted the Confederate supply lines like a huge python, blocking railroads and roads. About 112,000 reinforced Confederates in Corinth had built miles of rifle pits, artillery batteries and fortifications around the little town, moving tons of earth that was packed into big handmade wicker baskets that were stacked around cannons and rifle pits to stop enemy bullets and cannon shells.[72]

Inside the town, Corinth's poor water supply that adequately served only 1,200 residents was sucked dry by more than 100,000 thirsty Confederate soldiers. It shrank to a brackish, foul trickle. Wells went dry and the water that could be drawn was almost poisonous. After a rain, the most desperate men drank from gray puddles over shallow graves where horses, mules and men had been buried. Many fell sick with typhoid fever and dysentery and died.[73]

Colonel Manning Ferguson Force of Cincinnati wrote about Corinth after the war: "The surface waters, always unwholesome, were now poisonous. Many died every day."

---

72   Gabions, from the Italian for "big cage," dated back to the 16th century. A more sophisticated version is still used by the US Army today to protect operating bases.

73   The Confederates lost more men to sickness in Corinth than the nearly 3,000 killed and missing in battle at Shiloh. By one estimate, almost half of the Confederate Army camped at Corinth fell sick.

Confederate Commander Gen. P. T. Beauregard saw that the Union siege of Corinth could only end in disaster for his men and began making plans for one of the cleverest strategic retreats in the war.

*

When General Denver went into action again on May 17, he was in the thick of a battle against a Confederate brigade of more than 1,000 men. His three brigades of Ohio infantry, veterans of Shiloh,[74] were on the right of General Sherman's Fifth Division, which anchored the right flank of the Union Army. In front of them was an intersection of three roads shaped like an upside down "Y." As their pickets and scouts approached it, they were hit by withering fire from Confederates who were hidden behind the walls of a double-log house at the intersection—Russell's House.

The Confederates had cut loopholes in the walls to snipe at anyone who approached. As the Union troops took cover, General Sherman was ordered to "Drive the rebels from the house."

"Resistance was more obstinate than at any previous encounter," wrote Colonel Force. As a member of the Cincinnati Literary Society who served at Shiloh and Corinth in the 20th Ohio Infantry under Maj. Gen. Lew Wallace's Third Division, he had "Seen the elephant" many times and knew a tough battle when he saw it.[75]

At 8 a.m., Sherman led his men out quietly through the woods. Two teams of soldiers manhandled two 20-pounder Parrot rifled cannons, weighing more than one ton each, into concealed positions on the fringe of the woods where they could blow the walls of the Russell's House to sawdust. Denver was ordered to attack from the right, while Sherman hit the middle.

When they reached their position, General Denver ordered three companies of skirmishers—about 300 men—to advance on the log house. As the Confederates spotted Denver's men, the rip and pop of

---

74   The 53rd, the 57th and the 77th Ohio Infantries.

75   *Campaigns of the Civil War: Force, M.F. From Fort Henry to Corinth*, 1881. Among 41 generals buried in Cincinnati's Spring Grove Cemetery, General Force is the only recipient of the Medal of Honor.

rifle fire erupted, first like a pine log crackling in a fireplace, then like a bonfire, steady and roaring.

Denver stayed in the saddle and guided his horse through the narrow paths made by his men as they struggled and cursed their way through dense briars and thickets that seemed determined to grab them and hold them back. They were drenched in sweat and bleeding from thorns when they emerged from the woods.

Out in the open, the steady roar of gunfire was joined by a new note in the symphony of battle: Lead shot buzzed around them like a swarm of fat, deadly bees. But Denver remained on horseback. His six-feet-two frame presented a big, inviting target, but he wanted to stay high enough to see the whole action. It was the way of commanders during the Civil War to lead by courageous example.

As they said in those days, the battle was as savage as a meat axe. The Mississippians, led by Confederate Brig. Gen. James R. Chalmers, poured lead on the advancing men in Denver's brigade.

"The enemy stubbornly disputed every inch of the ground, but we steadily advanced," General Denver wrote later.

As they ducked and dashed for cover, there was the dull thud of lead hitting flesh and men fell in the Union lines, wounded or killed, while others took their places and furiously rammed home bullets, bit powder cartridges and poured powder into their muskets.

Then suddenly the rattle and crash of small arms fire was drowned out by huge blast that sent shockwaves across the open fields, making the grass bow and sway. The Parrot guns had opened up from the edge of the woods, hitting the log house at point-blank range. Their deep thunder made the men's big .60 caliber rifles sound feeble. The cannons sledgehammered the house with every shot, tearing holes in the thick log walls, sending jagged splinters in a flesh-tearing hurricane through the crowded rooms.

The Parrot was one of the most advanced weapons of its time. Grooves in the barrel spun the 20-pound projectile to make it more accurate and heavier than smoothbore cannons. The Parrot could reliably hit targets from more than a mile, delivering shrapnel rounds, fused shot or solid shot with a muzzle velocity of 1,250 feet per second. For Confederate snipers in Russell's House, it was deafening, deadly and terrifying.

**Confederate assault on Battery Robinette during
the second Battle of Corinth in October, 1862.**
The Century Illustrated Monthly Magazine, 1886.

"A quick, rapid fire quickly demolished the house," Colonel Force recalled.

As the cannons opened fire, that was the signal to advance. General Denver and his men ran forward across treeless fields. As they approached the house, the cannons ceased fire, and the men overran the wrecked house. They found it empty, except for a dozen Confederate corpses, some severely mangled by cannon shot.

General Denver lost seven men killed and 20 wounded. Among them were soldiers from his hometown of Wilmington and nearby New Vienna—young men whose faces and families he knew well.

Now, beyond the thick woods, they were only about a mile from the Confederate lines, within range of the enemy's cannons. They dug in, tended to their wounded and dead, and slept uneasily that night, expecting a counterattack. It came the next morning, when the Confederates poured out of their lines and drove General Denver and his men back.

General Sherman sent reinforcements, and the Confederates were driven back again to their lines in a furious firefight. This time, they stayed. Sherman's mission to "Drive the Rebels from the house" was done. But as they dug in again—their seventh camp since arriving—

Denver's men were perilously close to the Confederate lines and artillery, screened only by woods and a swamp.

As General Halleck thought about cautiously considering the possibility of a proposing a plan to take Corinth—then reconsidered and thought again—Confederate General Beauregard moved. Starting on May 27, he gave the order to evacuate.

As his frontline troops quietly pulled back, troops stationed in town made a commotion of cheering, as Beauregard ordered locomotives to move back and forth on the tracks to create an illusion that trains were arriving with fresh troops to reinforce his cheering soldiers. It worked. Halleck was grateful for any excuse to dither, and eagerly believed the odds against him were overwhelming.

Meanwhile, the Confederates escaped the noose of the siege and pulled out to fight another day. Halleck's chance to capture Beauregard's army and prevent a second battle for Corinth was lost.

On May 30, explosions and smoke rose from Corinth, as General Beauregard burned the supplies he could not take with him. When Union troops finally arrived to investigate, they found 3,000 sick and wounded Confederate soldiers in the town. General Beauregard had escaped with his army aboard trains loaded with tons of valuable supplies. The Confederates would return the following October to fight one of the bloodiest battles of the war at Corinth.[76]

Denver wrote to Louise, "Many buildings had been burned by the enemy upon evacuation…The heads of all the (Union) columns had entered the rebel lines about the same time and there was some rather foolish clamor for the first honors (to enter the town), but in fact there was no honor in the event, Beauregard had made a clean retreat to the south."

General Sherman commended his generals, including Denver. "Every officer and solider who lent his aid has just reason to be proud of his part."

---

76   The second battle took place the following October 3-4, when the Confederates returned with a healthy, larger army led by Gen. Earl Van Dorn. It was one of the bloodiest battles of the war. More than a thousand Confederates and Union men were killed and missing, and thousands more wounded. Gen. US Grant commanded in the second battle, which was won by the Union.

After Corinth was taken, General Denver and his Ohio brigades were sent to repair bridges and railroad tracks that had been torn up by Union cavalry to trap and starve the Confederates. He must have been good at it, because he spent most of the remainder of his service on the same duty.

Throughout that thankless work, he was harassed by politicians in Washington. The spider in the middle of that political web was his nemesis Senator Lane. With financial problems at home in Wilmington, and disgust over Lincoln's Emancipation Proclamation—which he believed was unconstitutional—Denver submitted his resignation in March 1863.[77]

"Well, I feel easier now that it is done," he wrote to Louise, "and yet it is impossible for me to escape the sharp pang of regret at parting with men whom I have been so long associated…. It is hard to leave them behind, but there are others who have the first and stronger claim on me, and these must be answered by love and affection."

Louise was waiting for him with his children,[78] including his new son James William Denver, born the previous December. He spent a year in Wilmington, then returned to Washington to join a law firm in 1864. Among his cases was a lawsuit by the Choctaw Tribe against the US Government, claiming the Indians had been swindled out of ten million acres in Mississippi by a drunken, crooked Indian agent. The case went all the way to the US Supreme Court, where the Choctaws were awarded $2.8 million.[79]

Denver served as president of the Mexican Veterans Association from 1878 until he died in 1892, and persuaded Congress to increase their paltry pensions.

---

77   Many agreed with James Denver that the president exceeded his authority and unconstitutionally bypassed Congress. As much as Denver agreed with the intent of the Emancipation Proclamation, he believed slavery should be ended through the law and the Constitution. Denver was especially worried by Lincoln's suspension of basic constitutional rights such as habeas corpus (due process protection from arbitrary imprisonment). He said Lincoln's "usurpation of power" presented "a great danger of the free government given us by our fathers being turned into a military despotism."

78   His children were Catherine St. Clair, 1861; James William, 1863; Mary Louise, 1868; and Mathew Rombach, 1870.

79   About $57 million in 2025.

In 1870, Denver ran for Congress in Ohio's 6th District, representing Brown, Clermont, Clinton, Fayette and Highland counties, but was defeated by a Republican.

He ran again in 1886 in Ohio's 12th District and lost again in the overwhelmingly Republican district. During that campaign, Edward Gilbert rose from the grave to haunt him again, almost 35 years after the duel. Even friends of Gilbert defended Denver against the scurrilous claims of his opponents, and a San Francisco newspaper published an editorial testifying to his honor and honesty when he served as a California state senator.

"It is a well-known fact that General Denver was offered $40,000 not to vote (for a fraudulent bill), and simply to absent himself when it was called up for the final reading. His answer was a scathing denunciation of the whole scheme."[80]

His speech was so effective, the bill was rejected. James Denver's true north was always honor.[81]

Mathew Brady photo of James W. Denver during the Civil War, 1863.

---

80   It was not the first or last time that James Denver made powerful enemies by following his own moral code of honor.

81   The newspaper didn't mention it, but as state senator James Denver also pushed through a law that gave property rights to women in California for the first time,

'HONORABLE PATRIOT AND SAGE'

When he fell ill with kidney problems and died in Washington on August 9, 1892, at age 75, both Republicans and Democrats lowered their flags to half-mast in Ohio.

His family was touched and proud to receive a letter from the city of Denver, Colorado:

"The great West laments with the East the close of his long and honorable career. He was both patriot and sage. He was a pioneer who saw and foretold the mighty possibilities of the West, and his name will be held in grateful remembrance as long as the proud city which bears his name shall endure."

He was buried in the family plot at Sugar Grove Cemetery in Wilmington.

In 1943, a Liberty Ship[82] was named the *SS James W. Denver*. It was sunk near Portugal on its maiden voyage. The crew escaped to lifeboats. One man died of exposure.

James Denver's life can be described by simple words that meant something in his time: courage, faith, grace, humility and duty. Above all, honor—which today seems as old fashioned as dueling pistols.

As Denver looked back on his life before he died in 1892, his honor was unblemished. He had fought the good fight, run the race to the end. He wished he had been present with his children during the years he was held hostage by politics in Washington, but he had done his best to impart his faith and philosophy to them in letters. He urged them to learn the satisfaction of hard work, to seek and do whatever honor demanded, to be courageous, strong in their faith and faithful to their families.

He revealed his frustrations and his ideals in his letter to Louise in 1863, when he was sick of war, pestered by political schemes and homesick for Wilmington.

---

82 Hastily built cargo ships that were rushed into production to move supplies and troops to Europe and the Pacific. Nearly 3,000 of the ships were built during the war, at a rate of three ships every two days. Because of the hurried pace of construction, the ships had problems such as mechanical failures and hull and deck cracks. The USS James W. Denver fell behind her convoy on the way to Casablanca because of overheated engine bearings and was torpedoed by a German U-Boat.

"I have become weary of this eternal—this lifelong—struggle for the public good, when met—as I have been at every step—by ingratitude on the part of the public to whom I have been a most disinterested and devoted servant, and the denunciations and enmities of the scoundrels whom I have so often thwarted in their rascalities."

Those "scoundrels" and "rascalities" included the crooked Jayhawker Jim Lane, political opponents in Ohio and Washington, and dozens of wild-eyed partisan newspaper editors who twisted Denver's courage and honor into bizarre scarecrows that mocked the truth.

After all he endured, he could hardly be blamed for saying he had no intention to ever seek "anything to do with public affairs again." But then he relented, perhaps recognizing in himself the man who could not resist the comet of destiny that beckoned him to new adventures:

"A man may find himself in a manner compelled to act almost against his will. I will not, therefore, pledge myself not to do my duty as a citizen or as the protector of my family."

Compelled to act almost against his will could have been a distant echo of that dawn in Sacramento in 1852, when he tried to spare the life of Edward Gilbert, then shot him to save his own life.

Nobody can say what Edward Gilbert may have become. But the United States should be grateful that James W. Denver walked away that day. He was a giant in his time. And he still casts a long shadow over American history today.

THREE

SNAKE IN THE GARDEN

The mystery that shook Shaker Village

Whitewater Shaker cemetery.

1877

1852   1878   1937   2008

A COUNTRY GRAVEYARD

The grass is mowed like any cemetery. A picket fence wearing fresh white paint lines a two-lane road that cuts like a causeway, connecting farmhouse islands in a sea of corn and soybeans.

But there is something odd in this rural burial ground: There are nearly two acres of empty space. There could be room for hundreds of graves, but not even two dozen headstones huddle along the rear fence in the shadows of a looming forest, as if they are too shy or too ashamed to be seen in the sunlight.

They tilt and lean like crooked teeth, stained by mold and time. More than 150 years of snow, wind and bleaching summer sun has almost erased the etched words and dates the way an incoming tide washes away names written in the sand. What's left puts entire lifetimes in a dash:

JOHN HOBART: 1792—1866
Our Mother SUSAN RUBUSH: 1804—1878
JOHN EASTBROOKS: 1787—1865

The dates when death came calling begin just before the Civil War, then abruptly stop in the early 1900s.

Two grave markers are blank, jagged pieces of slate stabbed in the ground like broken knife blades. If there were names carved there, time has erased them. The pair is set apart, as if shunned by the modest huddle of markers along the fence.

In the center of all that empty grass is a square monument, much bigger than the rest of the weathered, round-topped, white marble headstones. The answer to at least one mystery is written there in raised letters on the stained, gray granite:

Erected by the Society of Shakers
White Water Village
An Order of Celibate Christian Communists
To Honor the Memory of
The Members Whose Mortal Remains
Are Interred in This Lot
1827—1916
--
They That Have Done Good Unto The Resurrection of
Life Whose Abiding Place is Immortality

Visitors are rare. There are no fresh flowers, no flags to honor veterans, no gaudy plastic roses or other signs that anyone is left who cares. Time has hurried by without a nod, like the speeding traffic beyond the fence gate. But the few who do stop to read the inscription must pause in disbelief and read it again. Celibate communists?

Each grave has a story to tell. A life lived, full of sorrows, joys, hard work, dreams, adventures, illness, an allotted number of sunrises and sunsets, victories and defeats, love, faith, grief, mistakes and perseverance.

But the most interesting tale is about what's missing: The story of two women who are not buried here.

SHAME AND SUICIDE
WEDNESDAY, APRIL 25, 1877

It was a lovely late April morning. Bill Reany had one booted foot on the edge of his desk, his chair tilted back on two legs as he regaled a young, fresh-from-the-garden Cincinnati copper with the tale of a counterfeiting case.

"There were two of the mutts passing funny money," he recalled. "We nabbed one and sent him to the Ohio Penitentiary in Columbus, where he is now dining on stale bread and rainwater. But the other skilmalink dusted off. We caught up to him at the Ohio River just in time to see him throw something overboard from a small boat."

"Did you pinch him?" the young cop asked eagerly.

"No, without the counterfeiting plates there was not enough evidence, so says the boss. But I marked the spot up here," Reany tapped the side of his head, right where the gray was creeping up from his temples, "and as soon as the river went down to a trickle, as it always does in August, there they were, sticking out of the mud like tombstones—plates to print play-money fives, tens, fifties and hundreds—"

"Detective Reany!"

It was the boss, Captain Halliday, shouting from the broom closet he called an office. "I need you to take yourself off to the Farmer's Hotel quick as a bride's wink. Bad business there this morning." Halliday's Irish lilt made every statement sound like a question.

"The one on Colerain?"

"No," the captain said, emerging in his gartered shirtsleeves, his thick black mustache dusted with sugar from a German pastry. More of the snow flurry of sugar had sprinkled his vest where his ample paunch made a shelf as he sat at his desk. "The other one at the corner of Court and Race. They sent word there are two bodies on the third floor, room 21."

"What do we know?"

"Two women. Checked in last night. Take Fritz with you," Capt. Halliday said, pointing his pipestem at the young cop.

Reany stood and grabbed his bowler hat and coat. "Let's go, Fritz," he said.

"Sir, my name is Dietrich Muller," the cop protested, rushing to keep up.

"I will call you whatever you like as long as you keep up, Fritz."

At the Farmer's Hotel, Reany paused and looked up at the third floor of the brick building. The ornate woodwork needed a coat of fresh white paint. The windows were hazed with grime and coal soot. This homely hotel was no swank palace like the Burnett House or the Hotel Gibson. But it was named the Farmer's Hotel because that's who used it: farmers bringing pigs to slaughter and produce to Findlay Market. They only wanted a clean bed for the night, free of lice if possible, and a hearty breakfast at a reasonable price—meaning cheap.

As the detective stood there looking up, Muller shifted from foot to foot and finally asked, "Aren't we going up?"

"You will see more than enough soon enough," Reany replied, each word like a counted coin. He continued to gaze up, then turned to Muller and said, "Come along, Fritz."

The front desk was empty where the desk clerk should have been. The lobby was also empty except for the smell of cooking—sauerkraut, potatoes and pork, Reany guessed. They walked up the dark, wood-paneled stairs and found room 21 easily. It was the one with the small knot of people in the hallway, going in and out with an unnatural combination of jerky haste and indecision—as if they needed to do something quickly but didn't know what. They looked like the same crowd that gathered around every accident or crime scene, stretching their necks and wringing their hands.

Reany casually used two fingers of his left hand to pull back his jacket lapel and reveal the badge on his vest. The little crowd parted gratefully and he entered the room.

A nervous man in a black suit came forward to introduce himself as George Schiller,[83] proprietor. Reany nodded and turned to Muller. "Go downstairs and make sure nobody leaves."

Muller was staring as if hypnotized at the bed across the little room, and had to be grabbed by the arm and told again. "Fritz! Go

---

83   "Shame and Suicide: A Shakeress and Her Daughter Die Together," *The Cincinnati Enquirer*, April 26, 1877.

downstairs and make sure nobody leaves without they first provide a name and address."

The young copper came out of his trance looking dejected, but reluctantly left.

Reany spoke up to the people in the room, "Please wait outside. All of you except Mr. Schiller and the doctor."

"Dr. Forschbeimer," the man supplied.[84] He was holding the nearest woman's arm near the wrist, using his other hand to prop open her eyelid as he looked intently at her pupils through a pair of spectacles perched on his nose.

Reany took in the scene. Two women were on the bed. The one being examined was so pale she looked almost blue at the temples—a stark contrast against long hair as black as a raven's wing. She was about five feet five, he guessed. She wore a very simple homespun dress the color of faded cornflowers. The dress was somehow familiar to Reany, but he couldn't place it. He noted that it was identical to the dress worn by the smaller woman on the bed next to her.

As he drew closer, he was struck by the beauty of the first woman. He guessed her age to be about 22 to 25. It was the kind of loveliness you don't forget. Dark eyebrows, hazel green eyes and full, delicate lips that looked rosy against cheeks as pale as the pillow slip her head rested upon. The modest dress could not hide a figure that was trim and very attractive. It was the kind of beauty that makes women flex their cat claws, and makes men stutter and melt.

The only flaw on that porcelain face was a white froth around her mouth that bubbled with each slow and uneven breath. She was still alive but unconscious.

He turned to look at the second woman. "Too late for that one," the doctor said, noticing. "She must have died hours ago. But she felt no pain," he added, nodding at a small bottle on a stand next to the bed.

Reany picked up the bottle. The label said: "Sulphate of Morphia —½ ounce, Powers & Weightman, Philadelphia." An empty tumbler with a teaspoon of water pooled at the bottom stood next to it, alongside a pitcher of water, about half full.

---

84   Ibid.

He walked around the bed to look closer at the smaller woman. She was younger. About 15 he guessed. She also had white foam coming from her mouth like the head on a draft of beer. Her hands were neatly folded and she was on her side, facing away from the other woman, toward the wall. Her face was peaceful, no lines of worry or pain. And she was also beautiful— a smaller copy of the woman next to her.

He tried to steel himself against the beauty that made him want them to be innocent, pure. He failed.

He wondered: Sisters?

A second doctor came in just then and introduced himself as Dr. Eyemann.[85] He took in the scene as Reany had done, picked up the bottle next to the bed, then asked the first doctor, "Morphine poisoning?" It was as much of a statement as a question.

"It appears that way. This one is still alive."

Dr. Eyemann took a glass syringe from his bag, filled it from a bottle and used it to inject a clear liquid in the arm of the older woman, whose breathing was slow and labored. He looked up at Reany and answered the unasked question: "Antidote."

They waited. She seemed to stir slightly; the eyes fluttered but did not open, and she breathed more easily. Reany raised his eyebrows in a silent question. Both doctors shook their heads slowly from side to side, looking grim.

"Extremely dilated," the first doctor said to Dr. Eyemann, indicating her eyes.

"I agree," Dr. Eyemann said. "She is not going to make it. Not from a dose like that," he nodded toward the bottle and water glass. "But we need to get her to the hospital immediately."

As the doctors packed up their bags, taking their time now, Reany paused to look out the single narrow window that someone had opened to let in fresh air. The sunlight forced its way in through the dusty glass, yellow and warm, making beams that lit tiny specks of floating dust. Birds were singing outside. He smelled an apple tree in bloom. He pulled his pocket watch from a vest pocket and noted the time: 12:15 p.m.

---

85   "Weary of Life: A Mother and Daughter Die by Morphine," *The Cincinnati Daily Star,* April 26, 1877.

He put the pocket watch back and reached into an inside breast pocket in his jacket for a small black book and a pencil. He opened it and wrote down the time, followed by the date: April 25, 1877. He left a lot of blank space below it that he would need to fill with missing names, times and details that would add up to another sad story. His stories were all written backward: He knew the ending. But what led these women here, to this?

He turned to the proprietor and asked, "Mr. Schiller, what can you tell me?"

Where did they go?

"They checked in last evening at six o' clock," Schiller replied. "They had no baggage. Would you like to view the guest register?"

Reany took a last look around the room, then nodded and followed Schiller down to the front desk. Schiller flipped to a page and pointed. Their names were written in a very neat, flowing, feminine hand: "Sallie Dill and Ida May Dill."

"Did they have guests? Go anywhere?" Reany asked.

"No guests that I know of. They left together at nine o'clock last night for an hour. When they returned at ten, the mother—"

"How did you know she was the mother?"

"They introduced themselves that way."

Reany mentally revised his guess about the women's ages. "Go on," he said.

"When they returned at ten o'clock, the mother, Sallie, said they had experienced a very long day of travel and did not want to be disturbed until seven o'clock this morning."

"Travel from where?"

Mr. Schiller spun the guest book around and pointed at the page again. Next to the two names, written in the same script, was "Indianapolis."

Reany and Schiller heard commotion and looked toward the stairway, where the hollow clump of boots and shoes on the wooden steps was followed by two teams of men carrying two bodies on stretchers. The burdens appeared to be light. First was the mother, with her long black hair pouring over the edges of the stretcher like a spilled pitcher of darkness. Her too-white face made the sheet that was draped over her look almost gray.

The second, smaller body was shrouded as if for burial. Her head was covered, but her feet peeked defiantly out the bottom of the covering in white stockings and worn, cracked, brown leather shoes.

Both had still been wearing their shoes, Reany recalled. For some reason, it made him very sad. They did not even take off their shoes to get comfortable before taking those fatal doses mixed in a glass of water. Why?

Then something else came to him: The dresses. They were what the Shaker women wore in the Whitewater Village northwest of Cincinnati. They all wore the same thing: modest cornflower-blue dresses with white bonnets. Old women, young women, little girls—all in the same uniform like a women's brigade in the Union Army.

Mr. Schiller fidgeted and mumbled something about unwelcome publicity. Reany looked around. It was a hard-used hotel. Cheap, but clean. The wood floors showed the scuff marks of farm boots in places that were not covered by thin rugs. The rugs were nearly worn through to the backing around the front desk and through doorways.

"There is not much I can do about publicity," Reany said with a smile. "I don't boss the newspapers. From what I read, I'm not sure anyone does."

Schiller was not appeased. He wanted to say more, but Reany headed him off by asking, "Can you summon the maid who discovered the mother and daughter?"

Her name was Mary Peiper. She was in her 30s, a bit heavy but with a charming, dimpled smile and bright blue eyes that showed she was once pretty. A wedding ring was worn on red hands that were chapped by harsh lye soap, and she wore a green apron over her black dress with a round white cap trying to contain escaping strands of reddish hair. She told him she knocked on the door at nine o'clock and had no answer. When she came back at ten, she tried again. This time she knocked louder and called out, "Chambermaid!" She demonstrated for Reany. It made him want to open a door for her. It was a voice that could not be ignored. Cheerful, but all business.

There was still no answer, so she had climbed up on a hallway chair and looked in the transom. What she saw nearly made her fall off the chair. "They were so pale, so white, unnatural. I was sure they were dead. They were still dressed. Hadn't even slept in the bed or turned down the covers."

She had hurried down to the clerk on duty. "He didn't believe me," she said with a dismissive shake of the head, as if all desk clerks were ninnies. Finally, reluctantly, the clerk trudged upstairs to the third floor with her, looked through the transom and was shocked. They summoned Officer E.P. Higgins,[86] the beat copper patrolling the neighborhood. Higgins kicked the door open and the bodies were discovered. That was at eleven o' clock.

Reany found Higgins in the kitchen, a cup of coffee in one hand and a porkchop sandwich in the other. He mostly confirmed what the others had said, between mouthfuls and sips. "One more thing," Higgins added as he put down his coffee, reached in his tunic and handed Reany a small stack of letters tied in a black ribbon. "I found these on the table and picked them up so as to prevent unappropriate snooping," he said. "I figured those poor, lovely women have suffered enough without that."

Reany's spirits rose. Letters meant addresses and people to interview. Otherwise, he had no way to identify the women except the guest register, and he knew better than to trust that.

Higgins looked up at the taller detective and asked, "Suicide?"

Reany grudgingly lifted his eyes from the letters, raised his dark, bushy eyebrows and shrugged. "Too soon to tell," he said. "Looks that way. But then, maybe it was intended to look that way."

He paused, then asked, "Officer Higgins, does your wife take her shoes off after a long, hard day?"

"Can't say, sir."

"You never noticed?" Reany asked in disbelief.

"Never married."

Reany's next stop, thanks again to Officer Higgins, was a boarder at the hotel, Frances "Fannie" Lee,[87] who lived in the room next door to the one where the women had died. She said the two women were mostly very quiet. She heard no raised voices, no arguments.

---

86   "A Horror From Shaker Life," *The Cincinnati Commercial*, April 26, 1877.

87   Ibid.

But she heard them laughing and talking before she went to sleep. Later, she woke up and thought she heard sobbing, "But I might have been dreaming," she said. And then again, later, she thought she heard groans—of despair or agony, she could not say.

Reany found Officer Muller standing outside the hotel doors, hands behind his back, admiring a young woman who was passing on the sidewalk in a red-striped blouse and snug black skirt that reached her button shoes. Reany had to admit it was…interesting to see young women on the streets without their billowing bustles and hoopskirts that made them look like they were floating along on clouds of colorful fabric.

"Fritz!" he said, startling the young man, who almost jumped to attention. "You are dismissed. Tell the captain I am following some clues and will be back in a few hours."

"What do you think—"

Reany put a hand up. "Too soon, Dietrich," he said, making the young man smile at the sound of his name. "Grab yourself some lunch on the way back to the stationhouse. But first, what do you know about the Shakers?"

"I recognized them right away from their village," Muller said.

"You were a Shaker?"

"No," Muller said. "Our family farm is near New Haven. It was not unusual for hundreds of us to attend the Sunday meetings at Whitewater Village to hear the preaching and watch them dance. We used to go to the village for garden seeds and beer, but they stopped selling the seeds a few years ago.[88] And then there was too much noise and laughter from the crowds, so they closed their meetings."

"You recognized those two women in the hotel?"

"Who could forget them?" Muller asked.

Reany sent Muller back to the station and found a bench in the bright sunlight to sit down and read the letters.

The first one was dated April 15, sent from Whitewater Village, written to Sallie Dill by someone named Lucy. It was short, mostly news of day-to-day life in "Shakertown." But Reany noticed that Lucy closed with, "I hope Ida May is getting along."

---

88   The Whitewater Shakers discontinued their strong seed sales in 1875 when commercial seed companies took over the market.

The next was dated the same day, from Ettie Farraday, also a Shaker "sister" from Whitewater Village. "I miss you," it said. "Keep up the good spirits." A postscript warned Sallie to beware of Agnes Groves, who had asked to come back to Shaker Village but was denied. "We can never take her back. If you know what she is you will never be seen speaking to her, and I should have nothing to do with her."

Reany thought about that one. He guessed that Agnes had left the Shakers, fell on hard times and resorted to the oldest profession. She was now shamed. Fallen. Reany shook his head. Was this just gossip or was it a veiled warning to Sallie? Behave yourself or you will never be allowed to return?

Another letter from Ettie Farraday asked Sallie about her health. "You seemed so unwell," it said. "Ida must feel some homesick as she never spent one night from here."

From that he could tell these women were longtime members of the Shaker "family." From what he knew, children were taken from their mothers as soon as they stopped nursing and were raised by their Shaker "mothers." The Shakers followed a visionary named Ann Lee, who claimed she had seen the second coming and all sin was derived from desires of the flesh. They renounced private property and called themselves "communists," whatever that was. They shared everything but their beds. Celibacy was the iron rule.

What caused Sallie and Ida May to leave? Were they forced out, like Agnes, for some violation of the Shaker codes? Even the Shaker men—no, especially Shaker men—must have been smitten by Sallie and Ida May. Their beauty was something rare, to cherish and protect. He shook his head and told himself to focus on the facts. He was married with two sons of his own. Too old at 56 for such foolishness.

So Reany went over again what he had heard and read in the papers about the Shakers. Celibacy was their first commandment, yet they put the men's and women's bedrooms on the same floor in opposite ends of the same building. It was as if every night was meant to be a test of sleepless temptation. If they wanted to keep them apart without the torture of forbidden fruits, why not house them in separate buildings or at least on separate floors?

The Shaker Meeting House. Elders had private rooms above the first floor where the Shakers danced and worshipped. There were separate doors for men and for women. Joel M. Kozan, 2005

When they danced in concentric circles—women, men, women, men—they stomped the floors and made the old Meeting House boom until it could be heard for miles. They shuffled and marched, sometimes reaching for the sky and bringing their arms back into their chests as if gathering blessings from heaven. But they never touched; the women came and left in one door, the men used another at the opposite end of the Meeting House. They had to stay at least five feet apart at all times.[89]

In the women's bedroom at the end of their wing, there was a smaller reading and sewing room, lit by large windows. But there was something odd about that room: The door to that little space had locks on both sides. Were women locked in for protection or punishment? Was that where they ran to safety when men lost control, perhaps after "sampling" too much beer from their brewery?

He had heard the stories about how some Shakers spread flour on the floor of the hallway that separated the men's and women's bedrooms, to leave telltale footprints that would point to anyone who violated the taboo of intimacy.

What a sad life, he thought. How drab and frustrating to be constantly tested and accused of sin by your own natural thoughts.

As a detective, Reany had seen the strange and dark side of life more than most. He thought he had a pretty good grip on fallen human nature. He wondered how the Shakers made it work. He pic-

---

89   "The Shakers: A Visit to a Strange Community," *The Cincinnati Enquirer,* June 22, 1889.

tured a young woman like that girl swaying down the street outside the Farmer's Hotel—or the beautiful mother and daughter he saw upstairs. Add restless young men like Fritz and a lovely spring day when all of nature shouts in the voice of God, "Be fruitful and multiply."

Of course, he nodded to himself. Sometimes they didn't make it work. Maybe more often than anyone knew. He needed to learn more about their customs.

He turned to the next letters. These were Sallie's replies.

"Dear Ettie," she wrote on April 8. "I am thinking of home and the *dear* kind souls that I love so well. How little one thinks how they love another until they are parted."[90]

The letter showed heartbreak and desperation. "*You* must not forget me. Although miles may intervene, and circumstances have bereft me of a home, or my home, please reserve a place for me in your hearts," Sallie wrote. "May God help me is my prayer."

She did not leave voluntarily, Reany nodded to himself.

Then the next part: "Now to explain how I got here. I went to the Ladies' Christian Association; the Committee gave me a card; I came to 97 East Third Street, walked all the way. The lady liked our looks and hired me. She is a widow, with three children. She is as nice as she can be. She gives me $15 a month. She keeps a new kind of school, called kindergarten, for children."

Reany wrote the address in his book: "97 E. 3rd."

The next was addressed to Eldress Lucy, written by Ida May, dated April 17—just a week ago—with a new return address: 235 East Court Street.

TEARFUL LETTERS TO WHITEWATER

"I must confess I have been greatly mistaken in the world," Ida May wrote. "I thought I could have things to suit myself but I find I have been altogether wrong. I have not had a happy moment since I left *home*. No real, substantial pleasure: nothing but a perfect whirl of

---

90   "The Dill Tragedy: Letter from Ida May Dill Written a Week Before the Suicide," *The Cincinnati Daily Gazette*, April 27, 1877.

excitement. I know I was headstrong and unwilling to be taught but I have found that my way is *not* best but only leads into trouble.

"I know I caused you a great deal of trouble, but I did not do it intentionally. If you will let me come home I promise I will do differently from what I ever have done."

Reany paused. Thought again of the pretty young girl, hardly more than a child, with the folded hands, so peaceful in death. He read on.

"*I promise on my sacred word of honor* that I *will* conform to all the rules, no matter how hard it will be. Please answer as soon as possible for I will be in a fever of excitement until I hear from you."

It was signed, "Sincerely, your daughter, Ida May."

This Ettie must have been one of the "mothers" who raised Ida May. He pictured the women together, tending to children as they sewed, spun, cleaned, milked, cooked and did the men's laundry.

The next letter he picked up was the response from Eldress Lucy. It was kind but firm: No, they could not return. Sallie was welcome to come back, but Ida May was not. And Sallie was urged to stay with Ida May long enough to make sure she was safe and settled in her new life in the city.

Then he opened Sallie's reply: "I received your letter stating that Ida could not return. I was *very, very* sorry, for I had hoped you would give her another trial."

As drab and rigid as the Shaker Village was, Sallie and Ida May had pinned all their hopes and excitement on going back. It showed just how cruel and cold life in "the world" was for them, Reany thought.

The refusal was devastating. One line in Sallie's reply jumped out for Reany: "After due deliberation I have decided that death is preferable to the life of a dog. If she could have returned, I would have come back also. She must stay here, I stay also. You know a mother feels for her child, and it would not be human was it otherwise."

With each letter, Sallie and Ida May were getting more desperate.

Now he had clues to follow up. They were written on the front of the envelopes: The addresses where Sallie and Ida May had very recently lived.

As he got up to leave, he saw his friend and occasional drinking companion Tom Farrel. Tom was darkly handsome, a magnet for the ladies. His long black hair cascaded over his eyebrows and his vivid blue eyes were striking. He worked for The Cincinnati Enquirer and was a good reporter when he was not swizzled on whiskey or crapulous from the brown bottle flu. Reany knew all too well from years patrolling the wild side of town in "the Bottoms" that "Drunk Irishman" was like "hard-working German" or "dry Baptist"—the shoe might pinch, but it fit well enough.

"Well hello, Tom. Here it is Wednesday, the middle of the week, and you look like you just woke up on a slab and walked out of the morgue," Reany said.

"Head like a bag of chisels, but I'm still breathing," Tom said grimly. "I heard something happened here at the Farmer's Hotel. What can you tell me? It must be something big or they wouldn't have sent the city's finest detective."

"Buttering my bacon won't get you anywhere, I know your blather like a pig knows slop. Me, I'm just sitting here enjoying the sunshine. I have no idea what you are talking about."

"C'mon, Bill, I walked all the way from Vine Street. Take pity on me. Every step was a hammer on my skull."

Reany considered, then said, "Come along with me then if you're able to suffer a few more hammers on your thick skull and I will tell you what I can."

By the time they reached 97 East Third Street, several blocks south and east, Reany had sketched out most of what he knew and Farrel wanted to read the letters.

Reany knocked on the door of a large white house with a wrought iron fence and red brick path to the front steps. A housekeeper answered and said she would summon the mistress of the house, Mrs. Agnes Newlin.[91]

Mrs. Newlin was well dressed but looked harried, her pinned-up red-blond hair falling around her face and neck in wisps. She was in her early 50s, Reany guessed. She introduced herself and explained that there was no Mr. Newlin. Her husband had died many years ago and left her a comfortable income and the house she lived in. She

---

91   "A Horror From Shaker Life," *The Cincinnati Commercial*, April 26, 1877.

now ran the new "kindergarten" described by Sallie in her letter to her Shaker friend.

Mrs. Newlin was kind and gracious, just as Sallie had written. "I'm sorry I cannot help more. They were with me for only ten days," she said.

"What did you know about them?"

"Sallie, the mother, said she was also widowed. Her young husband died early in the war of rebellion—at Shiloh, I think. And that's when she sought the aid of the Shakers. She said she grew up in Indiana. They were both very neatly dressed in those Shaker-blue dresses, with white bonnets. They were both so pretty and very well spoken."

"Why did they leave your house?" Reany asked.

"Sallie told me they had a new place to stay and a new situation. I knew Ida May was unhappy here. She said as much to my other housemaids. It can be trying to manage these children," she waved a hand toward the back of the house. "She was a nursemaid for the kindergarten, and her mother was my upstairs housekeeper."

"Were there any problems you noticed, any visitors?"

"There was a young man who came to call for Ida May, but she sent him away in tears. I gathered he had left the Shaker settlement near Harrison to follow her. Lovestruck, I would guess. Easy to see why."

"Anything else?"

Mrs. Newlin hesitated, as if reluctant to say anything. Then said, "One day I had to scold Sallie. She went out at five in the morning and did not come back until noon. I let her know that she needed to get permission to be gone. I told her it was dismissible behavior. She apologized. Then the next day they packed their things—they didn't have much, just two trunks—and left."

"What day was that?"

Mrs. Newlin looked at the thick Persian carpet and put a finger to her lips as she worked it out. "They came to work on the eighth of April and stayed ten days. So, April seventeenth, I think."

"Anything else?"

"I almost forgot, there was another visitor, a young woman who knew them from the settlement. From what I overheard, she had also left the Shakers a few years ago and sympathized with Sallie and Ida May about entering a new, less sheltered world."

"Do you know her name?"

"That's easy. It was the kind you remember. Lamo Brooks. She said she was a seamstress at the Orphan Asylum on Mount Auburn."

Reany wrote it down, thanked her and they left.

They caught a hansom cab back to 235 E. Court Street, only a couple of blocks from the Farmer's Hotel: A wide, three-story townhome of solid bricks as dark as black coffee. It was a large, comfortable home in a wealthy neighborhood.

They were greeted at the door by William R. Brickley, a handsome young man, very sharply dressed in a black suit over a white shirt and black string tie. He told them he was a manager at one of the city's most popular dry goods emporiums, Louis Stix & Co.[92]

In spite of his veneer of self-assurance, Brickley seemed nervous. As they talked, Reany noticed a trickle of sweat creeping down from his hairline. As soon as they had introduced themselves, Brickley asked them to come with him to a saloon nearby where they could talk more freely.

Reany noticed that Farrel was very much in favor.

They walked to the Tom Johnson Tavern at Court and Vine, and took a place at the darkest end of the long bar, away from the other customers who were having an afternoon refreshment that, in some cases, would extend to an evening "day-ender" and a late journey home to an angry wife.

At first, Brickley was unwilling to talk freely, as he had promised, and answered questions with terse replies. He tried to stall by telling Reany, "I've heard of you. Aren't you the man who rounded up a bunch of clerks and fought Morgan's Raiders out near Miamitown?"

"They pulled up the center boards so Morgan's cavalry couldn't cross the bridge," Farrel supplied, helpfully.

Reany jabbed Farrel with a sharp elbow and steered the conversation back on track. "When did you hire the Dills?"

"They came to my house a week ago on Monday," Brickley said—which matched the day Mrs. Newlin said they left her home. "I agreed to employ the mother and keep the girl until she could find something

---

92   "A Horror From Shaker Life," *The Cincinnati Commercial*, April 26, 1877.

on her own. She was 16, more than able to work. My wife is an invalid, so we needed the help."[93]

As he discussed Ida May, either his resentment or the Irish whiskey loosened his tongue. "The next morning I threw her a copy of the *Enquirer* and said, 'Maybe you can find employment in that among the advertising columns.' But she would have none of it. She replied hotly, 'I don't want any work!'" Brickley still sounded incensed.

"How did you meet them," Reany asked.

"My brother brought them to the house."

Farrel asked, "Is your brother Fred Brickley? Stays at the Galt House?"

"Yes," Brickley replied. Reany jabbed Farrel again, who spilled his shot glass of whiskey, winced and mimed zipping his lip.

"Where does your brother work?" Reany asked.

"He's a ticket agent for the Cincinnati, Hamilton and Dayton Railroad."

"How did he happen to know Mrs. Dill and her daughter?"

Brickley looked uneasy and Reany could tell by his shifting eyes and furtive hands that he was about to make up a lie. "Don't try to sell me a dog," he growled, leaning in on Brickley, letting his coat fall open to display his badge and pearl handled revolver in a shoulder rig. "Until we are sure it's a suicide, we treat it as homicide. It doesn't get more serious."

Brickley's eyes got wide, he nodded, swallowed and answered. "He made their acquaintance at the Shaker Village in Whitewater. He knew them well, for he lived there two years."

"How long has he been away from that place?"

"He left five or six months ago."

"Where does he live now?"

"He boards at the Galt House, Sixth and Main."

"And why then is it necessary to talk here in the shadows about something so innocent?"

Brickley got that shifty-eyes look again, like a man whose wife has found perfumed letters in his coat pocket. He was going to lie, Reany knew it. "Never mind," he told him. "I will be in touch."

---

93   "Shame and Suicide," *The Cincinnati Enquirer*, April 26, 1877.

As they left, Brickley looked pale and shaken as he knocked back a stiff shot and rapped the bar for another.

On the sidewalk, back in the bright sunlight, Reany turned in the direction of the Farmer's Hotel and asked Farrel, "How did you know all that about Fred Brickley?"

"The man is a lushy ratbag, squifilated to the eyebrows."

"And you know this how?"

"I am a member in good standing in the brotherhood of lushy ratbags. We hold our meetings every afternoon on every day ending in 'Y' at any well-stocked tavern. But compared to me, Fred Brickley is the sultan of saloon shecoonery."

Reany leaned back and looked at Farrel in surprise but said nothing.

"Why are we going back to the hotel?" Farrel asked.

"I want to find out about Sallie Dill."

The news was not good. She had died at the hospital at 1:45— about the same time they were meeting William Brickley.

Reany felt deflated. The excitement of the case and the balmy spring day were bled away by the darkness of another tragic, unnecessary death. He told himself again that it shouldn't make a difference that the victims were so young and beautiful, but it did.

They took a bench in the shade at Piatt Park. Farrel began to nag and wheedle again to read the letters, and Reany gave in. He figured two of them could read them faster. He trusted Farrel's instincts—at least when he was more than half sober.

As they read, Farrel nudged Reany and said, "Listen to this, Detective Pinkerton."

Reany growled.

"It's from April 24, the day they left the Brickleys' house. It's written by Ida May, to someone named Nottie."

He read: "This is the last letter you will ever receive from me. I intend this night to sleep the sleep that knows no waking. I can not live, for all resources are at an end."

He paused and looked at Reany. "That sounds like a suicide note."

"Read on," Reany said, leaning back against the bench.

"I know if I had done better, I might have had at least another trial, for I have harmed no one but myself. Have they not allowed worse people than me to try it again? Didn't Lottie and hundreds of others? And why am I turned from the only place I can call home, to earn my bread or starve; to become a woman or a prostitute?"

"Let me see that," Reany said, taking the letter. He scanned it and read, "Notie, between heaven and all I hold dear, I rejoice at the thought of death."

Farrel nodded. "What did I say?"

"Hold that horse," Reany said. "There's also this: 'If *they* are there—you know who I mean—tell them all is forgotten and forgiven.' So who is 'they'?"

"Could be just the elders who threw her out?" Farrel guessed.

"Then why would she have to ask if they are there? Of course they would be there. No, this is someone else. Someone who wronged her."

"You suppose some celibate Shaker took advantage of that pretty girl?" Farrel asked.

"Let's put it this way. I would not be more surprised than I was hearing you call yourself a lushy ratbag."

"That was the hair of the dog barking," Farrel said.

"More like the dog itself," Reany said. "Let's go introduce ourselves to Fred Brickley."

At the Galt House, the clerk told them Fred Brickley's key was not in his slot, so he was either out or in his room.

"Well, that narrows it down," Reany said sarcastically. "Why don't you send someone up to find out?"

The clerk sent a bellboy to check. They waited. And waited. After about ten minutes, Reany headed for the stairs. The clerk protested, but Reany ignored him.

At room 87 they knocked. Then knocked again. Then pounded. No answer. "He was here," Reany said.

"The kid they sent up tipped him and he shinned off," Farrel nodded. "Perhaps we should look in a likely place?"

"Which would be?"

"The nearest saloon?"

"You go on, if you can force yourself," Reany laughed. "As for me, I need a quiet place to read these letters and think."

"Detectiv-ating?"

"So says the reportifier."

Before heading back to the stationhouse at 9th and Central, Reany hopped a cab to Cincinnati Hospital at Central and 14th, where the two women had been taken. He found their bodies in the morgue. Lit by flickering gaslight that made shadows dance on the walls, two men were preparing the mother for burial. They told him the girl had already been packed on ice.

The mother had been undressed, her dress and underclothes folded neatly. Reany looked and it was unmistakable: She showed clear signs of pregnancy. About four or five months, he guessed. The undertaker's assistants he questioned agreed.

They had seen no evidence that the girl was pregnant. "But I've never seen anything like it," one of the men said. "Of the thousands I have seen, never seen one like that."

"How?" Reany asked.

"Red," the man said. "Scarlet red all over. As if she was dipped in red dye."

"What do the doctors say?"

"They went on about blood pooling,[94] but they seemed unsure and a bit bewildered, if you want the truth."

Engraving of Shakers dancing, 1830.

---

94   Livor mortis, or postmortem lividity. Caused by pooling blood. It can be red at first, changing to a dark red or purple bruise color.

THURSDAY, APRIL 27, 1877

Reany read Farrel's report in the *Enquirer* the next morning. It was thorough. The reporter had interviewed a few more people and filled in some blanks. So it was apparent he did more than stop by a saloon—or he found his sources there, with well-oiled tongues. One of the headlines was especially interesting. Under the bold headline at the top, "Shame and Suicide," it said, "A Well-known Young Cincinnatian Probably Implicated."

The story said Fred Brickley had arrived at the Shaker Village two years ago, begging to be taken in as "a slave to liquor" who begged for a place to reform his ways.[95] The Shakers agreed, on the condition that he could not leave the Whitewater Village settlement. After months passed and he gained their trust, they sent him out to deliver strawberries to the city, a Shaker specialty. It was a mistake. Both times he came back stumbling drunk.[96]

The Shakers made him sign a covenant that he would not leave the settlement again and gave him another chance. He worked alongside the rest of the men on the farm; then, as he stayed sober, he was assigned to help with the bookkeeping for the Shaker businesses: sales of seeds, brooms and produce, milk and cheese, fabrics and, most popular, sturdy, plain furniture.

But the books were simple. It looked like Brickley had been given a cushy job that would allow him to avoid hard labor that raises sweat and calluses and strains the back.

Farrel reported that in May of 1876, a woman was ordered to leave Shaker Village for violations of the celibacy commandment, and Fred left immediately after, to follow her. Then the following October, he came back and was welcomed again with open arms.

Then on March 5, according to Farrel's source, as the bleak winter lingered, Fred Brickley was ordered to leave for good. Banished.

Reany compared that to the letters he had read the night before. Fred Brickley's troubles and ejection fit the same time period that

---

95   "The Double Death," *The Cincinnati Enquirer*, April 27, 1877.

96   Shaker men were sent on missions to sell garden and flower seeds as far west as Missouri, and were often gone for weeks or months at a time.

problems began for Sallie and Ida May.

Reany opened the morning *Daily Star* and smiled at their report. It was spoon-fed by a Shaker source, he guessed. "The daughter, a wayward, spoiled and stubborn girl, desired to go into the world and live in the city," the *Star* reported. "She could not be restrained and finally her mother consented to go with her."

Pure bosh. Wayward? Stubborn? Perhaps. But their letters clearly showed that Sallie and Ida May were forced to leave. And someone was using the Star to spread a lie that the women chose to leave. Who benefits? The Shakers, Reany decided. Also, Fred Brickley.

THE INQUEST

As he was getting ready to leave for the inquest at 10:00, he found Farrel waiting on the sidewalk in front of the Stationhouse. "Why didn't you come in?" he asked.

"I never know if I will be allowed to leave," Farrel replied, only half joking. Reany knew Farrel had slept more than once in the hard cells at the downtown stationhouses after a night out being mauled by John Barleycorn.

"So you learned a few things about our missing man Fred Brickley last night. I read your story, but I'm guessing there's more."

"You're right," Farrel said. "My source, who recently left Whitewater Village, told me Fred got to know Sallie Dill. In the biblical sense. And maybe the daughter too."

Reany winced. "Ratbag indeed. Why did they keep letting him come back so many times but deny the same forgiveness to Sallie and Ida May?"

"By my count, that's at least three strikes for drunkenness and corrupting women, and he was still allowed to come back."

"If I had to speculate, I would guess your source was the Orphan Asylum seamstress, Lamo Brooks?"

"I see that you didn't get that detective badge at a church raffle. Miss Brooks has no use for the Shakers—or Fred Brickley."

"Was she the woman he followed?"

"No, I think that must have been Agnes Grove, the women mentioned in the letter from Sallie's Shaker friend Lucy Woodward. The letter that said Agnes Grove 'must be avoided' for her life of shame."

"What else did you learn from Miss Brooks?"

"You know how the Shakers call themselves communists[97]? They share everything? Well, that includes secrets, apparently. They are not even allowed to keep the private property or their own personal privacy. They have to go through regular rituals of public confession to the elders."

"So they are *not* all created equal?" Reany asked, pretending to be surprised.

"Oh ye of little faith," Farrel laughed. "No, Miss Brooks described near mutinies against elders who were abusive tyrants. There is infighting, backbiting, even occasional violence among the pacifists at Shaker Village. And the confessions sound like the ones you persuade suspects to make in the stationhouse, but more personal and more detailed. Lamo—I mean my source—said Sallie broke down and confessed to them that she thought Ida May was pregnant. Then she confessed that she, too, had repeatedly violated her vows of celibacy."

"Fred was a very busy man."

"After that, Whitewater Village was like bumblebees in a teapot. It was quite a scandal. Old Fred must have been tracking flour in all directions of the compass. And he wasn't the only one. That man named Bishop mentioned in the letters? Miss Brooks said that's Charles Bishop, a young farmer who was also banished by the Shakers for too much attention to Ida May."

Reany said, "I can understand why they finally gave Fred the boot for good. He was trouble from the start. But Sallie and Ida May lived there 14 years. Ida May grew up in their Shaker family, raised by the whole village. Why wouldn't they get a second chance the way Fred

---

97   The Shakers called themselves "Celibate Christian Communists." Their version was more socialist than Marxist. But the ideas were not new. Some of the earliest theories that attempted to link communism and Christianity were offered in the 1516 book *Utopia*, by Thomas More. Later Christian communities followed the examples of his imaginary island Utopia, where there was no private property. Similar ideology was advanced during the French Revolution (1789-1799). The first Communist League was formed in 1847 by Karl Marx and Friedrich Engels. Those ideas, imported with German immigrants, found fertile soil in an era of Robber Barons, when there was no safety net for the poor, disabled, widows and orphans. Later in the century, anarchists grew out of the same soil.

Brickley did when he got drunk and compromised Agnes Grove?"

"I wondered the same thing. Especially in a Christian society that claims to hold women and men as equals," Farrel said.

"I'm beginning to understand why Sallie and Ida May felt so desperate and abandoned."

"The elders were not entirely heartless," Farrel said. "The Shakers sent them off with $15."

"That's less than a dollar a year for 14 years of work. Very generous," Reany said bitterly. "What else have your learned?"

Farrel said, "In addition to Miss Brooks, I talked to the editor at the *Harrison News*. They follow news of the Shakers very closely and have a good relationship with the village."

> **SHAME AND SUICIDE.**
>
> **A Shakeress and Her Daughter Die Together.**
>
> **The Mystery of the Tragedy and the Theories that It Excites.**
>
> **Did the Mother First Poison Her Child and Then Take Her Own Life!**
>
> **A Well-Known Young Cincinnatian Possibly Implicated.**
>
> A tragedy, unparalleled probably in its sadness, occurred at the Farmers' Hotel, corner of Court and Race street, yesterday morning. Mrs. Sallie Dill and her daughter, Ida May, were found in their room about eleven o'clock lying on the bed—the daughter dead and the mother dying from poison. The announcement of what was at first considered a double suicide did not excite the sensation that was raised when finally, after investigation, it became almost certain that one was a murder and the other a suicide. The two women were at first believed to be sisters; but later in the day the bodies were recognized as those of Sallie Dill, a Shakeress from the village in Whitewater Township, this county, and her sixteen-year-old daughter, Ida May Dill. HOW THEY DIED.

As they walked to the courthouse, Farrel pulled out a notebook and told Reany about the Shaker history and customs: Whitewater Shaker Village was established in 1823, amid the national Revivalist Movement of the early 1800s.[98] "They worship a British woman named Ann Lee, long dead, and they believe she was the second coming of Christ."

"Horsefeathers," Reany said.

"No, it's true. The proper name for their community is United Society of Believers in Christ's Second Appearing. Anna Lee, known as 'Mother,' apparently had trouble with her husband and claimed that God told her in a vision that the desires of the flesh were the root of all sin."

---

98   The Protestant religious revival called The Second Great Awakening swept through America from 1790 to 1840. The movement spread through Kentucky, Indiana, Tennessee and Ohio. Church attendance soared and many new denominations were born, including early Evangelical Christian Churches, Latter Day Saints, Jehovah's Witnesses, the Church of Christ and Seventh-day Adventists. Ann Lee emigrated from England to New York in 1774, spreading the Shaker church that reached a peak of about 4,000 sisters and brothers nationwide in the 1820s.

"That explains the celibacy," Reany nodded.

"And it explains why her husband ran off with another woman," Farrel quipped.

"What else," Reany asked.

Farrel flipped a page and said, "At their worship services in the Meeting House[99] they dance in concentric circles, segregated by the sexes. And sometimes a young women will shout out that she 'has it' and fall to the floor and shake and writhe like she's having a fit. Then she announces her vision to the chief elder. They talk in tongues, supposedly messages from Anna Lee and other spirits. And they have visions in dreams and they claim to receive invisible gifts that they receive and pass on to others—crowns, shields and imaginary swords, for battle in the spirit world."

"How does your friend know all this?"

"The Shakers invited their neighbors to their worship services, sometimes as many as 100 spectators. He told me that one Shaker meeting in 1838 is still talked about. The entire village was seized by an almighty power like a rushing wind and the brothers and sisters were seized by shaking, some for hours."[100]

At one point, Farrel explained, the visions caused concern to the male elders because the young women were taking control of village leadership. "And there have been more than a few scandals."

He told Reany about Elder Nathan Burlingame, who called himself a doctor. He was kicked out of the Shaker Village in 1829 after "corrupting the virtue" of several "sisters"—probably while playing doctor—and fled with a large amount of Shaker money.

In 1860, Second Elder John Strange Hobart was ejected from the Whitewater Village after he became so hostile to village rules that he gave lectures in Cincinnati on "The Mysteries and Cruelties of Degenerative Shakerism." He was dragged kicking and screaming to court

---

99   Built in 1827 of handmade bricks fired on the site, the Meeting House is 33 by 44 feet, and has an ingenious system of trusses that support the roof with no columns that could get in the way of dances. A half-story second floor had "retiring rooms" reserved for the elders and eldresses—segregated by gender.

100   Innis, James Robert, and Thomas L. Sakmyster. *The Shakers of White Water, Ohio, 1823-1916.* 2014.

in Cincinnati, where the elders tried to get him locked up in the local insane asylum, Farrel said, but the judge refused and said he was sane.[101] "And here's enough irony to make Shakespeare jealous," Farrel said. "During the recent war, the Shakers were among the first conscientious objectors[102] and paid a $300 fee to keep their young men from being drafted. Several went to fight anyway. But when Morgan's Raiders rode through Harrison and Cincinnati in 1863, General John Hunt Morgan[103] camped at Whitewater Village."[104]

Reany laughed. "I remember that. I was nearby at the Miamitown Bridge, less than ten miles from the Shaker Village. We killed two, wounded three and captured two of Morgan's Raiders, including his best scout. We lost a good man of our own. Just 24 of us against 500

We had to retreat.[105] So Morgan was at Shaker Village? I wonder how that went?"

"The elders said later that he was a gentleman, very respectful. He told them he had learned to respect the Shakers in Kentucky.[106] They even invited him to dine with them. But here's the irony: The Indiana Home Guard that was chasing Morgan arrived at the Shaker Village the next day and they were led by none other than Lt. John Strange Hobart."

"The same Hobart they tried to lock up in the lunatic asylum? Strange indeed," Reany said with a chuckle. "The Shakers would not go to war so the war came to them."

"The Shakers hid their good horses from Morgan, but Hobart

---

101   Innis, James Robert, and Thomas L. Sakmyster. *The Shakers of White Water, Ohio, 1823-1916.* 2014.

102   President Lincoln granted the exception from service for Shaker men.

103   Morgan arrived in New Haven south of the Whitewater Village on July 13, 1863, and looted the village.

104   Innis, James Robert, and Thomas L. Sakmyster. *The Shakers of White Water, Ohio, 1823-1916.* 2014.

105   Bill Reany was a major in Company S of the 7th Ohio Volunteer Cavalry, the "River Regiment." He faced General John Hunt Morgan and his raiders four times in battle and came out on the winning side three times. His sons William Reany Jr. and Lafayette Reany rode under his command. Kramer, Stephen, Lt. (ret.), "Detective William Henry Reany (1822-1874), Greater Cincinnati Police Museum.

106   There were two Shaker villages in Kentucky, Pleasant Hill near Harrodsburg and South Union near Bowling Green. Pleasant Hill is now a historic landmark.

must have known. He put a gun on one of the elders and threatened to shoot him and burn the village unless they turned the horses over to him."[107]

"He must have enjoyed that, getting his revenge after being dragged into court. But tell me more about the customs."

"Very strict. They rise with the morning bell at 4:30, have breakfast, then work until supper at 6:00.[108] Families and converts who join the village have to first give all their wealth and possessions to the Shakers. Each woman is matched to a man. They cannot meet, talk or laugh, but she does his mending, sewing and washing."

"Married without the benefits?" Reany laughed.

"Maybe more like some marriages in other ways," Farrel chuckled. "The men and women eat supper at separate tables. In silence. No talking allowed."

Reany laughed again. "That sounds like my parents."

"Mine too," Farrel said.

"What about the families who bring children to the village?"

"Children are taken away from their parents to live in the South School, about a mile from the North Village, where the parents live in a dormitory.[109] Did you know that the first school they built was burned down by the neighbors?"

"I've heard that they were not welcome, but I didn't know it went that far," Reany said.

"It was much worse at Union Village in Lebanon," Farrel said, flipping through his notebook again. "Let's see…here it is. In 1810 a mob of more than 500 gathered to persecute the Shakers, carrying guns, swords, bayonets and clubs.[110] And then at Whitewater, around that time, 20 young men were taken from the village and nearly lynched.

---

107   Innis, James Robert, and Thomas L. Sakmyster. *The Shakers of White Water, Ohio, 1823-1916.* 2014. Hobart took two of the Shakers' best horses. The Shakers were eventually reimbursed $300 by the state of Ohio.

108   "A Visit to a Strange Community," *The Cincinnati Enquirer,* June 22, 1889.

109   The three-story Dwelling House was built in 1844, 54 by 44 feet, with a 60x30 two-story extension. By 1846 it was filled with new converts.

110   Phillippi, J.M., *Shakerism: The Romance of a Religion,* 1912, United Brethren Publishing House.

The mobs called them 'children of the devil' and 'religious lunatics.' They have seen their share of oppression."

"Tell me more about the children. I'd like to know how Ida May grew up."

"Each child is assigned an adult caretaker—women for girls, men for boys, but not their parents. At least one caretaker was accused of whipping her child."[111]

"As a father I can't imagine tolerating such family separation," Reany said.

"There are benefits, especially for families in poverty and widows who cannot support their children. Shaker children are raised in a clean, sanitary home with good nutrition, hard work and an excellent education, even for the girls.[112] They're protected from the cholera and other epidemics that sweep through our city. But their life is cheerless and dreary, I was told. There are no pictures on the walls. Hopping, skipping and laughter are frowned upon. And Miss Brooks taught me a nursery rhyme the Shaker children memorize:

"Don't pick your teeth, or ears or nose,

Nor scratch your head, nor tonk[113] your toes

Nor belch, nor sniff, nor jest nor pun,

Nor have the least of play or fun."[114]

"No wonder so many leave as soon as they are able," Reany said. "Maybe that explains why Ida May was so keen for an adventure in the city."

"My friend at the *Harrison News* said that losing their young people has become a crisis," Farrel said, consulting his notes. "He said the population at Whitewater Village peaked in 1856 at 180. Part of that was a group of Millerites. Do you remember the Millerites?"

---

111   Innis, James Robert, and Thomas L. Sakmyster. *The Shakers of White Water, Ohio, 1823-1916.* 2014.

112   This was unusual in 1877, when education for girls was dismissed as foolish and unnecessary. Shaker children were taught to read and write well, to be proficient in arithmetic, and learned manners and many skills as they worked in the village.

113   Tap your toes.

114   Innis, James Robert, and Thomas L. Sakmyster. *The Shakers of White Water, Ohio, 1823-1916.* 2014.

"Yes," Reany said. "Weren't they the people who gave away everything they owned, put on white robes and climbed to the hilltops? They believed they would be raptured in the second coming on a specific date?"[115]

"Correct. After their great disappointment when Jesus did not arrive on time, about 70 joined the Shakers. But the population at Whitewater has steadily declined, especially among young men. Only 15 percent of them stay. In the Census of 1870, they had 124 residents, far more sisters than brothers and most of the brothers were very old or under age 12. They no longer have enough young men to run the farm, so they have hired outside labor."

Farrel described how George Amery had come to the Cincinnati Orphans Asylum asking for young boys to take in but was refused. "They've also taken indentured children from parents who cannot afford to raise them. "

THE OUTSIDE WORLD BECKONS

"That answers some riddles," Reany said. "The girls stay because there is little hope for them in the outside world unless they take the road to perdition chosen by Agnes Grove. But the boys want adventure and freedom to marry. If they are as well educated as you say, they must find work easily."

"Yes, especially since the growth of industry after the war. There have been big changes in the past few years," Farrel said. "The outside workers are controversial. The older elders warned that they would disrupt and corrupt the village."

"Sounds like they were right about at least one of them," Reany nodded.

"But since the coming of train service, they can't keep the sisters and brothers from visiting Cincinnati to see the outside world. They get books and newspapers to learn how people live in the outside world, where love and marriage are normal, not an abomination that sends you to hell. And the elders have been forced to stop censoring

---

115   The followers of William Miller, including a group in Cincinnati, believed his interpretation of the Bible that calculated that Christ would return on October 22, 1844.

books that they called 'pernicious.' They no longer read everyone's mail. Tobacco is permitted. They have a brewery to sell beer, and I can vouch that it is a fine ale that kicks like a bee-stung donkey."

"Hmmm," Reany said, tipping his bowler to an elderly woman who was stepping down from a carriage. "I think I would be derelict in my duty as a detective if I did not sample a growler or two of that Shaker ale."

"I would be glad to introduce you to an expert who could assist—a man so experienced in the field he is known as a professor of libational intoxicants—"

"Would this *professor* by chance be a dipsomaniac, ink-stained slang-whanger named Tom Farrel?"

"At your service," Farrel smiled with a little bow.

"Perhaps after the inquest," Reany said. "What else is new at Shaker Village?"

"Brace yourself: A church organ was added to services. Scandalous! And the women have planted decorative flowerbeds that were formerly forbidden as too frivolous."

"Flowers, music and literature? But still too hardfisted uppish to allow Sallie and Ida May to return." Reany shook his head.

"I discovered a possible reason for that," Farrel said. "Whitewater is under supervision by Union Village near Lebanon. And Union Village elders have been real sin-busters on Whitewater Village. Let's see, I wrote this down. Here it is. They said, 'We don't know of any place that there has been more outspoken contempt of separation of the sexes than at Whitewater."

"So the Whitewater elders are worried about far more than scandal in your headlines," Reany said.

Painting of a young Shaker woman in their traditional bonnet and dress. Courtesy of the Union Village Shaker museum at Marble Hall, Otterbein Senior Life.

✳

At the inquest in the Hamilton County Courthouse, they sat near the front and listened as the witnesses were called to testify. To their surprise, the missing man, Fred Brickley, was there, well dressed in a dark brown suit, but looking like he had climbed into a bottle last night and was sweating 90-proof red-eye trying to get back out. He was fur-tongued, bloodshot and shaky.

After the doctors testified that the cause of death was morphine poisoning, William Brickley took the stand and told an entirely different story than the version he told Reany at the saloon. This time he said the two women came to him at work and asked him for a job. He left his brother out of it entirely. He testified that he gave Sallie a job housekeeping at their Court Street house, but was surprised to see the daughter move in too.

"Bushwa," Farrel whispered.

Then Fred Brickley was sworn in. He was handsome but had the sallow complexion of a man who spent too much time in dark saloons. He struck Reany as the kind of blistering smooth-talker who might seem irresistibly charming to innocent, sheltered, unworldly women—such as Sallie and Ida May. Reany pictured him telling tales of the big city, in which he was always the hero, of course. Promising to take them there and show them the amazing sights and adventures.

In Cincinnati, he was just another lazy young drunk who never grew up to be a man. But in the Shaker Village he would be a lion among lambs.

"I haven't seen the bodies but I knew the two parties," he said. "They came to me and asked me to get them a situation and wanted to know if my brother couldn't take them in," he said. "I advised them not to go, as he had a house full now."

More bushwa, Reany thought. More likely, Fred sent Sallie and Ida May to William and urged his older brother to give them a job to avoid a family scandal. He had a debt to pay. They were on his conscience, if he had one. Or maybe the Brickleys were just afraid a secret might be exposed.

Fred continued, drawing himself up in the witness box as if what he had to impart was of great importance: "I became acquainted with them in April 1875 when I went out to the Shaker settlement. I would like to say one thing about the way the Shakers raise young children. They are kept just like house plants and are not allowed to learn nothing, so that when they are thrown out on the world, as in this case, they can do nothing to earn a livelihood.

"The regulations of the Shakers are, I fear, very hard upon young people. They take children of any age and bring them up in their own way of living. These children are required to work for the Society and are very restricted in their pleasures. Their services add a great deal to the wealth of the Society."[116]

Reany thought about the 'house plants' remark. There was truth in that. From what he knew and from their letters, Sallie and especially Ida May were thrown into the outside world after years in a cocoon, with no opportunity to stretch their wings. They must fly or die. And the predators were as certain as birds and butterflies.

As Farrel was scribbling notes furiously, Fred continued. "Ida May had a liking for what they called 'worldy pleasures,' and in her friendships probably sought too much attention from the young men of the Society."

Such as yourself, Reany thought.

"Ida May had incurred the displeasure of the Shaker community, and the mother concluded to take her away from there," Fred said.

Reany looked over and saw Farrel write "RATBAG" in large capitals.

Fred gained momentum as he spun his story. "There was no question of the mother's conduct while at the Shaker Village, only the daughter was looked upon as wild and reckless. Last Saturday, at my brother's house, she told me she intended to kill herself."

And you did nothing, Reany thought.

"I am satisfied that the girl was homesick, wanted to go back to the Shakers, and they not being willing to receive her, it preyed upon her mind to such an extent that she became weary of life."

After Fred, members of the Farmer's Hotel staff and Mr. Schiller testified, but there was nothing new to Reany.

---

116 The Double Death," *The Cincinnati Enquirer*, April 27, 1877.

Fred also submitted two letters that he claimed were written to him by Sallie Dill. Reany read them and passed them to Farrel with a raised eyebrow. They were dated April 24, the same day Sallie and Ida May had checked in at the Farmer's Hotel:

> "It seems like it has been my fate, and still is, to be an outcast. If I could recall the many harsh words I have spoken to you and obliterate them from your memory, it would be a happy moment to me. But please forgive all.

> "Fred, do take care of yourself. You have the ability and can fill a place that will make a man of you. I have felt interested in you and do still. If there is such a thing as a guardian spirit, mine shall endeavor to be yours.

> "Persons on whom I have relied would not extend a hand of charity as they promised they would. There is not any one who is really trustworthy. Mortals, oh mortals, how weak they are, making such loud professions and fulfilling none. If you only knew one half I have gone through you would shed tears of sympathy. But I do not expect any one to enter into my troubles and feel the true weight of them."

The second said:

> "I suppose *it* will surprise the folks some little when they hear of it. I have nothing to censure you for on this earth. I only hope you will take care of yourself and meet me in heaven.

> "My last thoughts will be of you, for Ida is going with me. Don't think me rash, for how could I see her go to ruin, as she certainly would if she staid here. And now a last farewell. For the last time, in reality, I say farewell."

Both were signed "Sallie."

Farrel finished reading and said, "That cramped handwriting in the second letter is nothing like her handwriting in the rest of her letters."

"I Pinkerton-ed that," Reany said. "The misspelled words are not like her, either. And isn't that second letter convenient for the Brickleys? Just enough of a suicide letter to leave no doubt, while it exonerates Fred."

"He lays it all on the Shakers," Farrel nodded. "Like all good lies, more than a tablespoon of truth."

The jury deliberated for half an hour and delivered their verdicts:

Sallie Dill: "Death from suicide by taking morphia."

Ida May Dill: "Came to her death from an overdose of morphia, by whom administered the jury are unable to determine."[117]

As the courtroom emptied, Farrel said to Reany, "Do you think we will ever know if Ida May took it herself, or did Sallie give it to her before taking her own dose?"

"Or if someone else supplied the morphine?" Reany added.

"If one or both were pregnant, that's a powerful motive," Farrel agreed. "Something like that can destroy a family's good name. The Shakers must be worried, too. Did you hear they sent one of their elders to town?"

"Tell me about it."

"I was sipping some anti-fogmatic last night with a clerk who works at the Indiana House. He said Fred Brickley staggered in smelling like rotten fruit from a whiskey tree. He demanded to leave a message for Elder George B. Amery, who was in town on business."

"The Dill business, no doubt," Reany said. "I don't suppose the clerk told you what the message said?"

"It cost me a dollar. You will owe me."

Reany just stared at Farrel. It was a look few could withstand.

"All right," Farrel wilted. "The message said, 'You must bury the Dill folks or I shall expose all I know!' With an exclamation point."

"'Bury the Dills?' I'm beginning to wonder why so many people are so eager to do that."

"Fred told the clerk it was urgent. He had to see Amery."

"Sounds like blackmail. What do you know about Amery."

---

117   "The Dill Tragedy," *The Cincinnati Daily Gazette*, April 27, 1877.

"He's interesting. Not orthodox. Maybe a bit heretical to the Shaker creed. He joined the Whitewater Village in 1870. Before that he was a printer. Why he came, I cannot say. Perhaps it was something like Fred Brickley, throwing himself on their mercy as a slave to liquor.

"He comes to Cincinnati often as their representative, and when he does he sometimes takes in lectures and concerts. He has written about his theory of a biblical foundation for socialism, so maybe it was the shared property and escape from materialism that attracted him. I don't think the other elders are aware of his secret life outside the village."

Reany thought about it, then started walking.

"Where are we going?"

"Indiana House, to see this clerk," Reany replied.

The clerk had more details to fill in some of the blank spaces in Reany's black book. He told them Amery had arrived that morning and was accosted by a friend of Fred Brickley, George Harbison, a young man from a well-known family who had also spent several months living at Whitewater Village with Brickley—and had likewise been forced to leave. The clerk said Harbison walked up to Amery and extended his hand in greeting—but Amery refused to shake it, saying he would have nothing to do with any friend of Brickley's.

Harbison kept at it, urging Amery to meet with Fred Brickley, the clerk said. "Mr. Amery told him, 'No, there is murder lying at someone's door on account of this Dill affair, and I will not shake hands with anyone who may in any way be connected with it."

"You're sure about that?" Reany asked the clerk. "He said murder?"

"Yes, it was very clear. His voice was raised. Very angry. It was a bit of a scene in the parlor."

Reany nodded. Amery had clearly accused Brickley of murder. "What happened next?"

"When Mr. Amery went out later, Fred Brickley was by the door, waiting for him. Again, voices were raised, so I heard it clearly. Brickley threatened Amery that if he didn't bury those two women in the Shaker Cemetery, he would tell things about them that would make it very unpleasant for the Shakers. Brickley said the Shakers would be disgraced."

"How did Mr. Amery respond?"

"He was very angry. Amery said, 'If you were to turn up the bottom stone of our Society I would not be intimidated from doing the right thing. Tell whatever you want.'"

After the interview of the clerk, Farrel was in a hurry to get back to the office and write his story. "This is a dirty business," he told Reany.

"I think it will get worse," the detective replied.

"Can you bring charges against Fred Brickley?"

"For what? There is no law here to enforce celibacy. Lord knows the evidence of that is all around us. And there's no statute to make a man do the honorable thing when he gets a woman in jeopardy."

"What about murder? Blackmail?"

"I'll speak to Mr. Amery. Someone needs to talk to him. The coroner did not. He should have been summoned to the inquest. But I'd say it looks doubtful. I imagine Amery wants to bury the Dills quickly too—as long as their graves are not on Shaker land."

"Have you seen their cemetery?" Farrel asked.

"No, tell me."

"They have about five acres and no more than a dozen headstones,[118] all crowded against the back fence, taking up space no bigger than a milkhouse. I guess they never thought it completely through that you cannot bury people who are never born. They have plenty of room for Sallie and Ida May."

Reany put a hand gently on Farrel's arm, looked him in the eye and said, "Tom, do yourself a favor and keep a clear head."

Farrel looked away, shrugged, and mumbled, "I will try." He left with his head down and his hands deep in his pockets.

'WILLFUL AND OBSTINATE'

Reany found Elder George B. Amery sitting in the private parlor at the Indiana House. He was a tall man, dressed in a black suit that was plain but well made. He wore a white shirt buttoned to the top, with no tie and no vest. He was slim and looked strong—farmer strong, with

---

118 McClure, Stanley, "A Record of the Inscriptions on the Tombstones of the Cemeteries of Crosby Township, Hamilton County, Ohio," June 6, 1991. From the earliest in 1852 to 1875, there were 12 burials.

an outdoor ruddiness in his cheeks. He was a handsome man, German blond, clean shaven, with even features, in his late 30s, Reany guessed.

His piercing blue eyes looked at you as straight and honest as a Dutch stone fence. He had a presence of command and a deep voice of authority. He introduced himself as the business manager and legal trustee of the Whitewater Village of Shakers. Reany got the impression of a man who, once decided, would be as hard to move as a cast-iron stove.

They took seats across from each other in comfortable, overstuffed chairs by a window that overlooked the busy street outdoors. Amery smoked a small cigar and spoke in the voice of reasonable, patient grievance. He wanted Reany to know the Shakers had been maligned.

"These people came to us destitute. When she arrived, the mother was holding the evidence of her bad judgment in her arms. The fruit of illicit love."[119]

Reany said, "I was told she was the widow of a soldier killed at Shiloh."

"'Oh, what a tangled web we weave when first we practice to deceive,'" Amery quoted from Sir Walter Scott's poem.[120] "She was abandoned by a young man who was the son of a wealthy Baptist preacher in Indianapolis. The young man joined the Union Army to escape his responsibilities. That he may have died in battle or by other means, I have no doubt.

"But you are right, it is a sad story. Her mother died young, and she was left without guidance as a young woman. Her father disowned her and sent her to us."

Reany wondered: If you have known them so well, why can't you speak their names?

Amery went on about how the Shakers did their best to guide the "willful and obstinate" daughter Ida May. "Her conduct was such as would prompt harsh treatment from those who strive to censure us," he said.

Reany noticed it sounded a lot like the story in the Star. "Willful." "Obstinate."

---

119   From Amery's public letter to Cincinnati defending the Whitewater Shakers.

120   *Marmion* by Sir Walter Scott, 1808.

Amery's cheeks blushed red as he tried to delicately explain the problem with Ida May. "When we remonstrated her for violating our most sacred rules of celibacy, she responded that 'I am only doing what my mother has done.'"[121]

"What did you take that to mean?" Reany asked.

"I think you know," Amery scoffed. "That man had no line he would not cross. I regret ever trusting him to help with our accounts."

"You mean Fred Brickley?"

"Yes," Amery snapped. He seemed to get angry at the mere mention of the name.

"Also, it was reported in the papers that we gave them $4," Amery said, indignant. "We gave them $15. And they took articles of clothing and possessions which my records show are valued at $200."[122]

Reany did not need to ask questions. Elder George Amery was a locomotive with a full boiler of steam.

"The women's letters seeking readmission made no mention of suicide. How could we know? And now this drunken derelict Brickley, who we generously took in, is threatening us if we don't violate our own foundational rules and bury the bodies in our cemetery."

"Did he threaten to blackmail you?"

"You could say that."

"Will you press charges."

"Oh, no, never. There is no reason to cause more trouble. He is already forgiven," Amery said.

"What did you mean by using the word 'murder' when you argued with Fred Brickley?"

"Who told you I said that?"

"What did you mean by it?" Reany persisted.

"My blood was up. I was intemperate. But if anyone drove those women to suicide…." Amery let the sentence trail off, suddenly aware that he could also be speaking of himself and the Shakers.

Reany let the silence hang for a moment, then asked, "What do

---

121   "The Double Suicide," *The Cincinnati Enquirer*, April 28, 1877.

122   The Dill Case: An Interesting Statement From the Financial Manager of the Shakers," *The Cincinnati Enquirer*, May 4, 1877.

you think Fred Brickley is prepared to tell that would damage your community?"

"I have no idea," Amery said too quickly.

"What about burial of Sallie and Ida May?" Reany saw Amery wince when he mentioned the women's names.

"As much as I might wish to, the elders decided that it would set a terrible precedent. It is our right to refuse burial to someone who has left our society. Where would we draw the line in the future? Would anyone be permitted burial in our cemetery?"

Reany wanted to say, "You certainly have room." But he did not. He was sure there was a lot more to the story. But he could tell Elder Amery was not going to fill in very many blanks in his black book.

FRIDAY, APRIL 28, 1877

The next morning was chilly and windy, as if winter was loitering in March, interrupted by brief flashes of June sunshine like a preview of summer—typical April. Reany stopped on his way to the station-house to pick up a stack of newspapers, eager to enjoy one of his favorite parts of the day. He got to work at 6:00, before it was busy. He propped his boots on the edge of his desk and picked up Tom Farrel's story in The Enquirer, under the headline THE DOUBLE DEATH.

It was a thorough report of the inquest testimony, including the letter from Sallie that Fred Brickley submitted, and a short one from Ida May:

"I trust we will meet on the other side where the reunion will not be broken. Fred, I can not leave you without saying goodby. Thank you for befriending me so often, and I trust we will meet some time to part no more. Farewell, Ida May."

Reading it a second time, Reany thought the tone was odd for a 16-year-old girl writing to a grown man of 29.

Then he picked up his morning copy of the *Cincinnati Daily Gazette*. The city had more than a dozen daily newspapers. The ones Reany had picked up were the *Enquirer*, the *Commercial*, the *Gazette* and the *Star*. He was often surprised at how much a detective could learn as local newshounds raced each other to catch the big story of the day, their headlines braying like dogs with a raccoon in a tree.

Oh-oh, he thought, as he read the *Gazette's* story, headlined "The Dill Tragedy." *Tom is going to be in a bad temper. He has been scooped—the only thing he hates worse than The American Temperance Society.*

One of the deck headlines caught his eye: "Letter From Ida May Dill Written a Week Before the Suicide; The Affair Still Clouded in Mystery."[123]

Reany knew the local papers never missed a chance to put "mystery" in a headline. They slugged it out every day for attention, and "mystery" was catnip for readers. But in this case, it was accurate.

As he read the story, it was obvious that Fred Brickley had given the *Gazette's* city editor an exclusive interview. And that meant that he had run to the paper to get his side of the story published either before or immediately after the inquest. It looked as if the Brickleys were scrambling to hide something.

The story was framed as if Fred had written it himself—if he had been sober enough. It said the inquest testimony "demonstrates that pleasure and companionship are not more dangerous to the mind than the immoderate severity which would exclude every emotion and excitement from human life."

Translated: The Shakers and their iron-rod rules drove those poor women to suicide.

Fred "had no other relations with them than as a friend," it said. *That's a lie*, Reany thought. "The mode of life at the village is described by Brickley as being entirely unsuitable for making the inmates useful members of society anywhere else. They are required to work, but there is a great amount of liberty enjoyed by the girls in that respect. They always become weary of the drudgery of work in families when they try to make a living in the 'world.'"

Interesting, Reany thought. *That's not at all what I have heard from former Shakers, who described the work as endless and relentless. But it serves Brickley's purpose to make it look like Ida May and Sallie were too weak and lazy to survive outside the Shaker Village.*

Fred also offered a reason why the Shakers would not take Ida May and Sallie back. "It was the policy, he said, of the Trustees, to reduce

---

123 The Cincinnati Daily Gazette, April 27.

the number of people in the village because they had met with losses during the year and were now in debt $3,000.[124] Every inmate who could be sent away would, by so much, reduce expenses. It was the news of the refusal that made the mother so despondent."

Brickley was smart. He had buried a seed of truth in an apple of lies. It was all very plausible and believable, but Reany wasn't buying it. There was more to the story than two idle, weak women who took their own lives because they couldn't return to the drab and restrictive life in Shaker Village.

Fred went on about how the Shakers were so strict, men and women could not even talk to each other unless it regarded business. Fred also let it be known, through the helpful *Gazette* editor, that Sallie had met with the brother of Ida May's father, who had come to Cincinnati but offered them no help.

To Reany, that explained her letter about people who promised to help and did nothing.

Fred Brickley insisted that there was "not a breath of suspicion" about Sallie, and described Ida May as "giddy, full of the natural longing of a young girl for the outside world. This had been increased and poisoned somewhat by an injudicious quantity of novel reading."

No *"breath of suspicion"? Well, that's another lie,* Reany thought. *Surely he knew that Sallie had confessed her celibacy violations to the Shakers and the hot breath of suspicion was scorching her neck until she left.*

But the other part about "injudicious reading" made the detective stop and put the paper down. He pictured the two women, sharing and discussing contraband novels that filled their imaginations with taboo dreams of love, passion and romance. The pages of those books opened a door to a whole new world—dashing knights and cavaliers, beautiful maidens in a fairyland where the desires and longings of the heart were not crushed under the millstone of Shaker doctrine; where young women could be flattered, courted and loved as God intended. And into that world steps Fred Brickley—a failure, a fool, an unre-

---

124   That amount would equal more than $91,000 in 2025. The debt was possible. Whitewater Village income declined from $5,700 in 1850 ($234,000 in 2025) to only $500 in 1874 ($14,000). By 1877, the exodus of young men had made finances worse.

markable loser in the game of life. But among the loved-starved Shaker women, he must have seemed like the dashing hero of their own romantic-novel dreams. They were under his spell. And of course, he chose the two most beautiful women in the village to corrupt.

Reany picked up the paper and read on. Through the pen of the editor, Brickley revealed how Ida May had confessed to improper conduct with the farmhand Charles Bishop, who was sent away. It was a cruel betrayal by Fred to expose the secrets of a young girl who could no longer defend herself.

But it served Fred's purpose to point the finger of suspicion at the Shakers instead of himself. It was as if a clever courthouse lawyer had written the whole story as Fred Brickley's defense for a crime that had not even been named.

The next paragraph made Reany laugh out loud. It said: "The fact that Fred Brickley was not an entirely homeless man, as most of them were, gave him superior opportunities for becoming acquainted with the inhabitants."

"I'm sure it did," Reany chuckled to himself. "*Intimately* acquainted. Big man from the big city. A wolf among sheep."

He scanned ahead to the letter from Ida May, "not heretofore published," according to the breathless boast of the Gazette.

If Fred Brickley had this letter, why was it not part of the inquest? Reany wondered. As he read it, he became more angry.

Ida May started out by informing Fred, "We have changed our place from 97 East Third to 235 Court Street. Perhaps you are acquainted with the gentleman with whom we reside, namely Mr. Wm. Brickley."

This kind of playful banter did not fit the Brickleys' version of events at all.

"Mother has retired (like a good child) and I am left alone, so I thought to while away the time, I would torment you a little."

Was this the teasing, bold Ida May who had the Shakers wound in knots?

"You came very near making me angry, vexed and mad Sabath evening by almost hooting at the idea of me going out with you. I went off and had a good cry, and thought I would rather die than write. But I changed my notion and here I am at it. Of course, you know, you have a terrible way of getting around a person, and I think you try your best to exert it at any favorable moment."

There it was again—that strange tone. This was no "indifferent friend" as Fred claimed. This was a young girl who was smitten, infatuated with Fred Brickley. A girl he toyed with by laughing at her "going out" with him. A girl he was manipulating—"getting around"—while he was no doubt playing the same games with her mother.

He looked back at the comment about "last Sabbath." Shaker Sabbath was Sunday. That made it April 17th. And that meant Fred Brickley had been with Sallie and Ida May that day—a week before their bodies were found—and yet he led the inquest jurors to believe he had almost nothing to do with the women and had scarcely seen them.

He read on. Ida May wrote, "Please do come down and cheer up muzzy, for she is very despondent, and I think your presence will dispel all gloom. To be sure, I won't have the benefit of yourself, nor do I expect it."

It ended, "Direct yourself to 235 Court."

At least as far as Ida May was concerned, Fred was much more than just a friend. As seen through the eyes of the girl, it was a romantic relationship—she even saw herself as her mother's—"muzzy"— rival for his affections. And both were lost and despondent without his attention.

Fred had managed to "get around" both women, whose innocence made them almost helpless to resist his worldly charms and big city experience.

At the end of the story, there was mention of a package that was left with Fred by Sallie on Tuesday, the day they checked in to the Farmer's Hotel. She had told him it was something to "remember me by," and insisted they would never see each other again. She was "going away."

The package contained a photograph album: pictures of Sallie, Ida May, Sallie's father, Charles Bishop and Fred Brickley.

Again, none of this was included at the inquest. Reany thought he could almost see the shadows of a powerful influence working behind the scenes, like an invisible wind that makes the trees bend together in the same direction.

Did the Brickleys have that kind of influence? The Shakers? If not, who did?

He set that question aside and moved to the remaining newspapers. From reports in the *Star* and *The Commercial Appeal*, he learned:

FRED BRICKLEY'S STORY

Brickley had also run to *The Commercial Appeal* on the day the bodies were discovered. It was no wonder that Reany and Farrel couldn't find him that day—he was busy telling lies to any editors who would listen. *The Commercial Appeal* boasted that "he saw fit to give to the city editor of the Commercial, and to no other journalist, on the day of the suicide, the most important matters in connection with the news of the same, which, of course, attracted general attention to the Commercial, as the only paper that had the complete news of this sad situation."

Reany scoffed. *Complete news? Or only what Fred decided was the complete news?*

He learned from the stories he read that Sallie was known and admired for her lovely contralto singing voice and was a leader in the Shaker choir. He thought back to the beautiful woman he had seen lying on the bed in the Farmer's Hotel and shook his head: What a waste.

He learned that the altercation between Elder George Amery and Fred Brickley had nearly come to blows, and the men had to be separated. Was Amery angry at Brickley's threats to "reveal everything"? No, he had already snubbed Brickley's friend Harbison and refused to see Fred before the threats. It had to be something else. Perhaps Amery detested Brickley for what had done to the Dills and at least one other woman at Shaker Village? Perhaps Amery was in love with Sallie too?

He learned that before Sallie and Ida May were told to leave the Shaker Village, the elders had tried to send Ida May to reform school. Sallie had recoiled in horror at the idea. She would not abandon her daughter to prison with criminals. She said in a letter, "To do such a thing, I feel as if it would kill me."

That was interesting. George Amery had insisted that sending Ida May to reform school was Sallie's idea.[125] And that could not be true.

Sallie knew enough from her life before the Shakers to understand and sympathize with Ida May's mistakes. She had arrived at the Shaker Village herself, abandoned at the same age, 16. Her daughter was no criminal.

And he learned that Sally and Ida May had been dismissed by the kindergarten teacher Agnes Newell because Sallie was gone one day between 5 a.m. and noon. In a way, Mrs. Newell's fib that they had suddenly left without notice was no surprise to Reany. Even good people often covered their tracks and minimized their own role in tragic events. Mrs. Newell did not want to be painted in headlines as the woman who sent Sallie and Ida May to die in desperation. Perhaps she had convinced herself that they left on their own, to ease her conscience.

He pulled out his pocket watch and checked the time. A group of doctors was gathering at the morgue to examine the bodies, especially Ida May's corpse. They were eager to investigate the strange color of her skin. He just had time to catch a cab to the hospital.

When he arrived, Farrel was already there, looking like a storm cloud. Reany joined him and said, "I read the *Gazette.*"

That drew a dark scowl from Farrel, so he added, "Seems to me, Fred Brickley knows somebody or paid somebody for a story like that."

That lifted Tom's spirits a bit. "Flummery and blusteration," Farrel said. "Their city editor couldn't write an obituary for a housefly if it drowned in his soup."

"It was nonetheless revealing," Reany said, making Tom Farrel's face go dark again like another passing thundercloud.

"Revealing of the coroner's incompetence," Tom snapped.

"Or worse," Reany said. "Money talks. And sometimes it speaks loudest with silence." He was about to say more when the three doctors emerged from the morgue to announce their findings.

After the small crowd became quiet, one of the doctors stepped

---

125   Letter to the editor from George Amery, *The Cincinnati Enquirer*, May 4, 1877. "Our first object was to secure for the girl, at the request of the mother, a place in the Reform School, and just as we were getting ready to effect this, we were notified by the mother that the girl was in a condition which precluded the possibility of placing her there."

forward. "I am privileged to report on behalf of my colleagues that we have examined the corpse of Ida May Dill thoroughly," said the tallest of the three. "It is our opinion that the remarkable scarlet color of her skin was caused by postmortem suggillation."

Farrel whispered, "Slug-you-what?"

"Pooling of blood after death. It usually looks like a bruise," Reany replied. He thought the doctor didn't sound very sure. And one of the three stood apart from the others, as if he had been outvoted.

Reany decided to ask him later. After a couple of questions from reporters for the *Gazette* and *Star* that more or less confirmed what Reany had told Farrel, he got his chance.

The third doctor was heading for the exit, in a hurry to leave. Reany caught up and introduced himself.

"I know who you are," said the young doctor, dressed in a tweed suit. "You're the policeman who singlehandedly stopped Morgan's Raiders. I'm Dr. William Gano."

"Well, you do me too much credit," Reany said. "More like Morgan and his Raiders stopped us, but we at least slowed them down. I would like to ask: Can you tell me, doctor, is there anything else that might cause such reddening of the body? It has been my experience that pooling of the blood after death is usually on just one side closest to the ground—which would be her right side—not the entire body."

"You are correct. That is why I was so curious about this case. To answer your question about what else could cause such a phenomenon…Well, there are a couple of things.

"I once saw something very similar in a man who died in his sleep. His death was caused by incomplete combustion in his coal furnace. The latest researchers call it heavy inflammable air,[126] or carbon monoxide poisoning."

Reany said, "But if that was the cause of Ida May's red skin, why wouldn't her mother have the same appearance? They were in the same room, breathing the same air."

---

126 Poisoning from coal combustion was first documented by a Swiss pathologist in the 1600s. English chemist Joseph Priestly isolated carbon monoxide in 1772 and gave it the name "heavy inflammable air." Both noted bright, cherry-red skin in victims.

"Yes," Dr. Gano said. "That's what my colleagues said. They dismissed my theory, in spite of the fact that it explains her appearance when their theory of suggillation does not. I can't prove my theory is correct, but I can definitely say theirs is not."

"Can you think of anything else that would do this?"

Dr. Gano stroked his full beard and dipped his head in thought. "Something keeps nagging me in the back of my mind, just out of reach. Something I learned in medical school." He looked up. "I'm sorry to hurry away, but I have patients to see."

"If it comes to mind, please inform me," Reany said, handing him a card with the address of the stationhouse.

Farrel was waiting for him at the exit. "Did you see the smirk on the face of that *Gazette* reporter?" he asked.

"Enlighten me, Tom," Reany said. "Today's story will be forgotten tomorrow, when it will be replaced by another story. There is always another story, another day, another newspaper with sensational headlines about something everyone has forgotten in a week or a month at most. Yesterday's news goes rancid like beer dregs in hot sunshine. So why do you treat this as life and death?"

Tom looked at him as if he thought the detective must be an imbecile. "It's *news*," he said. "There is only one chance to be first."

"And you need to be first because…?"

"Because I need to be first," Tom said, as if it were obvious. "Being second is hair in the butter."

Reany shook his head and gave Farrel a sideways squint. "Come with me, Tom, I will treat you to an early lunch. I promise there will be no hair in the butter."

Over lunch, reporter Tom Farrel and Detective Bill Reany compared notes on what they now called "The Dill Case."

"Share your theory," Reany invited, as they sat in a downtown hash-house and waited for their corned beef, potatoes and cabbage.

"Well, the way I see it, two poor, betrayed women, abandoned by those who brought them to shame, cast out of the home they loved so well, could not sink to the level of prostitutes, and so they took their fate in their own hands and rashly challenged the mercy of heaven, hoping to find it juster than the pity of earth."

"That's quite poetic," Reany said, "have you thought of putting it on paper somewhere?"

Farrel smiled. "Read tomorrow's *Enquirer*."[127]

"And the Brickleys?"

"The awful responsibility for the deaths of Sallie and Ida May rests at someone's door. This was no rash suicide in a moment of despair. It was premeditated and well considered, as their letters show. William Brickley is a worm who has been cleaning up his younger brother's messes probably since they learned to walk. Fred is a ratbag from eyebrows to heels. If he ever sobers up he may decide to kill the man he sees in the mirror and we will have a third suicide."

Farrel added, "Did you hear about the trunks?"

"What trunks?" Reany asked, eyebrows raised.

"There were two trunks containing all of the worldly possessions of Sallie and Ida May. The same ones they moved from Mrs. Newell's house to the Brickley house. Apparently, the coroner requested the trunks, but the Brickleys refused to give them up, and the coroner did not insist."

Reany thumped the table angrily with the handle end of the butter knife he had been using on a roll. "You mean that gutless excuse for a coroner did nothing? So the Brickleys, who may have contributed to their suicides, get to keep everything those women owned as well? I think we will see about that."

"I wonder if they are afraid something in those trunks might be incriminating. Letters we haven't seen, that kind of thing."

"And by the time we recover the trunks, anything of that sort will have been destroyed," Reany nodded with a frown.

"Sorry to upset your digestion," Farrel smiled, clearly not sorry at all that he knew something the detective did not.

"So what about the Shakers in all of this?" Reany asked, returning to their theories of the case.

"I haven't made up my mind. Why won't they take Sallie and Ida May back now that they're dead, and why is Fred so anxious to bury them as far away as possible in Whitewater Village?"

---

127   "The Double Suicide," *The Cincinnati Enquirer*, April 28, 1877.

"The way they tell it, they did all they could," Reany answered neutrally.

Tom laughed bitterly. "But those poor women were allowed only one mistake and they were thrown out. Fred came back drunk repeatedly, ruined at least one woman who was banished, and still they let him return. What is that in baseball, four strikes? Five?""

"Now you're getting close," Reany said.

"How so?"

"Why do you think the Shakers, who claim to treat men and women as equals, would be so lenient on Fred and so hard on Sallie and Ida May?"

The meal came and Tom thought about it as he buttered his roll, making a show of inspecting the butter dish for hair first, which made Reany laugh.

As they ate, Reany asked, "Remind me what you learned about the state of Whitewater Village."

Tom replied, "Well, they hit their biggest population in 1856, when they had 180. But since then, they have been on the skid."

"So I hear," Reany said. "Now down to fewer than 100, I think you said. So why would they send young women away and refuse to let them come back?"

"Miss Brooks says—"

"Oh, the lovely Miss Brooks again. Sounds like you may be seeing the former Shakeress who works at the orphans' asylum?"

"We had dinner," Tom blushed. "Once or twice. She *is* lovely."

"Good for you. Nothing like a good woman to keep a man out of the saloons. Or at least give him something to fear even more than a morning head like a bag of nails. As you were saying...."

"She says most of the departures from the village are young men. The elders don't have enough young men to work the 1,400 acre farm."

"They need young men so badly they brought in outsiders..." Reany teased.

"Like Fred Brickley," Farrel realized.

"And George Harbison," Reany added.

"And how many others?" Farrel said, getting excited.

"And some of these young men come from?"

"Wealthy, well-known Cincinnati families. Yes, I think I get it. It's like a Shaker Statue of Liberty." He raised his hand holding his water glass as if holding a torch. "Send us your drunks, your storm-tossed scoundrels, your black sheep who stain your family name, send these, your huddled ratbags yearning to meet innocent, pretty young Shaker maidens…"

Reany laughed. "I think you are on to something there. But even the most patient Christian forgiveness cannot explain why he would get so many chances. What could possibly motivate them to let him come back even after he disgraced Agnes Grove, who was abandoned to the streets?" As he said it, Reany took a gold coin from his vest and spun it on the table.

"Of course," Tom said, his eyes lighting up as he watched the coin spin like a top. "Money. Lamo said there were many uncomfortable discussions by the elders about declining revenues from their businesses."

"So perhaps that part of Fred Brickley's story about the $3,000 deficit could be true?"

"Probably the only words he said that were true—except perhaps his threat to tell all. Do you suppose this was what he was talking about?"

"Yes, he had access to the bookkeeping records. It's a theory I have considered," Reany replied. "I can see how it could easily be justified for all the right reasons. Christian charity toward wayward young men who need the strong moral guidance and hard work that the Shakers can provide. And their increasing need for young male converts to help carry the workload—and then perhaps a contribution of cash from the men's grateful families to keep the village in the black."

Tom shook his head, "And these young men are tossed into a society where women and men must be five feet apart at all times and cannot speak to each other unless business is the topic. Sharks among minnows."

"You even think in headlines, don't you?" Reany chuckled. Then his smile evaporated. "We laugh about it, but it's all very sad. Did you know Sallie was given the condition that she could stay if the Shakers sent Ida May to reform school?"

"They would send her to incarceration?" Tom was incredulous.

"Ida May was about the same age Sallie was when she was sent to the Shakers, disowned by her father. And then her daughter is disowned by her new family. Imagine how she felt."

Tom raised his index finger. "That brings to mind something else I meant to tell you. One of the doctors I talked to told me that their autopsy of Sallie showed she may have recently had an abortion. Or as they put it, her body had expelled a fetus."[128]

Reany put his head in his hands and almost wept. After a moment of silence, he said, "Perhaps that explains where she was that day from 5 a.m. to noon—the absence that got her fired from Mrs. Newell's home and packed off to the spider's web of the Brickleys."

"And who do you suppose arranged and paid for that?" Tom asked, as if the answer was obvious.

"Sallie would have no connections for that sort of thing," Reany agreed. "It can only be the Brickleys. I cannot imagine the Shakers would do such a thing, no matter how they wanted to smother the scandal."

"Yes, I believe George Amery when he said he would not be intimidated by threats. And I get the impression that he is not entirely in alignment with everything in Whitewater Village or the rigid Shaker rule books."

"You may be right," Reany said. "And yet, something tells me all the tracks are covered and nothing can be proved. The only two who could testify are at the morgue, abandoned again."

A few days later, On Sunday, April 29, Sallie and Ida May Dill were buried in Spring Grove Cemetery, side-by-side in unmarked graves,[129] at the expense of the Brickleys, the newspapers reported.[130] Reany read the story and nodded. It was the least they could do, he thought.

FRIDAY, MAY 4, 1877

Whitewater Shaker Elder George Amery got the last word when his statement was published in *The Cincinnati Enquirer* ten days after the suicides rocked Cincinnati and Whitewater Village.

---

128 *The Cincinnati Enquirer*, April 29, 1877. Sallie's body "presented every evidence of the recent discharge of a fetus. The daughter exhibited no signs of pregnancy, though there was positive evidence that she had not been true to her celibate vows."

129 Graves without stones or markers were not uncommon in the late 1800s, especially for two abandoned women who were tangled in suicide and scandal.

130 *The Cincinnati Enquirer*, Sunday, April 29, 1877.

"The Dill Case," the headline said. "An interesting Statement From the Financial Manager of the Shakers."

Among his comments on "the unfortunate Dill case," Amery said he had a duty to the public to "present the candid and thoughtful readers with Shaker views and Shaker standpoints."

"The public is often hasty in its judgment," he wrote. "Having carefully read all the accounts given by the various papers in this city," he made had a case to make. And he delivered his argument like a man playing prosecutor and defense in the same trial.

He pointed out that the Dills were dismissed by Mrs. Newlin for leaving without permission. "Our Shaker society has been treated much more contemptuously than this and has hundreds of times forgiven and borne acts of manifold greater transgression" by them, he wrote.

'A PERFECT EQUALITY'

"Notwithstanding the rules for the maintenance of our life of celibacy, there are strong bonds of friendship and love to be found among us, as the letters by these poor deluded women give abundant evidence."

He defended the decision to refuse their burial on Shaker property. Their covenant was to equally distribute the "manifold gifts of God, both of a spiritual and temporal nature, for the mutual protection, support, comfort and happiness of each other as brethren and sisters in the Gospel…thus abolishing poverty," but, "we can not be too careful in our dealings with those who either forfeit their right to membership or voluntarily relinquish it."

For those who honored the covenant, he said, "a perfect equality obtains and is enjoyed by every member…. We wear the same quality and style of clothing; eat the same kind of food at a common table; enjoy equal privileges of social intercourse with each other and have and hold equal right and title to a real and personal property, which has been and now is and forevermore shall remain dedicated to the sacred uses and purposes for which the Society was organized."

Then he got to Sallie and Ida May, whose names were conspicuously absent from his statement.

"These people had come to us not only in destitute circumstances, but even the mother, having in her arms evidence of her first unwise confidence, was almost helpless. The child was taken and carefully and prayerfully dealt by, guarded through infancy and childhood. … But in her willfulness and obstinacy she rejected all counsel and admonitions and her course finally became such as would have ejected her from any well-regulated family outside of our church."

He accused Sallie and Ida May of taking property worth $200. "There was not even a shadow of encouragement given to lead the mother to believe that the girl would be taken back," he wrote.

"We gladly draw the veil over this unfortunate occurrence," he closed. "We are devoted to what we believe to be a work to further the best interests of humanity."

Reany read it, crushed the paper into a tight ball and threw it across his desk so hard it hit a coffee cup that fell to the floor and shattered. Captain Halliday emerged from his office to investigate the commotion, took a look at Reany's scowl and asked, "What's got your saddle sideways, Bill?"

"Equality, strong bonds of Christian love and the best interests of humanity," Reany growled.

Captain Halliday stared at Reany, then looked at the wadded up newspaper on the floor in a pool of cold coffee. He scratched his head. "I warned you no good would come from reading those rags," he said pointing at the newspapers on Reany's desk. "They have turned you into a nominee for sultan of the lunatic asylum." He went back to his office, shaking his head. Reany got up, grabbed his coat and bowler and stomped out of the office for some fresh air.

A few months later, when the Dills had been long forgotten by everyone except Bill Reany, the detective was at the hospital to question a victim of a stabbing in The Bottoms, when he saw Dr. Gano in the hallway outside the ward.

Dr. Gano extended his hand and greeted him, "Detective Reany, what brings you to the Knife and Gun Club today?"

Reany smiled at the doctor's use of the street slang name for the hospital. "There was a stabbing in the Bottoms last night. I hope to get a description of the assailant from the victim."

"Then I have bad news for you. He died an hour ago. Too many leaks to seal. Exsanguinated."

Reany cursed.

Dr. Gano nodded. "I agree. But maybe I have some good news as well. I have been meaning to contact you. I did not forget that case of the two Shaker women. Whenever I had time, I searched my textbooks and finally found another cause of the syndrome we noticed in Ida May Dill."

Reany raised his eyebrows, immediately interested. "And what would that be?"

"When I discovered it, I thought, 'Of course!' I should have remembered it from medical school. It is cyanide poisoning," the doctor replied. "It can cause that same cherry-red skin coloring after death. Something about blocking the body's ability to use oxygen. Not my specialty, I'm afraid. I prefer to work with patients who are alive, so I can keep them that way."

"And how does cyanide poisoning compare to suggillation?"

"Suggillation is postmortem lividity, or livor mortis.[131] It occurs as blood pools from gravity, so it is on the bottom side of the body in repose after death. This coloring would occur over the entire body."

"Is that what you saw on Ida May?"

"Yes, I would say so. That's why I was troubled and disagreed with the suggillation finding. I wasn't sure why, but I knew there was a better explanation."

"Can morphine cause that color?"

"I suppose it is possible, but more likely it will cause a blueish or purple color."

"Is the red skin color always present in cases of cyanide poisoning?"

"No, it is not. Only in some cases. In others, there may be no change in skin color, or they may look almost blue."

"How fast does it act?"

"It can be very fast."

Reany thought, *Maybe that explains why they did not even remove their shoes.* He asked, "What about the foaming around their mouths that I noticed?"

"That can be caused by morphia poisoning or by cyanide poisoning.

---

131   Discovered in the 1860s, first reported in the *Medical Times & Gazette* in 1866.

It would definitely occur if both were ingested."

Reany thanked the doctor, who seemed in a hurry to get back to his patients. They wished each other well, and Reany left. On the walk back to his desk in the stationhouse, he thought about what he had just learned. If cyanide was the cause of Ida May's mysterious scarlet skin—"as if dipped in red dye"—it could mean many things.

Did Sallie add cyanide to Ida May's dose of morphine to make her death fast and certain? That made no sense. It didn't fit with all that he had learned about Sallie's character.

Did Ida May somehow add cyanide to her own fatal dose? Was it possible that she took cyanide while Sallie took morphine? No, that made no sense, either. And there was no need to explain why Ida May's body was bright red and Sallie's was ghost white. They may have both taken morphine and cyanide, with different reactions.

And neither woman would have known how to go about getting such poisons in the city. They had only left the sheltered Shaker Village three weeks before and did not know anyone who could do that—except Fred Brickley.

He gathered from the letters that Fred wanted nothing to do with Sallie after she became pregnant. He may have arranged an abortion, then jilted her, driving her to suicidal despondency—"weary of life," as the headlines said. It would not be the first suicide that Reany had seen after an illegal abortion. For some, the guilt and shame were too much to bear.

Did Fred also supply the fatal cocktail? Was it possible that he added cyanide without their knowledge to make sure the women's doses would be completely fatal?

That made sense, but without a confession by Fred Brickley, there was no way to prove it.

That led to another question: Did Fred act alone, or was he guided by his older brother, William? Or were others involved—families whose sons had also caused scandals at Whitewater Shaker Village, who feared exposure and disgrace?

He came back to his initial version: It was Fred, with help from William. Both lied and acted guilty. They were hiding something, Reany was sure of it.

✳

In October 1878, newly promoted Cincinnati Police Officer Dietrich Muller stopped by the stationhouse at Ninth and Central to visit Detective Bill Reany. He found Reany at his littered desk and asked, "Did you hear the news?"

"I read the newspapers every day, but I am beginning to think they only make me more ignorant, if that is possible. All scandal and skulduggery. So tell me something I don't know, Fritz," Reany replied, standing to pull over a chair for Muller.

"That's *Officer Fritz* to you," Muller laughed. "I thought you might be interested to learn something I heard about when I was in Harrison yesterday. Remember Elder George Amery?"

"I could not forget him. He seemed like a man torn between right and wrong, who was not putting up much of a fight against wrong. He couldn't wait to bury Sallie and Ida May under someone else's barn."

"He's gone. Absquatulated. Vamoosed." Muller used the street slang proudly, with a German accent. "It's the talk of the town in Harrison and Whitewater Village. He left for Madison, Indiana, where he aims to start a new religious community or communist kleptocracy or some such hooey."

Reany looked surprised. "And what's the cause of that? He seemed like such a devout and earnest Shaker."

"From what I heard, he fell in love with one of the sisters, Alice Grey. The elders got wind of it and accused him of being overly familiar, violating the rule of celibacy. Sound familiar?"[132]

"That's the same reason they banished Sallie and Ida May."

"Apparently, that sad affair changed George Amery," Muller said, sitting forward with his forearms across his thighs, spinning his hat in his hands. "I was told he began to believe that the strongest passion of mankind is love. How radical! Union Village elders in Lebanon stepped in and relieved him of his duties as elder and legal trustee. He was ordered to move to the South Village, away from Alice."

---

132 Innis, James Robert, and Thomas L. Sakmyster. *The Shakers of White Water, Ohio, 1823-1916.* 2014.

"The George Amery I met would not take that very lightly."

"He did not. He left and three women followed him. Alice, whom he married, and two others: Marietta Faraday and Lucy Woodward."

Reany's chair, carefully balanced on two legs, hit the floor as he leaned forward on his desk and said, "Repeat those names?"

"Ettie and Lucy. The good friends Sallie and Ida May wrote to in those letters that were in the papers."

"I see that you followed the case very closely."

"I could not get those two sad women out of my mind after I saw the bodies. So beautiful, so young, so much promise. So tragic."

"I agree. I still think of them," Reany said. "So, *Detective* Fritz, what do you make of it?"

"Did you see this?" he asked Reany, dropping a newspaper on the detective's desk.

Reany looked at a Cincinnati newspaper called *Westlich Blatter* and shook his head. "I can hardly read newspapers that are supposed to be in English, and I don't read German. What does it say?"

"This would be the *Western Pages* in English," Muller said, picking up the paper and pointing to the masthead. "The headline says, 'The Shakers: A Day Among the Communalists of the Whitewater Valley.' The writer visited the Shaker Village for a few days and did a thorough report."[133]

"All the other papers wrote about the Dill case, even in New York, so I guess it makes sense," Reany said. "What did the reporter discover?"

"He compares the village to 'a great feudal estate that is managed by expert agronomists,' meaning farmers—I looked it up," Muller said proudly, reading from the story. "He says they have something called union meetings twice a week where the Shaker sisters and brothers get to talk and socialize in small groups.

"He describes 'painstaking cleanliness, hard work and self-discipline.' It's very flattering. Listen to this: 'The life of a Shaker is vastly more comfortable and pleasant than that of a typical farmer or artisan. They ate well, were well-clothed and had comfortable dwelling places.

---

133 Sakmyster, Thomas, "The White Water, Ohio, Shaker Community: An Newly Discovered 1977 Visitor's Account," *American Communal Societies Quarterly*, Jan. 1, 2020.

Not even the smallest signs of decay.'"

"Then why do so many leave?" Reany asked, shaking his head.

"I wondered the same thing," Muller said. "This man was especially smitten by the women. He says they have a natural appearance, trim and nice and are far above most other women in their intelligence and knowledge."

"I guess that explains why the letters from Sallie and Ida May were so well written," Reany nodded. He looked at Muller as Muller studied the *Westlich Blatter* and asked, "What do you think about it all?"

Muller looked up, eager to share his thoughts. "I think those women Lucy and Ettie, with help from Amery, tried to intercede for the Dills. They did what they could. And when the Shaker Village elders turned their backs on Sallie and Ida May, George and his Shakeress friends were angry."

"That's good," Reany said. "But don't let Captain Halliday hear you thinking like that or he will pin a detective badge on you. What else?"

"I think all three of them, George included, resented what happened, and they could stand the hypocrisy no more."

"Hypocrisy how?"

"They are a society founded on Christian love, but they showed no love and grace to those women and rejected true Christian forgiveness. Instead, they punished the most natural, God-given kind of love, between a man and a woman. They claim to summon spirits, but I sometimes wonder if some spirits who answer are heaven sent."

"I have been troubled by that too," Reany said. "Something Tom Farrel told me. He said the children sometimes writhe in torment[134] and cry out when they go into trances. Whatever is doing that, it is not angels."

Muller gave an exaggerated shiver. "That raises the hair on my arms."

Both sat in thought for a moment, then Reany said, "Never mind the *Western Blabber*. What do people say about George Amery in Whitewater Village?"

"*Western Blatter*," Muller said with a chuckle, correcting Reany's fractured translation. "Some of the elders are passing rumors that he

____

134 Bauer, Cheryl, and Robert Jones Portman. *Wisdom's Paradise*, 2004.

left behind a deficiency in the books of $9,000. But Elder Henry Bear wrote a letter to the local paper. I tore it out for you."

Muller pulled a scrap of newspaper from his hat and read: "We hold no ill will against him, and feel it is our bounden duty to correct, whenever we can, all untruthful reports against his character to do him injury."[135]

"Elder Bear should watch out," Reany laughed. "He might be the next to be cast out like Cain into the Land of Nod if he's not careful."

"Not likely. They are desperate for men. Only about 90 sisters and brothers live there now, and nearly all the males are over 60 or under 16. And George Amery was not only the Whitewater Shakers' man to negotiate with Cincinnati businesses, he was a great preacher and one of the most skilled at making brooms."

Reany thought it over for a moment. Then shook his head and said, "So Amery jumped the broom. I reckon you're right. His conscience finally got to him."

"Did you know every Shaker village has a name within their society?" Muller said. "The name for Whitewater is 'The Lonely Plain of Tribulation.'"[136]

Reany said, "As I understand it, tribulation is a time of suffering, judgment and persecution. I'd say that fits them like a Shaker bonnet. You and I are not the only ones who are haunted by Sallie and Ida May Dill."

"Ghosts of Shakertown," a drawing of Whitewater Shaker Village by Cincinnati artist Carolyn Williams in 1935.

---

135 Innis, James Robert, and Thomas L. Sakmyster. *The Shakers of White Water, Ohio, 1823-1916.* 2014.

136 MacLean, John P, *Shakers of Ohio,* F. J. Heer Printing Co. Columbus, Ohio, 1907.

EPILOGUE

William Brickley died in 1885, at the age of 38, just eight years after the "Double Death Shaker Horror" that rocked Cincinnati and left Whitewater Shaker Village under a cloud of scandal.

Fred Brickley died six years later in 1891, at age 43. When Reany read the news of Fred Brickley's death, he was surprised that Fred and his pickled liver had outlived his brother William.

Both of the Brickleys were buried in family plots not far from the graves they had purchased for Sarah "Sallie" Dill and Ida May Dill.[137]

The Shakers never recovered. Their population steadily declined, and their jealously guarded cemetery was destined to remain nearly empty, as most brothers and sisters elected to leave Whitewater Shaker Village.

In 1907, three women eldresses were killed in a fire that burned their dormitory while they slept. By then, the village was down to fewer than 50 residents. Income had almost dried up, with too few men to farm the land or make furniture, beer or brooms.[138]

In 1909, the village made headlines again when *The Cincinnati Enquirer* reported a search for a missing boy, Eddie Brown, who had escaped the Shaker Whitewater Village after a severe beating by Dr. John Ludwig. Ludwig was jailed on a charge of kidnapping.

The boy was found. Ludwig accused him of a "serious charge" in connection with his own young son, but Brown insisted he had confessed only to avoid being killed by Ludwig in the woods.

---

137 Only William Brickley's grave is marked. The graves of his brother Fred and the rest of the Brickley family are unmarked or the markers have been lost to time.

138 Among other sources of income, the Shakers had a grist mill to make flour. At one time the village had four acres of mulberry trees and 20,000 silkworms were raised by the women, to make scarves, capes and bonnets for sale. They had a brewery to produce beer and sold it along with brooms, seeds, produce, cheese and dairy products, honey, grapes, applesauce and cider. Bornemann, Jennifer, "Celebrating 200 Years of Whitewater Shaker Village," *The Local Historian*, November/December 2023. Burress, Marjorie B., "Whitewater, Ohio Village of Shakers, 1824-1916: It's History and Its People." 1979.

In 1898, a newspaper report described the sad decline of Union Shaker Village near Lebanon, which was once the second largest Shaker village in the nation and ruled all Shaker communities in Ohio and Kentucky. "Fear of extinction has seized Union Village," it said, "and its great buildings may fall to decay."

The Cincinnati Enquirer reported, "Only forty of the queer sect are left at Lebanon and they are feeble with age." By 1910, Union Village was just a memory that haunted a few abandoned buildings.

Whitewater Shaker Village managed to hang on longer, until finally it became a ghost town in 1916, with only six elderly Shakers left to sell their last parcel of land.

Today, Union Village is gone except for the stately main house called Marble Hall, that rises at the side of State Route 741 like a land-locked lighthouse, with twin turreted towers at each end and a Gothic windowed cupola rising from the center. The old Shaker house is now a museum and assisted-living apartments for Otterbein Senior Life. The Shaker land was sold to the United Brethren in Christ in 1912.

The smaller Whitewater Village, about 40 miles southwest of Union Village and 25 miles northwest of Cincinnati, near Harrison, is mostly intact. Ten remaining buildings on the site have been preserved as a National Historic Site by the Friends of White Water Shaker Village since 2007. Great Parks of Hamilton County bought 600 acres of Whitewater Shaker land. The rest of the original 1,400 acres was sold to nearby farmers.

Compared to the ornate, elegant Marble Hall at Union Village, the former Whitewater Village home of Sallie and Ida May Dill looks as plain and humble as an austere ladder-back Shaker chair next to an overstuffed, plush velvet Victorian fainting couch.

The 1898 newspaper description of Union Village could be written about Whitewater Shaker Village today:

"There is something so strange, weird and pathetic about it as it stands in all its splendor today, as to cause the weariest wanderer to halt and go around, rather than across the acres of fertile land which is included in their domain."

"Now more like a tomb than a town."

FOUR

BIG TOM AND THE BLACK WIDOW

The trial and execution of Anna Hahn

Cincinnati's first convicted serial killer.
Page 1 of the *Cincinnati Enquirer*, November 7, 1937

1937

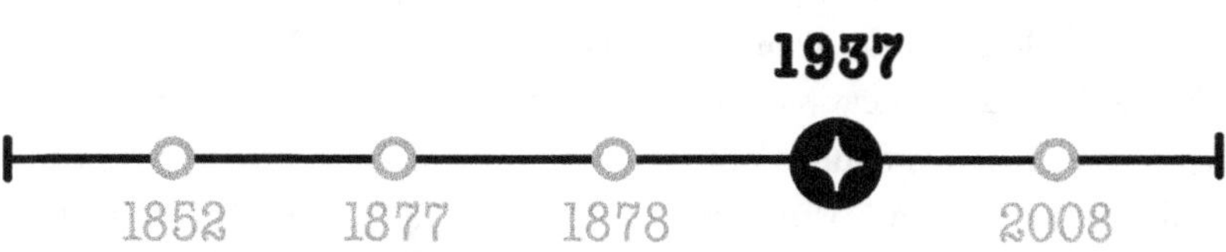

OCTOBER 1937

Cincinnati

Police Detective Tom Faragher's big right hand nearly covered the black leather-bound Bible as the bailiff held it out to him and asked, "Do you swear to tell the truth, the whole truth and nothing but the truth, so help you God?"

"I do," Faragher replied with a nod.

The courtroom was lit by October afternoon sunshine that peeked through the tall, narrow windows as if it wanted to push its way in and take a seat. But no seats were left. Spectators filled the courtroom church pews, shoulder to shoulder like longneck bottles in a case of beer. More were lined up in the hallway outside. The trial had been moved to the biggest courtroom in the Hamilton County Courthouse, but it still was not big enough.

Common Pleas Judge Charles S. Bell rapped his gavel sharply like a conductor tapping his baton to silence the tune-up of coughs, sniffles and chatter. "Mr. Outcalt, your witness. You may begin."

Faragher liked and respected Hamilton County Prosecutor Dudley Outcalt well enough to be just "Tom" and "Dudley" outside the courthouse. But today would be all "Yes-sir" and "No-sir." The jury would probably be surprised to learn that they had ever met.

"Detective Faragher, you joined the Cincinnati Police when?" the prosecutor asked, rising to stand near a table that was stacked with paperwork, notes and a battered, overflowing expanding-file.

"That was 1927, sir," Tom replied.

"So, ten years ago. And how long have you been investigating homicides?"

"Three years, sir. Since the Homicide Squad was created in 1934." Tom shifted on the hard oak chair and settled in. He made the witness box look too small but still managed to look comfortable and at ease. Big Tom, as he was known to friends in his police bowling league, had a receding tide of short, dark hair, a full face and sad eyes behind glasses with dark, heavy frames. He looked like an overworked manager at a Kroger's supermarket, or the kind doctor who delivers the bad news outside a hospital room. He wore his courtroom suit: dark gray with a white shirt and dark maroon tie.

He had testified so many times in court, the cases were as uncountable as the motley parade of mopes he had pinched. His presentation was low-key, dry, the voice of experienced authority—a man who knew who he was, who could be relied on to speak the truth no matter how sharp its edges or which way the knife cut.

"Can you tell the jury why that special Homicide Squad was created?"

"Yes, sir. It was set up to take advantage of the best experts at the University of Cincinnati Institute of Legal Medicine,[139] to enable us to apply scientific and medical knowledge to solve our cases."

"This was a new approach?"

"Yes, sir. Our city now leads the nation in using forensic science for homicide investigations."

"How many men were assigned to this elite team?"

"Five."

"Quite an achievement to be selected from hundreds of police officers."

THE BARREL CASE

It was not a question so Tom just waited. Yes, he remembered well how excited he was to be promoted from patrolman to plainclothes detective, then to the new murder squad. It was easy to recall the squad's first day: Two years ago, on the Monday after Thanksgiving in 1934. It was as if the Grim Reaper was eagerly waiting in the shadows to ambush them with one of the most sensational murders in local history.

Headlines called it "The Cask Murder" or "The Barrel Case." What should have been a slow Monday morning began with a stomach-churning visit to a grisly scene in a dim little garage attached to an apartment in Avondale. The property owner, Jacob Fischoff, had rented out the empty garage to a stranger for $2, then called the police the next morning after he became suspicious and took a look at the contents. He would probably regret that look for the rest of his life.

In the garage, the detectives found an oak barrel, standing alone—leaking the unmistakable fragrance of death. Inside was the twisted, broken, naked body of a man. His knees were folded up to his chin like a stacked chair at a church social. His hands were folded neatly

---

139 It no longer exists.

across his chest as if placed there by an undertaker. His paper-white face looked up through the top of the barrel with wide, empty eyes searching for help that never came. Detectives soon discovered he was Alvin Brunner, a diamond salesman who was educated in England and listed his last address as Brooklyn, New York.

It took four strong cops to remove the body. Rigor mortis had set in, and the corpse was wedged in as tight as a size 11 foot in a size 8 shoe. Two men tried to hold the barrel while another pair who had drawn the short straws played tug-of-war with the clammy, slippery corpse.

The Homicide Squad members shook their heads in amazement. It was almost like a macabre carnival trick to find a grown man's entire five-foot-six body wedged inside a wooden barrel that was not even waist high. Stuffed in with the dead man were a blanket, a pillow, a white belt—the only item of clothing—two towels and a sheet. All of the items were soaked or stained with blood.

A leaking bullet hole in the back of Bruner's head made it clear that he had been shot. At the bottom of the barrel, detectives found a blood-stained ribbon with the name of a Columbus jewelry store. They traced Brunner to the store, where he had stayed overnight in a room behind the shop.

When they searched the jewelry store, they found that a safe had been left open. The jewels Brunner had been carrying and a .32 caliber handgun that matched the bullet in his head were missing from the safe. Next door to the store was a bakery where the owner reported that an empty flour barrel had been stolen from the alley outside his back door. A large blood stain darkened the pavement where the missing barrel should have been.

The owner of the jewelry store had come in to open up and found that the room behind the shop was a bloody mess. He called Columbus Police, who found what looked like a murder scene without a body.

Cincinnati provided the corpse.

The salesman had been shot to death for $12,000[140] in diamonds. The killer had crammed his body in the barrel, hammered the lid tight, strapped the barrel to the back of Brunner's car and drove to

------

140   Worth $287,000 in 2025.

Cincinnati, where he asked around until he found garage space to rent. Witnesses said the stranger talked as if he knew the neighborhood. Police figured he was from Cincinnati or he would have dumped the barrel in Columbus.

The Cincinnati Homicide Squad investigated for weeks and came up with two suspects: The dead man's secretary, who usually traveled with him, was missing; and witnesses said the jewelry salesman had picked up a hitchhiker. Did Brunner make the fatal mistake of telling a hitchhiker about the diamonds? Did the secretary decide to kill his boss and take them? Were they both the same man?

A woman who met Brunner shortly before he was murdered told police she had received a letter from him in which he described a premonition that something terrible would happen to him because of his kindness to strangers. That may have come true. Police soon suspected that the "hitchhiker" was probably his "secretary" who killed him—the man Brunner met in Hamilton, Ohio.

The car was last seen heading south. Then the case went cold. It still bothered Detective Faragher. Brunner's sad, tangled body and staring eyes haunted the back of his mind where he kept unsolved cases in a mental file cabinet. That was a dark place he tried not to visit.

And now he was testifying in a case that eclipsed all the headlines of the Cask Murder. But first, the prosecutor asked him about another big case from last June: "Were you asked to assist in what became known as the 'Head and Hands Murder'?"

"Yes, sir," Faragher nodded.

"This one also made sensational headlines nationally, but can you describe it for any jurors who are not familiar with it?"

"Yes, sir. Two boys were fishing near Carrollton, Kentucky one day when they snagged a heavy straw box. When they opened it, they found a human head and a pair of hands."

There were a few gasps in the courtroom and Faragher heard a woman moan something about "poor boys." He continued.

"The local sheriff asked us for assistance. A week later, a headless body of a large man, missing both hands, was found in a culvert near Eminence, Kentucky, about 25 miles south of Carrollton."

Faragher remembered the jokes about putting two and two together:

two hands and two arms. Big Tom didn't like to joke about such things. He was unfailingly polite and respectful of the dead and their grieving families.

He said, "We were able to identify the victim as Capt. Harry Miller, a retired Cincinnati fireman. We discovered the murder scene at Captain Miller's summer home in West Harrison, Indiana, which showed signs of a violent struggle—copious blood stains, broken furniture, overturned tables."

"That case was solved?"

"Yes, the fireman's sister had a chauffeur—an ex-con from Kentucky who killed Captain Miller as part of a plot to steal $100,000 in securities. The killer, Heber 'Jimmy' Hicks, is now on Death Row in Indiana."[141]

"And you were instrumental in solving that case?"

"We were able to examine the victim's remains and discovered fragments of a .32 caliber bullet in his brain. We found a matchbook that led us to a bar where witnesses identified Hicks."

"Objection," said defense attorney Joseph Hoodin, not bothering to stand. "Relevance?"

Outcalt turned and smiled regretfully at the jury as if they would all have to be patient while he indulged the rude interruption. With thinning gray hair and a dapper light-gray vested suit flashing a gold watch chain, the prosecutor was handsome, charming and reassuring. He looked like a trusted banker. "Outcalt" was the Americanized German name Altgeld—literally "old money." But Tom knew that under the polished surface of old-money manners, Dudley Outcalt was as tough as a boiled combat boot.

He had been a hero of World War I, one of the dashing pilots who flew in Captain Eddie Rickenbacker's famous "Hat in the Ring" Squad-

---

141 The fireman did not go gently. He was beaten in the head with a metal bar, then shot, and still may have been alive when his hands and head were chopped off with an axe. The bloody axe and crimson rags were found near the lake where the head and hands were discovered, along with a matchbook from a West Harrison bar. The sister was described as a "spinster opera singer." She was a suspect until Hicks confessed. He had been released on parole from a life sentence for murdering a young woman in Kentucky. He admitted to hiring three men for $400 to help murder Captain Miller.

The famous insignia of the "Hat in the Ring" squadron led by World War I ace Eddie Rickenbacker. This one is on the side of Rickenbacker's Spad XIII biplane.

ron.[142] He could do no less coming from a family tree whose branches were hung with the flags of military service. His great-grandfather had served in the Civil War and in the Ohio General Assembly.[143]

After World War I, Outcalt came home and joined another family tradition, practicing law. His grandfather Miller Outcalt had been a Hamilton County judge, and his father, Dudley Clifton Outcalt, became a prominent lawyer and leader of the Republican Party.

Dudley Miller Outcalt Jr. followed their footsteps in public service and went to work as an assistant for Hamilton County Prosecutor Charles Bell—the same Judge Bell now presiding over Cincinnati's "trial of the century."

The prosecutor was no stranger to tragedy. One Saturday morning in late May 1931, he dropped his father off near

Attorney Outcalt Sought In Cin'ti

(Associated Press)

Cincinnati, O., April 2.—Dudley C. Outcalt, 60, one of the prominent members of the Hamilton county bar, who disappeared last Saturday while enroute to his office, was the object of a search today by police and county authorities.

His son, D. M. Outcalt, former assistant county prosecutor, said relatives were without a motive to explain the disappearance. No trace of the man has been found.

---

142   Rickenbacker, of Columbus, was awarded the Medal of Honor. He was an Ace of Aces, shooting down 26 enemy planes, flying the biplane Spad XIII. The 94th Aero Squadron he led produced eight aces in the First Pursuit Group. The unit was one of the first in what is now the United States Air Force. One of the pilots was William "Billy" Mitchell, credited with the birth of American air power. The B-25 Mitchell bomber used in the Doolittle Raid on Tokyo in WWII was named after him.

143   Oliver Outcalt committed suicide in the cellar of his Cincinnati home by cutting his own throat "almost from ear to ear" out of "despondency," the *Wilmington Journal-Republican* reported on October 30, 1895. Another member of the family, Richard Outcalt Joyce, was the pilot of Crew 10 for the Doolittle Raiders' daring attack on Tokyo in 1943. And Col. Dudley Miller Outcalt's grandson, Capt. Dudley Miller Outcalt (1951-2024), attended the US Naval Academy after graduating from Western Hills High School in 1969.

his law office in Norwood and his father disappeared, never seen by his family again. For weeks and months, the Outcalts ran notices, classified ads and descriptions, seeking any information about Dudley Clifton Outcalt, 61, five feet five, gray hair, blue eyes, well dressed in a brown topcoat, gray hat and black shoes.

His family said he had been having some health problems natural to his age but was otherwise cheerful and in good spirits. He had made plans for the following week. It seemed unbelievable that he would take his own life or suddenly choose to vanish.

A body was found in the Ohio River that matched his description. His son drove down to Kentucky to take a look, but it was not his father.

Then came the strange reports. Several friends and acquaintances said they had seen him walking the streets of Cincinnati. Some said he seemed dazed, lost. Others said they asked if he was okay and he told them he was fine.

Faragher knew what many in Cincinnati did not: The missing man had nearly been disbarred the year before he disappeared. A complaint accused him of "a breach of legal ethics with respect to funds invested for a client." The senior Outcalt denied any wrongdoing, but a committee was appointed to investigate, and that dark cloud was still casting shadows on his reputation when he vanished.

The missing man was also involved in a suspicious property sale not long before he vanished, Faragher had heard. A valuable parcel of land that had gone unclaimed for 15 years was being sold by Outcalt when the owner suddenly showed up.

Another angle the Homicide Squad detectives had to keep in mind was just across the river: "Sin City." Strange things happened to men who visited Newport, Kentucky for gambling, hookers and bootleg booze. Even prominent citizens sometimes got in trouble, were beaten or vanished without a trace after getting tangled in the tentacles of the Cleveland mob that bossed Northern Kentucky's casinos, brothels and bars.

Now, six years had passed, and the mystery of the disappearance was still unsolved. But the son had moved on, and was now the new prosecutor, elected just last November in 1936. He was still dashing, handsome and charming, giving no hint of the sadness within.

Tom watched as the prosecutor turned his full wattage of charm on the jury like a spotlight as he replied to Hoodin's objection.

"Mr. Outcalt?" the judge asked.

"Your honor, may it please the court and our lovely jury, I am merely establishing this outstanding detective's impressive record of resolving more than *90 percent* of the cases he has investigated—that is, I am laying a foundation for his testimony to come."

The "lovely" remark was a deft touch, Tom thought. This jury was like none he had ever seen: 11 women and one man. He could tell Outcalt's flattery had hit the mark. Eleven ladies were blushing and smiling; the solitary man on the jury was smirking.

"Overruled," the judge said, with another light rap of his gavel and a pointed look at the defense table, where lead counsel Joseph Hoodin tossed down his pencil dramatically, took off his glasses and rubbed the bridge of his nose to signal his weary disgust.

Judge Bell said, "You may continue, Mr. Outcalt, but let's move along."

BURIED IN WITNESSES, EXHIBITS

Tom hid a smile. They finally were getting to the case that filled the courtroom today, known in headlines as the "Blond Killer" and "Black Widow Murders." And Outcalt was loaded for battle as if he was flying a mission to fight the Red Baron in the skies over France. He had submitted more than 100 witnesses and 137 exhibits, including 50 large glass jars that contained livers, hearts and kidneys floating in formaldehyde like nightmares in snow globes—the macabre viscera of murder victims.

They were already well into the second week of the trial, with at least another week to go.

"Certainly, your honor," Outcalt nodded to the judge. He strolled over to the defense table and pointed at a small, well dressed, attractive blonde woman sitting next to Hoodin. Her face remained as still as a marble statue, blank and unreadable as an empty page. She was no Hollywood beauty, but her even features, trim figure and relative youth, at 31, must have made her irresistible to the old men she killed, Faragher thought.

"When did the accused first come to your attention?" Outcalt asked Faragher.

"She was arrested on August 11, but our investigation had been under way for two months by then."

Seven killed and another five who were crippled for life, lucky to be alive, Faragher thought. *And there she sits, as cold as March rain.*

The investigation had been one of the most bizarre yet for the Homicide Squad. In addition to a spree of murders, Anna Marie Hahn was suspected of insurance fraud in three fires—two homes and a restaurant she ran with her husband, Philip Hahn. And she had robbed her elderly victims of more than $70,000[144] in homes, securities, "loans," personal property and cash. The detectives had interviewed scores of neighbors and witnesses, exhumed four bodies for autopsies and done dozens of lab tests with the help of the University of Cincinnati Institute of Legal Medicine.

During interrogations, Hahn talked and talked as if every word was another brick in a wall around her castle of lies. She had an answer for everything, often anticipating their next questions. She was a smart one, a former schoolteacher in Germany. And she seemed unshakable. She had nearly gotten away with a shocking string of terrible murders.

But then one day in the summer of 1937, Fritz Grafemeyer, owner of a restaurant in Over-the-Rhine, came into the police station with a story to tell.

Grafemeyer had started to worry in late May when he realized that his good friend and loyal, daily customer Jacob Wagner had not been in for days. He asked around the neighborhood and was stunned to find out that Wagner had died suddenly on June 3.

Grafemeyer didn't understand how his healthy, happy friend, a retired bachelor and gardener who was well known for lovely plantings at some of the finest homes in the city, could be gone so quickly. So he kept knocking on doors and asking his customers if anyone knew what happened to Jacob Wagner.

What he learned disturbed him so badly he could not sleep at night. He finally went to the police with the story. But instead of sending

---

144   In 2025 dollars, about $1.5 million.

detectives to investigate, the desk sergeant gave him the brush-off. Four times he went back to the police, and each time he was treated like a crank with a barking-dog complaint. On his final visit, Fritz lost his temper. He shouted in a mix of angry German and English and pounded the table until finally, the sergeant agreed to pass along a report to detectives.

Unlike the stationhouse cops, the Homicide Squad was immediately interested. Detective Faragher took the case. He found Wagner's apartment on the third floor of a narrow brick building next door to Findlay Market in Over-The-Rhine and began to knock on doors in the building.

The neighbors in the closeknit German community all remembered Jacob Wagner fondly as a kind and quiet old gentleman who lived alone.

Then Faragher got a break. A woman on the second floor clearly remembered a little blonde woman who spoke German, who went through the building asking Wagner's neighbors, "Are there any old German men who live here?" The woman told Faragher she thought that was odd. He agreed.

Neighbors on the third floor in the apartment next to Wagner's said they overheard Wagner and Hahn through the thin walls as she introduced herself as Wagner's niece from Germany. The old man told her he had no niece, but she insisted. She told him a large sum of money had been left to him from an estate in Germany, and she could help him recover it.

After that, they said, she visited often. One day, they overheard a loud argument as Wagner angrily accused her of stealing his bankbook. She denied it, and promised to look for it. When she found it, she gave it back to him and invited him to dinner, but he insisted she could cook for him at his apartment instead.

And that was Wagner's fatal mistake.

Outcalt asked, "What did you learn about his state of health, Detective Faragher?"

"Mr. Wagner was 78, but his neighbors agreed that he seemed healthy until he was visited by Mrs. Hahn," Faragher told the jury.

"You mean the accused, Anna Marie Hahn?" Outcalt clarified,

pointing at her. She looked straight ahead, ignoring the prosecutor, the detective, the judge and the crowded courtroom.

"Yes, sir."

"What were you told?"

"We learned that he became violently ill and died immediately after her visit on June 2."

"What else?"

"After he fell ill, she brought him oranges to help him recover, but he got much worse and had to be taken to Good Samaritan Hospital, where he died the next day, on June 3."

"How did she claim they were related?"

"At his funeral, she was heard to say, 'Isn't it sad. This is the second old uncle I have buried this month.'"

This time Hoodin jumped to his feet, pushing his chair back and making it screech in protest as it scraped across the marble floor. "Objection! Hearsay!"

"Sustained," said Judge Bell.

It would be struck from the trial record, and the jury would be told to disregard it, Faragher knew, but they would not forget it.

Outcalt resumed as if nothing had happened. "Mr. Wagner lived alone?"

"Yes. The neighbors said he had no other visitors. He told them, 'I have a new girl, but I had to sign everything over to her.'"

"And what was everything—all the savings of this lonely, elderly man of age 78?"

"He had an estate of about $3,000."[145]

"What became of that?"

"She filed a claim for it on the day he died. She produced a will that left everything to her, but when we had it examined by handwriting analysts at the FBI, they agreed it was a forgery. She also immediately tried to cash a $1,000 check on his account. That was also forged and the bank rejected it."

"So you became interested in her as a suspect in his death?"

"Yes, sir. We learned that she had cooked for him immediately

---

145   About $70,000 in 2025.

before he died. So we had his body exhumed."

"And what did you find when the body was dug up?" Outcalt asked, clarifying "exhumed" for the puzzled looks on some of the jurors faces.

"Fatal amounts of arsenic. During the autopsy, there was a strong garlic smell—a positive indication of arsenic poisoning. Analysis of his internal organs found enough arsenic to kill 20 men."

The crowd gasped and turned its eyes to the glass jars of organs.

Outcalt said, "Let the record show that Detective Faragher is referring to Exhibits 28, 29 and 30, glass jars containing the arsenic-poisoned kidney, liver and heart of Mr. Wagner."

The Homicide Squad partnership with the University of Cincinnati School of Medicine had paid off, Faragher told the jury. Men in lab coats with advanced degrees as physiologists and toxicologists would take the stand to testify later, but Big Tom had a calm and steady presence that made his words as trustworthy as a kind grandfather's advice.

So Outcalt asked him, "Based on what you have learned about arsenic poisoning, how would you summarize Jacob Wagner's final hours?"

"Torture. Hell. Agony. Unbearable pain and suffering."

Outcalt turned to Judge Bell. "Your Honor, what follows may be disturbing for some in the courtroom."

Faragher looked at the jury. They were riveted. The whole courtroom seemed to hold its breath, quiet enough to hear a butterfly land on a rose petal. They wouldn't leave and lose their seats if the courthouse was on fire, Tom thought.

"Ladies and gentlemen, you've been warned," the judge said. "If anyone would like to exit, we will pause." He waited. As Faragher expected, nobody moved. Faces in the gallery looked eager, hungry, wide-eyed, like gawkers gathered around a fatal car wreck.

"Continue," the judge said at last, turning back to Outcalt.

The homicide detective was asked to share what he had learned from the university's medical experts about death by arsenic poisoning. He started with some history.

"Arsenic has been known as the king of poisons since the time of the Roman Emperor Nero, because it has no telltale odor, no color, no taste," he said. "A dose the size of a pea dissolved in water is almost immediately fatal."

"And what are the symptoms of poisoning?" Outcalt asked.

"Victims feel shortness of breath, a sore throat, pins and needles in the hands and feet. They may have chest pains and irregular heartbeats. They begin to cough. Their skin becomes red and swollen, with hard white patches on their palms and the soles of their feet.

"Next come racking seizures and terrible abdominal cramps that twist the body, followed by nausea, violent vomiting and uncontrollable diarrhea."

"And death?"

"Death finally comes from multiple organ failure and shock, but the agony can be prolonged for many hours, even days," Faragher told the wide-eyed jury.

He heard small moans in the crowd as he recited the torments of arsenic poisoning. He looked at Anna Marie Hahn. Nothing. She looked as if she was bored. No, not even that. More like the vacant stare of someone waiting at a bus stop or sitting through a long, tedious speech. She was there in court, but she was somewhere else.

"Are there any obvious outward signs of poisoning?" Outcalt asked.

"Extreme salivation and a strong odor of garlic from breath and body fluids."

"What about milder doses?"

"A non-fatal dose can cause delirium, confusion, loss of strength and paralysis of arms and legs."

Outcalt turned to the judge. "Your Honor, may I approach the bench?"

Judge Bell nodded and used two hooked fingers to summon Hoodin as well. Faragher eavesdropped from the witness box.

Outcalt: "I would like to question the detective about poisoning victims who survived. It could be unpleasant, but perhaps we should deal with it now and get through it all at once."

Judge Bell: "Mr. Hoodin?"

Hoodin: "You have already ruled to admit alleged victims who were not part of the indictment. Over my adamant objections—"

Judge Bell: "I am very aware of your objections. You have made them flash like neon lights over a Newport casino." He turned to the prosecutor. "I have given you wide latitude, Mr. Outcalt. Charles Heis can testify on his own behalf. The others are inadmissible."

Faragher was not surprised, but he was disappointed. The Homicide Squad's investigation had turned up a startling pattern that removed any doubt about Anna Hahn's guilt: People who met her died suddenly and painfully.

Mr. and Mrs. Johannes Oswald, her elderly aunt and uncle, took her in after she arrived in Cincinnati from Bavaria in 1929. They became suspicious of her luxurious clothes and frequent visits to the horse-betting parlors in Elmwood Place—all on her small income working as a chambermaid at the Alms Hotel. They must have asked too many questions, Faragher thought, because both died shortly after she moved in. She claimed their house was left to her.

Then an elderly German man, Ernest Kohler, died in 1933 after telling his friends he had "a new girl." As soon as he was buried, Hahn produced a will in which Kohler left his home at 2070 Colerain Avenue to "my wife," Anna Marie Hahn.

There was Julia Kresckay, the landlady in the building where Jacob Wagner lived. When Faragher visited to investigate, one of the renters in the building who was a friend of Kresckay told him that Hahn had borrowed $800 from Kresckay, then offered her some medicine.

"Every time she received the medicine, she became violently ill," said the roomer. He told Faragher how he had confronted Hahn after Kresckay was hospitalized, and demanded that she pay the loan back. Hahn stubbornly refused until he threatened to go to the police. Then she quickly returned the $800.

The roomer said something else that got the attention of the detectives as he described Julia Kresckay's attacks of sickness: "When the matter from her mouth touched her flesh it raised white blisters."[146]

Dudley Outcalt resumed his questions: "Tell us about croton oil, Detective Faragher."

"Yes, sir," Faragher said. "Croton oil is a lethal poison made from a colorful, common houseplant. The Latin name is Codieaeum Variega-

---

146   Mercer, Tom, "Blond is Linked With Another Poisoning; Indicted on Charges of Murdering Two," *The Cincinnati Enquirer*, August 17, 1937.

tum. More commonly known as a coleus plant. The leaves are shaped like a spearpoint, striped in bright red-orange and green, often with a blood-red streak down the middle. Oil made from the seeds was used as a laxative 50 years ago, but only in extremely small amounts. Just two drops can be fatal. Contact with the skin causes blisters and peeling."[147]

Outcalt picked up a small square paper from his desk and said, "Let the record show, we have introduced as Exhibit 47 through 52, prescriptions filled by a pharmacist for Anna Marie Hahn. Among these are croton oil."

As the written prescriptions were given to the jurors, Faragher thought of all the victims such as Julia Kresckay, whose suffering would not be admissible in court.

Mrs. Kresckay had been taken to the hospital where a doctor diagnosed croton oil poisoning. The woman was severely disabled, her legs paralyzed by the "medicine" she had been given by Hahn. Unable to take care of herself, she had been forced to returned to her family in Hungary, where she was still unable to use her legs.

Olive Kohler—not related to Ernest Kohler—was another sad story. Elderly, poor, unemployed and desperate for a job, Olive Kohler met Anna Hahn in a café. Hahn seemed sympathetic and offered to get Olive a good government job in return for a fee of $100. The job never came, but demands for more money continued. Then on June 22 and 23, Hahn brought ice cream to Mrs. Kohler.

Neighbors said Hahn claimed she was from the Salvation Army and wanted to make Mrs. Kohler "comfy."

Instead, both times she ate ice cream served by Hahn, Olive Kohler became violently ill. The effects were so severe, she became mentally deranged and had to be committed to Longview Asylum. Within four months she was dead.

'IS THAT YOU, LILLIAN?'

Hahn then knocked on the door of Olive Kohler's sister, Mary Arnold, 95, who lived above the ice cream store. Mrs. Arnold was

---

147   Croton oil is still used as the active ingredient in skin peel treatments by dermatologists.

almost blind, living on a meager widow's pension from her husband's service in the Civil War.

When Mrs. Arnold went to the door, she asked, "Is that you, Lillian?" mistaking Hahn for a dear friend.

"Yes," Hahn lied. She offered to buy Mrs. Arnold a beer, but the blind woman got suspicious and declined—a decision that probably saved her life. Her case was inadmissible too.

But Judge Bell would allow George Heis to testify. He met Hahn in the summer of 1936. She owed him money for coal deliveries, so she offered to cook for him. A dinner of spinach and beer, prepared by Hahn, nearly killed him. He spent a year in bed recuperating. He had to be carried on a stretcher to the police station to file charges of theft against Hahn. And he pledged to come to court in his wheelchair to describe how his healthy and robust life had been destroyed by the woman who was being called "the Black Widow."

Heis made good on his promise, and Faragher was there to watch as he pointed at Hahn across the courtroom and shouted, "You did this to me!" The jurors were shaken. But Hahn was unfazed, a sphynx. She didn't even blink.

"Detective Faragher, you were there when Mrs. Hahn was arrested and you searched her home?"

"Yes, sir. That was on August 11. I accompanied Homicide Squad Commander Captain Pat Hayes."

"Was there anything unusual about Mrs. Hahn's behavior that day?"

"There was. When Captain Hayes announced he would search the cellar, she became very upset. She shouted, 'What are you going down there for?' Her face was red and she was flustered. This was very unusual. She is normally very composed."

The jury looked at Hahn, who confirmed the description, looking straight ahead, refusing to meet their eyes.

"So this was one of the few times detectives had seen her lose her composure? Tell us what happened next."

"As we went down the stairs to search the cellar, we didn't find anything at first. Then Captain Hayes reached up and felt around on top of some rafters that would have been within her reach. He found a clear glass bottle containing about a quarter inch of a whitish substance."

"Were the rafters dusty?"

"Yes, sir."

"But the bottle was clean?"

"Yes. It had no dust on it. It had not been there long."

"How did she react when the bottle was found?" Outcalt asked, pointedly looking at Hahn.

"She got very agitated and demanded that he give her the bottle. Captain Hays refused. She kept demanding. Her voice rose and she was flushed and angry."

Outcalt let that linger for a moment so the jury could think about it. Then he asked, "Did you have the contents of the bottle analyzed?"

"Yes, sir, we did. The analysis was done by scientists at the University of Cincinnati."

"And what did it contain.

"Arsenic."

The gallery made a little "oh!" of satisfied surprise, like the sound someone makes when they finally find a missing wallet under a bed. Faragher looked at Hoodin and almost felt sorry for the defense lawyer. He was still young enough to believe he could win, although his glasses and stocky, round face made him look much older than 29. But he also knew his task was like threading a needle while blindfolded. Hahn was too icy to be sympathetic. A jury of women would see right through her where men might be swayed by her looks or unable to condemn a woman. And the evidence was stacked as deep as those jars of blood-red remains of the victims.

The Black Widow tag in headlines was a good fit, Faragher thought. One of the survivors of her poisons was the man who married her in 1930, the year after she arrived from Germany as Anna Filser. Philip Hahn, a telegraph operator, worked nights and seemed unaware or didn't care about her absences as she "nursed" her elderly victims.

His relatives told detectives Philip Hahn had experienced several severe and mysterious illnesses during their marriage. Twice she tried to insure him with double-indemnity policies that would have paid $10,000[148] upon his death, but she could not afford the premiums.

Philip was lucky. Hahn's son from a previous marriage, Oscar, 11,

____

148   More than $231,000 today.

found a bottle of croton oil she had hidden in the cushions of a chair in their home. Oscar said his mother got mad at him when he gave it to his stepfather Philip. But now it was a key piece of evidence. Philip

Anna Marie Hahn in court, with a picture of her son, Oscar. Courtesy of *The Cincinnati Enquirer*.

still had it in his locker at work when Faragher came to question him.

Faragher found out Hahn had at least two husbands: her first was a doctor in Vienna she left when she immigrated to Cincinnati. He was the father of Oscar, she claimed, but she wouldn't say anything else about him except that he died in 1929, the same year she arrived in Cincinnati. Faragher wondered if he had been poisoned too.

She also had claimed she was married to Ernest Kohler, so she could take his estate when she killed him, but that marriage was a sham like the forged will, Faragher believed.

Faragher passed a hand over the smooth rail in front of him, where the nervous, sweating hands of guilty defendants had worn the varnish off in places, exposing lighter oak underneath. As he touched the rail, he imagined he could feel their desperation linger like stale smoke. He never mentioned it to anyone, but he sometimes felt that same invisible presence when he picked up a gun, knife or rope that had been used to inflict evil.

He thought of the Oswalds. Ernest Kohler. Julie Kresckay. Olive Kohler. Mary Arnold. All elderly. All Germans. Defenseless women and lonely old men. How many had this little blond killed that were not discovered?

Most murderers were like that butcher Jimmy Hicks who killed the fireman. They had no conscience. They were as rabid as snarling dogs. But this woman sat there like she was made of stone, impassive, untouched by the dark swirling cloud of death around her. She seemed to have no soul.

He was brought back to the present as the judge leaned over in his direction and asked softly, "Do you need a break, Tom?"

"No, sir. I'm fine."

So was the case against Hahn, he thought. Dudley Outcalt still had four murders that were admissible. One was in the indictment. Three more were allowed by Judge Bell, over the loud and angry objections of Hoodin.[149]

Faragher testified about the first: Albert Palmer, 72, an immigrant from Paris. He was a retired railroad watchman who lived alone in a shoebox-shaped two-story apartment building on Central Parkway. He had met Hahn in December 1936 and died three months later, on March 27, 1937. His sister told detectives he was in good health before he met her. Hahn visited him at least six times to prepare his meals and he visited her home frequently, according to a grocer on the second floor of Palmer's building, Peter Toner. Albert Palmer died in agony.[150]

His sister recalled, "After he visited her, he looked funny in the face, suffered terribly in his stomach and hurt all over."

When Faragher and his partner Walter Hart went to Palmer's grim, small apartment, they found stained wallpaper, sparse furnishings, a thin mattress—all the sad emptiness left behind by a lonely man. A nephew had gone through his property and discovered a stack of treasured letters from Hahn, addressing him as "Dear Sweet Dady," and signed "with love and kisses."

Neighbors told the detectives that Hahn and Palmer had often been seen together at the Elmwood Place betting parlors. "She played the horses," one said.

149　The Ohio Supreme Court and the US Supreme Court affirmed Judge Bell's ruling the following year when the Hahn verdict was appealed. Her appeal was denied.

150　On Saturday, October 23, 1937, the *Cincinnati Post* reported, "The Palmer Phase of the case will be handled for the state by Assistant Prosecutor Simon Leis. He was the father of longtime Hamilton County Prosecutor and Sheriff Simon Leis Jr.

Palmer's sister said, "When they returned, he looked stupefied."

Faragher believed that was caused by morphine that Hahn had obtained from a drugstore by claiming it was needed to nurse her elderly friends. She was "An angel of mercy, trapped by unfortunate circumstances," Hoodin told the jury.

Palmer's family said he had $2,000[151] saved up before he met Hahn. It was all gone.

One of Hahn's letters to Palmer that was introduced as evidence said, "Honey, I have to have $100 in the bank for that check I gave that fellow. I hope you won't turn me down." It was signed, "Love, Anna."

Another said, "I looked all over the place for your pocketbook and couldn't find it. This sure is terrible, you won't have no money now."

The poisonings began to accelerate during the summer of 1937 as Hahn became desperate for money to pay her gambling debts. Two months after Palmer died, Wagner was poisoned to death and died on June 3.

While Wagner was slowly dying, Hahn was already lining up her next victim, George Gsellman, who died on July 5. His tiny attic apartment was bleak. It was squeezed under the roof like a cramped attic at the top of a three-and-a-half story brick building at 1717 Elm Steet, with squashed rectangular windows like gun slits and ceilings so low Big Tom had to duck through the doorway.

A good detective used all of his senses at a crime scene. Faragher started by standing in the middle of the room to listen. He heard the ordinary sounds of life in the streets outside. Traffic, honking horns, shouts. Then, under that, nearby apartments. A thump of a dropped shoe, the bump and click of a closed door. Shuffling feet. A faucet. Muffled voices from the floor below as if people were talking under a layer of blankets. Then he heard voices from next door. They were talking about the policeman who had just gone into Mr. Gsellman's apartment. Every word was clear through the cheap plaster walls.

Witnesses, he thought. *They might have heard something.*

Next he used his eyes to look slowly and carefully around the room. The floors were bare. The furniture was crude—two old wood-

---

151 In 2025, $46,000.

en chairs, chipped and scuffed, next to a tiny table set for two, with food still on the plates. A rumpled, unmade bed with filthy, unwashed sheets. Pegs on the wall held two shirts and two pairs of trousers. There was no chest of drawers, no cozy reading lamp, no table beside the bed. The room radiated loneliness and sadness. But it had a secret to tell.

Faragher was used to death scenes and the smells that lingered. The butcher-shop stink of fresh blood. Decay and its old friend excrement. Sometimes he thought he could smell fear the way you could smell a woman's perfume when she has left a room. He had learned to get past the reek that could gag a corpse and look for what was beneath it. In Gsellman's apartment, the first impression was death, vomit and incontinence. His deathbed reeked like an outhouse in July. Then another layer. The smell of hopelessness and filth. Cockroaches, bedbugs, unwashed laundry, garbage, mold, rats, stale sweat. And just underneath that, the sick-sweet garbage odor of rancid food.

He imagined he could taste it. Spinach? Sauerkraut? Boiled cabbage?

In the shadows, against a wall that was away from the tiny windows, there was a two-burner gas stove. He saw pans and picked them up to find the remains of a meal. He looked again at the little table. Two places set for dinner, with uneaten food still on the plates—attended by an honor guard of dead flies.

Something sudden and terrible had interrupted that meal.

He touched the chairs. The table. Then he picked up one of the cooking pans again. There it was. Something he couldn't explain. More of a feeling than a picture. A foreboding, a hunch as fleeting as a shadow crossing the moon. The person who held the pan had used it as an instrument of murder.

The plates and pans were taken to the university crime lab for analysis. The results showed that Faragher was right: The meal was loaded with fatal doses of arsenic.

George Gsellman had been murdered. The question was why? The poor man lived on such a paltry annuity he could barely afford to feed himself, much less take Anna Hahn to the betting parlors or lend her money. She had taken his last $100.

He knocked on doors again and learned more. On July 5, the

neighbors said, she visited and cooked Gsellman a meal. They heard him moaning, retching, crying out. And they heard a woman's voice with a German accent, telling him she would get help. He was found dead the next morning, surrounded by the filth of his final hours of excruciating sickness as his body emptied itself in a futile attempt to expel the poison.

When they interviewed Anna Hahn later, she denied even knowing Gsellman. But two witnesses said they saw her at his apartment the night he died. Confronted with their statements, she responded as if she had merely forgotten someone's name. "Oh, him. Of course."

After Gsellman died, she chose her next victim within a week. He was a cobbler who owned a small shoe-repair shop. George Obendorfer—her third victim named George—was 67. He was alone in his shop when Anna Hahn came in off the street and asked him if he could fix a broken heel on her shoe.

Faragher pictured the scene. Another lonely old man, repairing shoes that are as broken down and worn out as he is. The bell above his shop door tinkles and an attractive young blond walks in. She lifts the hem of her skirt to show him the broken heel of her shoe, smiles and flirts with him as he admires the slim, shapely leg. "Yes, of course," he says with a smile, "I can help you."

He's too eager, too easy for her. Things are getting too hot in Cincinnati. And this old man might be her ticket out of town.

They talk about the old country. She lays on the German accent and touches his arm as they talk. He is smitten. She talks about going to Colorado with her son and says she is afraid to travel alone. If only a kind gentleman like Mr. Obendorfer would come along to provide company and protection…

"Colorado? Yes," he says, "of course I would. I have a sister in Denver. Business is slow. What's a few days?"

Those would be the last days of his life.

Obendorfer was thrilled and excited as he packed for the trip out West. He told his friends about his young and pretty "new woman." He even dipped into his savings to buy a new suit.

Before they boarded a train in late July, Obendorfer wrote his new girlfriend a check for $5,000 to pay off her mortgage. But the money never made it to the bank. The mortgage payment was another lie.

On the train to Colorado, she was with him whenever they dined, salting his food with a shaker she carried in her white, knitted handbag.

That's when George Obendorfer began having problems. He had severe stomach pain, cramps, nausea, sudden diarrhea and insatiable thirst.

Outcalt asked, "Detective Faragher, what did Mrs. Hahn's son, Oscar, tell you about taking glasses of water to the suffering old man?"

"Yes, he told us his mother sent him with water at least 18 times."

By the time they got to Denver, Obendorfer was feeble and very sick, unable to walk without help. But after a few days, in spite of his condition, Hahn insisted they had to move on to Colorado Springs. The owner of the Hotel was asking too many questions.

"Was this the same hotel owner who was a member of the Denver City Council?"

"Yes, sir."

"The one who told you she denied knowing Mr. Obendorfer, and said she met him on the train?"

"Yes, sir, that is correct."

"No further questions, Your Honor," Outcalt said.

"I have no questions," Hoodin said.

"You are dismissed. We will take a ten-minute recess," Judge Bell said with a bang of his gavel that ignited a brushfire of chatter through the courtroom.

Faragher's testimony was finished, but he stayed to listen to the next witnesses.

THE WESTERN DUDE

First was a railroad mechanic who testified that on the train he heard Anna Hahn tell her son, "Oscar, bring me that medicine" for Obendorfer, who looked feeble and very sick.

A Denver banker said Mrs. Hahn had come in to request a bank draft from George Obendorfer's savings account in Cincinnati. Hahn had introduced herself as "Mrs. Obendorfer," and wanted a check for $2,000 to $3,000 so they could buy a small farm.

When the banker told her Obendorfer would have to endorse the draft, she argued, then gave up and left. "I thought her story was suspicious, the banker said. But before he could follow up with the police, she skipped town and took Obendorfer and Oscar to Colorado Springs.

"The state calls P.P. Turner," Dudley announced.

Turner was the owner of the Park Hotel in Colorado Springs. He was tall, lean, well dressed, with an impressive mustache, a brown suit, a string tie and shiny black Western boots that echoed through the subdued courtroom as he walked to the stand across the hard marble floor.

After introducing his witness to the jury, Outcalt asked, "Please tell us, Mr. Turner, when you first met the defendant, Mrs. Hahn."

"Yes, sir. At about 7 o'clock on the night of July 30, Mrs. Hahn, her son and an old man, came to my hotel. She registered for all three of them, signing his name as G.G. Obendorfer. They all were registered from Chicago."

"Chicago?" Outcalt asked sharply, to make sure the jury did not miss the lie by Hahn.

"Yes, sir, Chicago. I assisted Mrs. Hahn in helping Mr. Obendorfer to his room. He seemed to be a very sick man. His face was yellow, he was perspiring freely and breathing heavily."

"And what occurred the following day?"

"In the morning, I passed his room and heard him moaning and groaning on his bed. I told Mrs. Hahn that I wasn't running a hospital, that the man was in very bad condition, and that she would have to get him in a hospital."

"How did she react?"

"She was very indignant, but nevertheless, a few minutes later she asked me to recommend a hospital. She called a cab and took him there."

"What did she tell you about her relationship with Mr. Obendorfer."

"I asked her who the man was and she told me she didn't know. She said she met him on the train but had never seen him before then. She said he was sick and she had taken care of him, but now she washed her hands of him, that it was the city's job to take care of him."[152]

"Mr. Turner, what was the condition of the room?"

"It was all mussed up, to put it politely. The bed linens, rugs and

---

152   Garretson, Joseph Jr., "Love Letters Are Bared In Anna Hahn Trial," *The Cincinnati Enquirer,* October 23, 1937.

furniture were soiled. It was in such a terrible condition the hotel staff would not go in to clean it."

Dudley let that image linger for a moment before asking, "Can you tell us how she reacted to the news of his death?"

"Yes, sir. The morning after Obendorfer's death, I told her that he had died and she said, 'Why tell me? I never saw him in my life until I met him on the train.' The following day she checked out."

Faragher recalled what Hahn had said during an interrogation when she was told Obendorfer had bragged to his friends about his "new woman."

"That is to laugh," she had said harshly. "I should be interested in a man like him! He was such a stupid old man."

Big Tom, Pat Hayes and Walter Hart had seen a body in a barrel, a headless corpse and too many grisly scenes to count that could not be erased from their vivid, disturbing dreams. But her scornful laugh at that "stupid old man," hard as slate, cold as a grave, gave them chills.

Faragher remembered the day they interviewed the son. For an 11-year-old, he was unusually

Oscar Hahn in court. Courtesy of
The Cincinnati Enquirer.

mature and articulate. He admitted that his mother had told him to lie. And he described the train ride with Obendorfer.

"The old man believed in witches," the boy said. "He called my mother a witch on the train and she told him to hush, that people would hear him. Once I drew a picture of a skeleton and laid it on the seat beside him. When he saw it he gasped, 'Ach!' like that, and drew his hand across his throat. 'Witches!' he said to my mother."[153]

---

153   Garretson, Joseph Jr., "'Lies, All Lies!' Anna Hahn Exclaims Under State Grilling in Murder Case." *The Cincinnati Enquirer*, November 2, 1937.

They showed Oscar a picture of the skull and bones warning on a bottle of poison. "Is this what you drew?" they asked.

"Yes," he answered. The boy thought it was funny.

Obendorfer had frugally saved for many years to build his bank account in Cincinnati, but he died in a charity hospital and was buried in a thin pine coffin in a pauper's cemetery in Colorado Springs, far from his home in Cincinnati and farther still from his family in Germany.

That's when Anna Marie Hahn made her biggest mistake. Before she left Colorado Springs for Cincinnati, she pawned rings she had stripped from Obendorfer while he was too sick and feeble to resist, along with a $300[154] diamond ring that was reported stolen from the Park Hotel by the owner's wife.

Oscar admitted that his mother coached him to lie that he had found the diamond ring in the dirt outside the hotel, but Colorado Springs detectives did not believe him. After she left, they traced her back to Cincinnati and contacted Cincinnati Police with a warrant for the arrest of Anna Marie Hahn for grand larceny.

On August 10, Homicide Squad Detective George Schattle looked in during a police lineup and was surprised to see someone familiar among the faces. It was the same woman the Homicide Squad was investigating for the Wagner murder: Anna Marie Hahn.

He alerted the team and she was arrested the next day. The pawn ticket for the stolen diamond ring and jewelry taken from George Obendorfer was found in Hahn's Cincinnati home, filled out under the alias "Marie Fisher."

Homicide Squad detectives compared notes with Colorado Springs Police, who immediately sent a team to exhume the body of Obendorfer.

They say dead men can't testify, Faragher thought. *But Obendorfer did.*

Three autopsies were done on Obendorfer's remains, but at first no evidence of poisoning was found. Then a toxicologist for the city of Denver did a closer study of his liver, heart and kidneys and found it: Like Wagner, Palmer and Gsellman, Obendorfer's death was ruled to be caused by arsenic poisoning.

---

154 In 2025, $2,300.

The poison in his organs matched the composition of arsenic in a saltshaker that was found in Obendorfer's weatherbeaten straw satchel.

The saltshaker contained 82 percent arsenic trioxide and 14 percent table salt, the analysis showed. And that saltshaker was identical to the one that witnesses saw Anna Hahn use to salt Obendorfer's food as they dined on the train from Cincinnati to Denver.

Prosecutor Dudley Outcalt holds the saltshaker that contained arsenic, a key piece of evidence in the trial. Courtesy of Andrew Outcalt.

Then the Homicide Squad and their scientists at the University of Cincinnati had another breakthrough in the case. Dr. William Machle, a physiology professor, took the stand and described his discovery when he examined the white knitted purse that Anna Marie Hahn had carried to Colorado.

Lint in a corner of the purse contained arsenic, and more was found in the lining of the purse.

The evidence in the purse hit home with the nearly all-women jury. "A woman always knows what's in her purse," Faragher's wife explained to him. "That proves the saltshaker was hers."

For his defense, the best witness Hoodin could find was Oscar, who lied again for his mother. But he had already admitted lying for her, so nobody believed him when he claimed the arsenic bottle in the cellar was something he found behind the neighborhood pharmacy.

With nothing left to lose, Hahn took the stand. Faragher figured she believed she could talk her way out of a guilty verdict the same way she talked her way into the lives of those lonely old men and women.

As expected, she had an explanation for everything. All those old men dying after meeting her—just a coincidence. "Isn't that strange?"

she remarked. She only nursed them and tried to make them comfortable. "This is what I get for being kind," she snapped.

All those witnesses who saw her with the victims before they died? All of them were lying or mistaken, she said.[155]

Her unexplained income of thousands of dollars taken from her victims? It was from betting the horses—although she couldn't recall the name of a single winning horse.

She insisted she had never seen the bottle of arsenic in her cellar until the detectives found it there.

"I never saw Mr. Gsellman eat or drink anything in my life," she said. And the trip to Colorado was Obendorfer's idea, not hers.

Hoodin was in tears during his closing argument. He asked the jury to believe that she was a kind, compassionate woman who was caught in a malicious tangle of coincidence. The women on the jury were as unmoved as Hahn had been throughout the trial.

And Outcalt had the last word.

It was late in the evening of Friday, November 5, 1937. The jury was tired. The spectators were dull-eyed. The case that was so big it made headlines in London was finally winding to a close after all those exhibits and witnesses and jars of floating viscera that were already haunting the dreams of some of the jurors. Even Judge Bell looked worn and exhausted.

Then Prosecutor Dudley Outcalt stood to give his closing argument and woke everyone up again. He shot his right hand out, pointing his finger to the corner of the courtroom and shouted, "In the four corners of this courtroom there stand four dead men!"

"Gsellman!" he said, moving his pointing finger around the corners, "Palmer! Wagner! Obendorfer! From the four corners, bony fingers point at her and they say: 'That woman poisoned me! That woman made my last moments an agony! That woman tortured me with the tortures of the damned!'"[156]

He had the court's stunned attention. Anna Marie Hahn, he

---

155   Garretson, Joseph Jr., "'Lies, All Lies!' Anna Hahn Exclaims Under State Grilling in Murder Case." *The Cincinnati Enquirer*, November 2, 1937.

156   *The Cincinnati Post*, Saturday, November 6, 1937, Page 2.

noticed, was glaring at him with undiluted hatred that could blister the skin like croton oil, anger like arsenic.

He paused, lowered his voice and walked to the rail in front of the jury, where he looked them in the eyes, one by one, as he spoke. "And then, turning to you, they say, 'Let my death be not entirely in vain. My life cannot be brought back, but through my death and the punishment to be inflicted on her, you can prevent such a death coming to another old man.' From the four corners of this room, those old men say to you: 'Do your duty!'

"I ask of you for the state of Ohio," he finished, "that you withhold any recommendation of mercy."

As he spoke those final words, he pointed at Hahn, whose face was hard and white as the marble floor. But her eyes betrayed her, burning with venomous rage.

The jury was shaken, the spectators were shocked to silence. Outcalt took his seat. Hoodin shook his head, fuming.

Judge Bell read his instructions to the jury and sent them to deliberate.

As the jury of 11 women and one man filed out of the courtroom at 9:21 p.m., they looked down or straight ahead. None would look at Anna Marie Hahn. She had been the center of morbid and curious attention for weeks. Now, as far as they were concerned, she was already dead.

No woman had ever been executed in Ohio. But Outcalt's instinct was right: The women jurors did their duty where men might have flinched.

After just two hours and 13 minutes, they returned. The only man on the jury had been chosen to be foreman. He handed the jury's verdict to the bailiff, who read the fatal words: "Guilty…No mercy."

As the crowded courtroom erupted in chatter and reporters banged out the doors, Judge Bell banged his gavel for order. As Hahn was escorted from the courtroom by deputies, she kept on her mask of chilling indifference—until she reached her cell, where she ran in, slammed the door behind her, threw herself onto her cot and burst into sobs.

---

157   Justice was swift in those days. In 2025, it is not unusual for two years to pass between indictment, arrest and trial.

From her arrest on August 11 to the guilty verdict on November 6, less than three months had passed.[157] On December 1, she was taken by car to Columbus and delivered to a prison cell on Death Row at the Ohio Penitentiary.[158] She was the only woman on Death Row.

Joe Hoodin filed appeals on her behalf to the Ohio Supreme Court and the US Supreme Court. He accused Prosecutor Dudley Outcalt of "flagrant misconduct." He protested that the crowded courtroom made a fair trial impossible, and that Outcalt inflamed the emotions of the jury with his "séance" closing argument that summoned the dead.

The appeals were rejected. The verdict and sentencing were affirmed by the Ohio Supreme Court and the US Supreme Court.

On December 7, 1938, a year and one month after her sentencing, Anna Hahn was dragged and carried to the electric chair.[159] Her last appeal to the governor was rejected in the final hour before her death.

"Her usually beautifully groomed golden-brown hair was disheveled. Her tear-swollen face was the color of ashes," *The Cincinnati Enquirer* reported.[160]

She refused her last meal of fried chicken cooked by the warden's wife. She would not get dressed.

"Appearing almost child-like in blue cotton pajamas, a brown and tan flowered silk robe,

Hahn is escorted from court. Courtesy of *The Cincinnati Enquirer.*

---

158   It was built in 1830 on Spring Street in Columbus, as the state's primary prison and place for all executions. The "Ohio Pen" was closed in 1984. The buildings were demolished in 1997. Ohio History Connection.

159   Between her arrest and execution was 16 months. In 2025, the time between a death sentence and execution is indefinite or sometimes infinite. The last execution in Ohio was 2018. As of January 2025 there were 114 inmates on Death Row, including one woman. Ohio Department of Corrections.

160   Dush, Sarah, *The Cincinnati Enquirer*, December 8, 1938, Page 1

black oxfords and tan silk hose rolled to the ankle, she clung to the women [guards] in mute appeal for help and courage," the *Enquirer* reported.

As she passed their cells, dragged and carried by guards, men on Death Row called out encouragement and farewells. "Goodbye, boys," she replied.

Then she looked ahead down the queasy green hallways to the darkness that waited and she fell apart.

Her icy stoicism evaporated as she approached the Death House,[161] a small brick building with darkened, caged windows and one small chimney, home of "Old Sparky"—the ancient, skeletal electric chair with its tentacles of wires, unforgiving steel clamps and rough, black wooden frame saturated with fear and death.

Her knees wobbled, then gave way and finally she collapsed. A doctor revived her with ammonia, but she had to be picked up and carried to the chair.

"Old Sparky," the Ohio Electric Chair, as it looked in 1938.

As she was strapped in she moaned, "Don't do that to me. Oh, no, no, no." She pleaded with the warden, who told her, with tears on his cheeks, "No, Anna, it's too late now."

A FINAL, UNFINISHED PRAYER

She tried to reach out to the reporters, prison guards and witnesses who were seated to view the execution, and screamed, "You can't do this to me! Won't somebody help me?"

How many times did those poor old men cry out in the same words? Tom

---

161 Built in 1913, it was used to house the electric chair that was introduced in 1897 to remedy botched hangings. Between 1897 and 1963, 315 Death Row inmates were executed in the electric chair, including three women. Anna Hahn was the first. Next was Dovie Blanche Dean, 55, of Columbus, described as the gray-haired grandmother who poisoned her husband's milk. She was executed in the electric chair in 1954. That same year, six months later, Betty Eveyln Butler, 26, was executed for beating and drowning a woman she lived with in Cincinnati.

Faragher thought as he read the story.

Steel and leather straps holding wet sponges were buckled to her head, arms and legs to conduct 1,950 volts of current. She called for Father John A. Sullivan to come closer. He whispered in her ear, then led her in the Lord's Prayer.

"…Forgive us our trespasses as we forgive those who trespass against us," he said.

She repeated the words, "…as we forgive those who trespass against us," her voice muffled behind a black leather hood.

"…Lead us not into temptation but deliver us from the evil one," he said.

Hahn repeated, "Deliver us—"

And those were her last words. At that moment, two prison guards pushed identical buttons that opened circuit breakers that surged the fatal jolt of crackling electricity through her jerking, shaking body. [162]

It was 8:09 p.m.

The current was turned off one minute later. She was declared dead at 8:13, as a fine layer of smoke drifted toward the chimney and lingered near the harsh ceiling lights. Witnesses said it had a metallic odor.[163]

Nobody claimed the body. Her husband refused comment. He had visited her twice in prison but wanted nothing to do with the execution. Asked if Oscar was being sent back to Germany to live with relatives, Philip Hahn said, "I never adopted him," and hung up the phone.

Cincinnati and the rest of the world moved on from Anna Hahn. There was Christmas shopping. Car wrecks. An armed robbery downtown in broad daylight. Warnings of deadly bootleg whiskey. News that illegal slots were operating in the county. A report from Berlin said that the Nazis had imposed a 20 percent tax on Jews leaving Germany and quoted a Vatican spokesman's warning that worse "provisions of the utmost severity" were to come from Hitler.

---

162   Designed so that neither man would know which of them was the executioner. The lights did not dim. That's a Hollywood myth. The prison had ample power supply.

163   Dush, Sarah L.., "Anna Hahn Falls And Is Carried to Chair," The Cincinnati Enquirer, December 8, 1938.

A few days later, a small news item, "Trip Unlikely for Hahn Boy," said Oscar Hahn, 13, had been invited to Hollywood by film star George Raft, but Joe Hoodin declined on the boy's behalf. "Our idea now is to get the boy out of the limelight as much as possible," the defense lawyer said.

Then on December 19, the Hahn story erupted again. A headline at the top of the front page of *The Cincinnati Enquirer* shouted, "Anna Hahn's Death Cell Confession! Four Cincinnati Murders are Laid Bare."

As if speaking from the grave, her confession said, "I couldn't have been in my right mind… God will judge me."

She had been paid for the exclusive story, with a promise that the money would go to Oscar.

Like her interviews with detectives, the confession went on for pages, a stone wall of words. She described her normal girlhood life in a comfortable family. She admitted killing four men: Palmer ("poison in the oysters"), Wagner, Gsellman and Obendorfer. But she defiantly denied the rest.

"I don't know how I could have done the thing I did in my life, only God knows what came over me when I gave Albert Palmer that first one, that poison that caused his death. … I never knew myself afterwards and I don't know now; when those poor men got sick I tried to do everything for them. I sat at their bedsides nursing them."

She said the trial was like listening to a story about someone else. "I couldn't have been in my right mind when I did them. I loved all people so much. Now I am so close to death. Death is all around me."

*

The day after Anna Marie Hahn's execution, December 8, 1938, was dark, overcast and drizzly like the day before and many more days to come in the Cincinnati winter. The sun that was so eager to get into the courtroom in late October had turned its back. Now it hid behind a purple bruise of low clouds as Faragher went up the long, wide steps to enter the heavy brass doors of the courthouse, on his way to obtain a warrant.

While he was there, he dropped in on newly elected Common Pleas Judge Dudley Outcalt.

174

"I see they gave you a very nice office," Faragher said, taking a seat in a deep chair covered in cracked and comfortable leather that was the color of Kentucky bourbon. It was a good chair for thinking and smoking, he thought, looking out the windows behind Outcalt. The rain outside was trying to decide whether it would punish the city with an ice storm or give it probation with a light dusting of snow.

"Do you miss the prosecutor's office?" the detective asked.

"It was bigger, more exciting, more people to supervise, but I don't miss the furniture that went with it."

"I see you brought this chair along."

"I mean a different kind of furniture," Outcalt said, shaking his head.

"You mean the pressure," Faragher nodded. It was a statement, not a question. He had seen the toll that trials took.

"Yes. Months and months of preparation for trial. Life and death in the balance. The heartbreaking duty to speak for victims that everyone wants to forget. I find it's less stressful to stand behind the plate and call balls and strikes than to pitch nine innings. I don't know how you put up with all of it, Tom."

"I wonder myself sometimes. Most of the day-to-day stuff is jewel thieves, armed robberies, drunken manslaughter, the same things you see in court every day. Aggravated Nitwittery."

Outcalt chuckled. "Maybe we can get that codified in the lawbooks. First-degree Aggravated Nitwittery: Ninety days in the Workhouse. I would throw in Felony Jackassery."

"We would run out of cells, sir," Faragher said. "And a lot of our friends who run this city would fill them up."

Outcalt laughed. "Too true, Tom."

"To answer your question about pressure, most cases are the kind I can leave at the precinct. But there are three kinds of homicides that follow me home. Too young, too old and too female. Those are the ones I can't let go of."

Outcalt nodded and waited as Faragher lit a cigarette, shook the match out and dropped it in the ashtray. Faragher looked up and continued.

"The other day I was driving home after a long day and I was about to lay on the horn at this old flivver in front of me, puttering along, holding up traffic. But something stopped me. As I passed it, I looked over. It was an old couple. Very old. A little white-haired lady, driving with her chin up, trying to see over the steering wheel. Her husband was slumped over against the other door. I could barely see his head over the door sill. But he was doing his best to watch the road and help her.

"And for some reason, that's when it really hit me. Those lonely old men and women. I don't know if I was more angry or more sad. But I knew at that moment we did the right thing. Anna Hahn got what she had coming."

"I understand," Outcalt said. "It feels like you want to punch someone and cry at the same time?"

Faragher nodded.

Outcalt blew a fragrant bluish ring of cigar smoke and said, "That's why I called out the dead men to testify and told the jury those old men were pointing their fingers at her in court. While we all focus on the murderer, the victims get left behind. It's all about the 'Black Widow' and the 'Blond Killer,' with pictures of her on page one every day. The victims and their lives are buried, six feet under. I had to speak up for them, exhume them again, put them in the room."

Faragher nodded. "Have you wondered when they realized what she was doing? Obendorfer figured it out. That's why he talked about witches. But what about the others?"

"At some point they had to know," Outcalt answered. "But by then they were too weak, too sick to do anything about it. Maybe that's why she dosed Gsellman with enough poison to kill him overnight."

After a pause while they smoked, each to his own thoughts, Faragher said, "It's never really over, is it? Even when we close a case like this one, as closed as a case can be, there's a lot we never will know. It hangs around like the rank stink of Gsellman's little attic room. I've had that jacket cleaned twice and I still smell it when I put it on."

Outcalt said, "You should burn it."

"On a detective's salary?" Faragher laughed. Then, "You're probably right."

"Submit it as evidence and I will get the county to reimburse you."

Faragher laughed again. "The guys in the Homicide Squad would never let me live it down. By the way, I saw your quote in the papers about how she murdered those old men to cover her gambling habit. Is that what you think?"

"I wanted to say more," Outcalt said, "but they probably wouldn't print it anyway. Simple motives are what the Janes and Joes who read the papers can understand. It puts a neat ending on the story and closes the book."

"There's plenty of truth in it, though," Faragher said. "My first big case as a detective was horse betting. I saw plenty of gambling fools and their jackassery felonies when I worked vice. Nothing good comes of slots, dice and horses. Look at Newport. An empire of thieves ruled by knuckle-dragging goons."

"But we both know it was more than the horses with her," Outcalt replied, leaning back in his high-backed swivel chair behind a big walnut desk that looked like a survivor of the courthouse fire in 1884. Snow was gently falling outside the windows now. For some reason, that lifted Faragher's spirits, in spite of the sloppy drive home. Everything would be clean and white again—for a while. He nodded and knocked ash from his cigarette into a standing chrome ashtray next to his chair.

He said, "That woman was like a trainload of words. Her train never stopped and when she did, there was no room to get a word aboard for all the stampede of words getting off."

"That reminds me of a joke," Outcalt said. "My wife and I had words—but I didn't get to use any of mine."

Faragher laughed. "That's a good description of her testimony. She was a cool one until you brought the dead men into the courtroom. I have to admit, it gave me chills."

"And it made Joe Hoodin steam like a leaking radiator," Outcalt replied. "What was it he said in his appeals? 'Flagrant misconduct.' When we were in France, the answer for insults like that was revolvers at dawn. And the way she looked at me..." Outcalt shook his head. "That look could scare the hair off a cat."

"I noticed she wore that gold cross every day during the trial," Faragher said. "I thought that was curious. When we asked her about her faith during our interrogations in August, she told us, 'I don't believe in anything.' She seemed defiant, proud of it. But it looks like she might have changed her mind there at the end."

"Don't they all?" Outcalt said as he blew another small cloud of cigar smoke at the high white ceiling. "She was a strange bird. As they say, God only knows. The paper said she died saying a prayer. Sounds like it was rough."

"I've witnessed a few," Faragher said. "I've never seen anything quite like the Death House. All those bright lights and it still feels dark. The chair. The smoke. The strange smell…" He paused. "Some go quiet, some go hard. She went hard."

Outcalt nodded. "As I said in court, I believe there was not another human being like her on the face of the earth."

"Let's hope not. But I believe there are more out there," he waved his cigarette at the windows. "People who are not satisfied with one murder. The kind who kill not for passion or money but because they get some twisted thrill from it, the power to play God, the power over life and death. Gambling, greed—just bushwa. An excuse they use to justify it."

"Lord, I hope you are wrong," Outcalt said. "But yes, there were a few like that in the flying circus. Men who actually *enjoyed* killing. The ones who left the formation to strafe the trenches. Sometimes I wondered if they even cared whose trenches."

They sat in silence, pondering the unknowable. After a pause, Outcalt said, "You're certainly right about one thing, Tom."

Faragher sat back in feigned surprise. "Will you put that on the record in a court of matrimonial law? My bride Marguerite won't believe it."

Outcalt laughed and leaned forward. "I think you're right that we will never get bored. There are more than enough people with darkness in their hearts and violence in their blood. We will be busy at this for a long time."

Big Tom nodded, crushed his cigarette and put on his raincoat as he stood to leave. "Blessed are they who maintain justice," he quoted.[164]

"Amen," Outcalt nodded. "Sleep well, Tom."

Faragher gave him a doubtful look and said, "You too, Judge."

✻

Big Tom Faragher was busy at justice for a long time.

---

164   Psalm 106:3

Dudley Outcalt Jr. was not so fortunate.

Faragher served the city of Cincinnati for 33 years until he retired in 1960 at age 57. During his career he met death in its multitude of ugly masks: murders, suicides, accidents. He investigated more than 1,250 cases—the most ever by one detective in Cincinnati, and probably a record for the state of Ohio.[165]

In 1934 he assisted the FBI and worked with Melvin Pervis, the agent who shot and killed the infamous bank robber John Dillinger. In 1941, he investigated 43 murders and solved 41. That caseload and success rate was typical for Big Tom.

He and his longtime partner Walter Hart founded the Holy Name Society and its mission to "raise strong men in the name of Jesus." Hart and Faragher organized and served at annual masses at St. Peter in Chains, including a 1943 mass to honor the Cincinnati Police officers who were serving and lost in World War II.

DEATH FINDS THE DETECTIVE

In 1952, Walter Hart was run off the road on the Beechmont Viaduct and his car dangled in the air, snared in the bridge guardrails and cables for hours before he could be rescued. The difficult recovery from his accident injuries and the accumulated toll of more than a thousand murders, kidnappings and tragic deaths led him to request a transfer in 1955. The slender, bookish detective with the wireframed glasses and fedora had seen enough. He transferred to a desk job. But death had the last word.

A few months later, Detective Hart stopped at the Gray Eagle Café at Elm and Sixth on his way home from work, to discuss plans for his daughter's wedding reception. Three ex-cons burst into the store with guns and announced a holdup.

Hart and the other customers were pushed into a restroom during the robbery. Hart could have stayed there. Instead, he pulled his concealed revolver and charged back into the café. He shot one of the robbers, wounding him. As the robbers returned fire, he was shot

---

165 Kramer, Steve, *Detective Thomas Joseph "Big Tom" Faragher Jr. The King of Homicide Detectives*, Greater Cincinnati Police Museum.

through the heart and killed almost instantly.

That night, Big Tom's phone rang. He was accustomed to such late-night calls, always bad news, the worst kind. Death did not keep office hours from 8:00 to 5:00. It preferred to do its work after dark.

"I've got a hell of a job for you," the police lieutenant told him on the phone. Faragher expected bad news, but nothing like this.

"Then the lieutenant told me who it was," he told *The Cincinnati Enquirer*. "I couldn't believe it."

He was sent to break the news to Hart's wife. "As soon as she saw me, Mrs. Hart froze," he recalled. "She didn't cry. She just asked 'What happened?' I told her. She didn't say much. You know, at times like that you just go numb."

Faragher worked day and night to investigate the murder of his best friend and partner for 20 years. It seemed as if death had finally caught up to them like a deadly poison they had been forced to handle too many times.

Two of the holdup men, Robert Lee Jackson and Willie "Chin" Barnett, were both caught quickly, but the third, Lemual Trotter, fled and was finally tracked down in Alabama. Jackson and Trotter both said "Chin" Barnett shot Hart.

Asked by reporters if the men should be executed, Hart's wife, Lillian, showed remarkable grace. She said their punishment would be up to a jury. "Walter was a wonderful father and a good husband," she said. "We miss him terribly."

The jury for each man decided his fate. Barnett, the killer of Hart, was sent to the state prison for the insane, where he eventually died. Trotter and Jackson were each executed in the electric chair.

Big Tom Faragher worked on after losing his friend and partner. One of his final cases before he retired was the sensationally grim killing of Louise Bergen by Edythe Klumpp, the lover of Bergen's husband.

Faragher was able to determine that Klumpp shot Louise Bergen through the throat, then burned her on the shore of Cowan Lake. Mrs. Bergen may still have been alive when she was burned, patholo-gists said. Her body was found on November 1, 1959.

Klumpp was defended by Cincinnati lawyer Fosse Hopkins, who was known in his day as one of the best any defendant could hope for. But Faragher had done his job thoroughly. The evidence was clear.

She was convicted and sentenced to death in the electric chair.

As she waited on Death Row, Ohio Governor Michael DiSalle, an opponent of capital punishment, conducted his own investigation, including an interview of her in prison using "Truth Serum." DiSalle decided the jury was wrong and overturned her sentence with clemency. Although Klumpp had confessed, DiSalle believed her revised story, that Bill Bergen killed his wife and made Klumpp take the blame by threatening her children.[166]

On Friday morning, March 15, 1974, 14 years after his retirement, the King of Detectives, Big Tom Faragher, was found in his bed, dead of a heart attack. He was 68.

✱

The day after the surprise attack at Pearl Harbor by Japan on December 7, 1941, Judge Dudley Outcalt reported for duty in the Army Air Corps. He was 44. As commanding officer of the Air Corps Reserve Squadron at Lunken Airport, Colonel Outcalt expected to get "cleared for takeoff" immediately.

But a health issue was discovered during his induction physical exam and he was rejected.

He had surgery to correct the problem, waited the required six months, then applied again on the same day his waiting period expired. This time he was accepted and rejoined the service. After winning reelection as Hamilton County Common Pleas judge in 1942, he took his oath of office, then immediately took a leave of absence and was sworn into the Army Air Corps the next day.

He missed his beloved Indianapolis 500 on Memorial Day that year, where he often worked in the pit crew and occasionally rode in the race.[167] The Indy 500 race was canceled that year because of the war.

In the Army Air Corps, Outcalt was given the rank of major and assigned to Ferrying Command, to fly new aircraft from factory pro-

---

166 She was paroled in 1971, remarried and moved to Kentucky where she died in 1999. DiSalle was defeated in his bid for reelection, mainly because of public outrage over his decision to spare Klumpp from execution.

167 Probably with his old commander Eddie Rickenbacker, who founded the Rickenbacker Motorcar Co. and raced several times in the Indy 500.

duction lines to the bases where pilots were trained, or to ports where they could be shipped or flown to Europe and the Pacific.

He was soon promoted to lieutenant colonel and sent to Washington; then he was promoted again to colonel and chief investigator in the Office of Special Air investigations. He also was awarded his wings as a command pilot, the highest pilot rating in the Air Corps at that time.

On May 26, 1945, shortly after the VE Day celebration of victory in Europe, as the war was grinding to an end, Col. Outcalt took off from Biloxi, Mississippi as the pilot of a twin-engine B-25 Mitchell[168] bomber. Over a farm in Silver Spring, Maryland, almost within sight of the Washington, DC airfield where they would have land-

ed, the plane exploded in midair, crashed and burned. The cause was unknown. There was no trace of the four men aboard. Col. Outcalt was identified by remains of a uniform coat with his name stenciled on it, found in the wreckage.

The news was splashed across Page 1 of *The Cincinnati Enquirer.* **DUDLEY M. OUTCALT KILLED IN PLANE BLAST**[170]

The Hamilton County courts were closed for his funeral. The glamorous WWI hero, barnstormer, daredevil car-racer, tough prosecutor, judge and Army Air Corps pilot who dropped everything to serve his country, was gone—vanished overnight like his father.[170]

---

168 Named after William "Billy" Mitchell, one of his fellow pilots in the celebrated "Hat in Ring" squadron that served in World War I.

169 *The Cincinnati Enquirer*, Sunday, May 27, 1945.

170 In both cases, the family had no body to bury.

171 *The Cincinnati Enquirer,* "Outcalt Rites," May 28, 1945.

Presiding Judge Alfred Mack said the tragic death was "a great loss." He recalled Outcalt's cross examination of experts in the Anna Marie Hahn trial as "marvelous, a great credit to the profession."[171]

The US Army Reserve Center on Mosteller Road in Sharonville is named The Dudley M. Outcalt US Army Reserve Center in his honor. His grave is in Rest Haven Memorial Park in Evandale.

FEEDING FRENZY

Dying to Lose Weight

Even cigarettes were once advertised for weight loss. This 1930s ad urged women to "reach for a Lucky" to "maintain that modern, youthful figure."

JUNE 2008

Jim was looking over the menu at Otto's in the gingerbread Old German Mainstrasse Village in Covington. His eyes lingered longingly on the Kentucky hot brown: "Ham, turkey and bacon on sourdough, smothered in cheese and brown gravy…."

No, he thought, turning to the salads. Jim was "watching his waist." Watching it swell like *The Blob* in that goofy 1958 movie. His slacks seemed shorter and tighter lately. The well-worn holes in his belt had moved overnight, replaced by new ones. Shirts he used to wear were pushed to the back of the closet, so snug he was afraid he would pop a button and put someone's eye out. *Must be shrinking in the laundry*, he thought, his eyes wandering back to the hot brown.

He shook his head. No again. Susan would ask when he got home, "What did you have for lunch?" If he said, "Hot brown at Otto's," she would give him that look—part eyeroll, part "heaven help me" and part "thirty days on fish and broccoli for you." It might be accompanied by one of those soft sighs that women used to condense an encyclopedia of grievances into a puff of air. *How can they say so much just by breathing?* he wondered.

He summoned all his feeble, weakening willpower and ordered the Cobb salad.

It was impossible to eat healthy as a newspaper columnist. Everyone wanted to go to lunch three or four times a week. Or he might be out of the office, like today, covering a council meeting or a court case, and had to go to a restaurant or starve. The menus were always like browsing through yearbook pictures of old friends you had fun with: Good old pastrami on rye and his paisano rigatoni Bolognese; all-American double cheeseburger; cute little chicken pot pie—

Loud laughter made him look up as two men were escorted to the booth next to his. He caught a quick glimpse of them before they were seated on the other side of a thin, walnut-stained plywood divider.

"…Not enough sand!" one of the men said as they neared the table, sparking the outburst of guffaws. The joke-teller was well dressed, maybe early 30s, trim like a runner, with styled blond hair and rimless glasses. He wore a tan poplin suit with an expensive red striped tie over a light blue oxford button-down. It looked like everything he wore was lifted out of a display window at Sak's.

Jim recognized the punchline from a current lawyer joke: "What do you call a thousand lawyers buried up to their necks in the desert?"

As the two men were seated, the second man asked, "Did you hear about the busload of lawyers that ran off a cliff in California?" This one was bigger and older, perhaps early 50s, solid, square-jawed, built like a guy who might have been a lineman in high school before linemen became 350-pound freaks. He was dressed in a charcoal suit that looked like lightweight wool, very expensive. He wore a white shirt and a cheerful yellow tie with a light blue pattern. His dark brown hair was cop-short—not a brush-cut, but not long enough to comb—and graying at the temples.

"It was tragic," he said, setting up the punchline. "There were five empty seats."

Both men laughed again.

Lawyers telling lawyer jokes, Jim guessed. He had a theory that lawyers secretly loved the popular insults because the fear behind the humor was an implicit genuflection to their godlike power. No sparrow could fall without a liability class-action lawsuit, followed by optic-yellow warning labels on twigs: "Caution: Not intended for use as a ladder, stepstool or perch."

As the men spoke, he could hear every word on the other side of the divider between the booths. He couldn't see them, but he could place the voices.

"Did you hear God had to dismiss his defamation suit against Satan?" younger tan suit asked. He waited a beat. "He couldn't find a lawyer who didn't have a conflict of interest. They all had clients in hell."

"Ouch, that stings," gray suit chuckled. After a pause, he asked, "What do you like here?"

"When in Rome…." tan suit answered.

"Oh, I get it. The Kentucky hot brown. Sounds like something that was on the menu when Robert E. Lee was still a private. What is it, pork belly on hard tack, marinated in bourbon?"

As they laughed, Jim looked up to see his server approach with a salad bowl the size of a Cadillac hubcap, overflowing with bacon, boiled eggs, ham, turkey and cheese. Puny scraps of lettuce peeked out from the shores of a creamy lake of thick ranch dressing. He felt virtuous. When Susan asked about his lunch he could honestly say, "Just a salad."

He thanked the waitress, asked for a refill of his iced tea—unsweetened, of course—and tuned back in to the booth next door. As he listened, he had a nagging feeling that the two men looked familiar. He had seen them somewhere.

"So how did you get dragged into the diet drug circus?" tan suit was asking.

That's it, they were in court, Jim realized.

"Long story," gray suit said. "I was a detective in Phoenix. I got a nice offer for more money and regular hours, so I put in my retirement papers and took a job with one of the big law firms. They sent me to Philadelphia where the Fen-Phen class action was consolidated. If Hell is populated with lawyers—and their clients—it must be empty because all the lawyers were in Philadelphia. They could have wallpapered the Vatican with all their writs and motions. They swarmed like a plague of locusts in Egypt—no offense."

"None taken. But the Locust Protection Union might demand an apology."

"When they figured out that 70 percent of the claims were going to people who had never been injured—more than $6 billion in fraud—they sent me to investigate some of the worst cases."

"Like this one?"

"Correct. I hear your local talent might win gold in the fraud Olympics."

Jim put down his fork, realizing he had not taken a second bite. He reached for his notebook and Bic ballpoint and started jotting notes. These guys might spill a lot of inside dope he would never pry loose on the record.

"And how did you get stuck being my tour guide?" older gray suit asked.

"I was already camping out in the courtroom, trial-watching for the Kentucky Bar," tan suit replied. "When your office called them, they offered my name."

"I imagine the Kentucky Bar ethics referees will wear out their whistles before the dust settles?"

Tan suit chuckled. "I expect some very distinguished attorneys to exit their law careers at high altitude, and this flight is fresh out of parachutes."

"Even the Master of Disaster? I've heard he has enough juice to light up Los Angeles. And the extension cord goes all the way to the White House."

Jim wrote down, "Stan Chesley." He was Cincinnati's nationally famous apex predator in the litigation food chain: father of the class action, one of Ohio's premier fundraisers for the Democratic Party, close friend of Bill and Hillary Clinton, husband of a federal judge, owner of the most expensive home in the city's most wealthy neighborhood, Indian Hill—and he was now caught in the Fen-Phen scandal like a tyrannosaurus with both feet in the tarpit and arms too short to pull himself out.

"Well, he was an overnight guest at the Clinton White House, but I imagine those circuits have gone dead since George Bush moved in. This diet-pill litigation could be the second Great American Gold Rush. What's the worst corruption you've seen in—what, ten years of lawsuits now?" tan suit asked.

"Do lawyers always answer a question with a question? Okay, I'll play. We had a Kansas cardiologist who was paid $1,000 per case by the plaintiffs' lawyers to review 725 claims of alleged heart damage. It took her about three minutes each to find nearly all were victims of the diet pill. I'll spare you the arithmetic. That's nearly a million dollars for less than 40 hours of work. She was so good at finding victims, another group of plaintiff lawyers hired her to review 10,000 more cases."[172]

"I should've been a doctor."

"Then we had a Louisiana preacher who must have used five gallons of Wite Out to forge new names on medical charts so he

---

172 Frankel, Alison. "The Fen-Phen Follies." American Lawyer, March 1, 2005. "(Cardiologist Linda) Crouse testified that she generally spent only about two or three minutes looking over these echocardiograms. And she usually approved them for submission to the trust: Crouse found that the echocardiograms of 60-70 percent of the Napoli and Hariton clients her office tested exhibited disease sufficient to qualify them for payments from the trust-compared to the 5 percent she found in a blinded clinical study in 1998." The judge called it "a mass production operation that would have been the envy of Henry Ford."

could round up phony victims.[173] He was paid $230,000—which was a bargain for the lawyers who sued for millions.

FAKE PILL BOTTLES, REAL CASH

"We caught a guy who was forging Fen-Phen labels on pill bottles to collect jackpots. Show up with the phony pill bottle, get a fat check. And we've had law firms that submitted claims with false heart tests—EKGs done in hotel rooms, law offices and mobile fraud-mobiles, done by lawyers' assistants who were not even nurses, much less cardiologists. Some law firms rigged the diagnostic machines to show false heart damage on every test. They could hook you up and find out you have leaky heart valves, yet you are as healthy as Michael Phelps. Why do you ask?"

Tan suit said, "Because if what I've heard comes out in court, this case could put all that in the shade. There's the same fraud and fudged tests, but this one takes it to the next level. Lawyers are fighting lawyers like courtroom Kung Fu. Instead of collecting fees at one-third of the $200 million settlement, they took two-thirds and hid it from their clients.[174] The federal judge says the whole legal profession is on trial, and I'd say the verdict is guilty."

"I wouldn't bet on it yet," gray suit said. "Funny things happen when hundreds of millions are in play."

"Like what?"

"There are high-dollar courtroom consultants who can break into any jury. Hold that thought, here comes our lunch," gray suit said.

Jim heard plates thump onto the table as the server asked, "Is there anything else I can get you gentlemen?" They said no, and after a pause, the ex-cop asked, "Will I need to chase this with some Fen-Phen diet pills?"

Tan suit answered, "No, you'll get all the heart damage you can

---

173   Forbes Magazine. "The $22 Billion Gold Rush," March 24, 2006.

174   "According to the U.S. Department of Justice, the plaintiffs only received about $74.2 million [of the $200 million settlement]. Gallion, Cunningham and Mills split an estimated $74.8 million, while other attorneys received $30 million and the Kentucky Fund for Healthy Living received $20 million." Carey, Liz, "Lexington history: Lawyers stole millions from clients in diet drug settlement," *Lexington Herald Leader, May 20,* 2025.

handle the way nature intended—gravy and cheese." They both laughed.

✷

It was early June 2008. Jim had spent nearly two weeks covering the case they were talking about. It was being tried in the US District Court on Fifth Street in Covington, Kentucky—about five blocks south of where they sat.

Each day Jim walked into the courtroom he felt like he was stepping into a paperback by Tom Wolfe.

There was a racehorse. A stripper. Exotic cars. A drunk. A University of Kentucky blueblood lawyer. The swaggering "Master of Disaster" who compared himself to the Tiger Woods of class-action litigation. And an acerbic, "the baloney stops here" judge who held everyone in contempt.

Today there was also a disbarred judge on the witness stand, testifying against lawyers who were on trial for sponging up $120 million of a $200 million settlement. As if that was not absurd enough, an expert witness testified that the diet-pill victims should have been more grateful because the lawyers were "underpaid."

All but invisible during the trial were 440 sad victims—mostly women—who took deadly diet pills. Their heartbreak was physical as well as figurative. As their health declined and their medical bills went from stout to obese, they had been given a few crumbs from the $200 million cake after the lawyers had eaten everything else.

Looming in the background were multibillion-dollar pharmaceutical companies, thousands of doctors who had become eager pill pushers, FDA regulators who were stooges for the drug companies, and reporters and editors whose news stories read like promotional ads for a deadly, untested "miracle drug."

The local case was like an epilogue to the national Fen-Phen scandal that was called a "one of the biggest tort scams ever" and the biggest medical liability settlement in history. The lawyer feeding frenzy began the same day the drug was recalled in 1997, and there was still blood in the water 11 years later when the local trial began in May 2008.[175]

---

175 The ultimate cost was pegged at more than $22 billion. "The $22 Billion Gold Rush," Forbes Magazine, March 24, 2006. It was surpassed by the tobacco industry master settlement (1998, $206 billion) and the opioid settlement (2021, $50 billion).

Four well-known, distinguished members of the Kentucky Bar were accused of looting a $200 million settlement that had been approved by a crooked judge. Now the disbarred judge was ratting out the lawyers, the lawyers were ratting on each other and all of them were ratting on Chesley as the "mastermind" of the settlement.

One of the Kentucky lawyers was Melbourne Mills Jr., whose sweptback white hair and buttery Southern drawl fit his name like honey on a biscuit. He looked and sounded like he had been sent by central casting to play the oily lawyer on a soap opera. He had used his popular "Call The Man" TV ads in Lexington to fish for hundreds of Fen-Phen victims. He took $25 million from the $200 million settlement, but claimed that his daily half-gallon dose of Old Crow bourbon had made him too soused and senseless to understand how the victims were robbed. Jim joked that he "took the Fifth" with a new twist of lemon.

A Lexington male attorney with the unfortunate but very Kentucky name of "Shirley," Shirley Cunningham Jr., used his $21 million share to build a polished reputation as a community leader and philanthropist, while he maintained an office he never visited on a Florida college campus where he claimed to be a professor. Most figured he was added to the Fen-Phen team by affirmative action, to bring in black victims of Fen-Phen diet pills.

William Gallion, the ringleader, grabbed more than $31 million from the settlement, then ordered a clerk to destroy records when the Kentucky Bar started to investigate why he had collected his attorneys' fees twice. As the lawyer for the University of Kentucky Medical School, he was a wealthy VIP in Lexington, a true blueblood in a city that bleeds Kentucky Wildcat blue.

And there was Chesley, who had somehow extracted immunity from prosecution in return for testimony against the others. He took $20 million as a "consultant" who seized control and gave orders, according to Gallion. It was Chesley's idea to set up a separate $20 million slush fund, ironically named a "trust," that was hidden from the drug victims. It was used to pay the judge $50,000 for his cooperation; the rest was paid out to Mills, Cunningham, Gallion and Chesley.

As the men in the next booth talked about the Cincinnati Reds and ate, Jim looked down at the crisp white tablecloth in Otto's. There was an indigo-blue glass vase in the middle with real spring lilacs. The flatware was spotless and the napkin was thick cloth, not paper, as white as a clean sheet on a clothesline. He was reminded of the grease-streaked, hard-plastic table in the food court at Florence Mall, where he met one of the Fen-Phen victims for an interview a few years back. Her name was Willma with two Ls. She was from Eastern Kentucky coal country, and she drove hours to the trial in Covington three or four times a week, with her husband Alvin, dragging along her wheeled oxygen bottle like a dog on a leash, wheezing like she had swallowed a Cracker Jack whistle.

As they sat on cheap red plastic chairs at the food court, he saw her doughy legs sticking out below her bright flowered house dress, and her puffy ankles bulging out of her shoes, heavy and thick. The flesh looked soft, spongy, unhealthy, as pale as the belly of a dead fish. It was "the water," she explained.

"Mah leaky heart can't keep up no more. The doctor tells me I have a bad valve."

"Like that Ford what burned oil," Alvin added with a knowing nod. He wore pressed Wranglers and a white pearl-snap shirt, buttoned to the top.

Willma gave him a hard look that said more than a thousand sighs. Then she continued, "Mah lungs, they's the worst of it. Some kinda pole-man… pole-man—"

"Pulmonary hypertension?" Jim supplied.

"There, that's it," Willma said, smiling as if he had just solved the final clue on *Jeopardy*. She was in her early 50s, but her seamed face and pallor made her look 30 years older.

They told him how their credit cards were way beyond maxed out, all their meager savings and Alvin's pension gone, bled dry by doctors, tests, drugs and treatments that only slowed her steady slide toward an ICU unit and an early grave.

Her two-strike diagnosis was fatal. The heart-valve damage *might* be fatal, but pulmonary hypertension certainly was. She might even have another side-effect: death of brain cells that produce serotonin, the chemical that makes people happy. Fen-Phen overstimulated serotonin production for a feeling of euphoria—until it killed the cells that released it, and the "feel-good" effect evaporated forever, replaced by numb dread.

Willma was slowly drowning like a leaky riverboat and her heart and lungs couldn't pump away the water. The drug had robbed her future and taken what little joy and happiness she had left. She could not even remember the good times because the drug cause a neurotoxic memory loss.[176]

She had insisted on meeting at the food court because that's where she had been summoned to collect her share of the settlement, "Right at this here table," she said, clicking a fingernail with chipped crimson polish on the streaked yellow plastic. She had been given a check for $25,000. When Herb asked why she had to sign off without seeing the final settlement agreement, the young woman in a business suit and heels who represented the class-action lawyers threatened Willma and Alvin with a $50,000 fine, or even jail time, if the judge found out they were "jeopardizing the agreement for everyone" by asking too many questions. They were warned they could not tell anyone about the check and were not allowed to see the total amount of the settlement.

Jim's attention was brought back to Otto's as the cop in the gray suit spoke. The soft clicking of forks on plates had stopped. "I will have to suffer for this hot mess in my next workout, but it was worth it."

"Hot brown," tan suit laughed.

Gray suit pretended to grumble, "You won't laugh when you get to be my age. Once you get past 40, the Fat Fairy visits every night to leave a deposit. Burning it off is like trying to whittle a redwood with a plastic spoon."

Tan suit offered a sympathetic chuckle, then returned to their earlier topic. "You've been at this a long time. How did we get here?"

"We walked."

"No, I mean the case."

"I know," gray suit laughed. "Seriously? From the beginning?

"Yeah, sure. The court clerk said she'd call if court resumes, but

---

176   Mundy, Alicia. Dispensing with the Truth. Macmillan + ORM, 2010.

it looks like there will be conferences in the judge's chambers for the rest of the day."

"I got that impression too. Okay, here goes. From the beginning."

Jim turned to a new page and was glad he had grabbed a fresh notebook that morning. He took another bite of his neglected salad and thought, *No more court today? Should I go back to the office? Nah. This is more interesting.*

BIRTH OF A 'MIRACLE' PILL

"It started with a weight-loss pill called Pondimin. Hardly anyone used it because it put people to sleep. The active chemical was fenfluramine—the first 'fen' in Fen-Phen. It was discovered in 1979 by some M.I.T. genius named Richard Wurtman. They sold the license to France and got a whole country to take it for a test drive."

"Sort of like getting your little brother to try the new cereal," tan suit joked.

"Right. Then another white-coat wizard named Michael Weintraub got a bright idea. Mix fenfluramine with amphetamines to keep users awake. That was the second 'phen,' phentermine."

"Amphetamines? Speed?"

"Yes. They give users more energy."

Tan suit asked, "How does it keep people from gaining weight?"

"Wurtman's wife was also doing research for M.I.T. and discovered that people overeat for the chemical high. Carbohydrates stimulate serotonin production, which makes you feel happy and satisfied. More carbohydrates, more happy vibrations. Fenfluramine stimulates serotonin production without the carbs. Abracadabra: less appetite, more euphoria."[177]

"Playing the lottery with brain chemistry? What could possibly go wrong?" tan suit laughed.

"Plenty. The new weight-loss magic pill Pondimin was a dying dog in the drug market—until Weintraub released his study. Overnight the dog turned into a racehorse. Weintraub showed how Pondimin could

---

177 *MIT News*, February 5, 1997.

be prescribed off-label with amphetamines, and thousands of doctors started writing prescriptions. American Home Products, which had Pondimin—"

"Now they're Wyeth?"

"Wyeth, AHP, same thing. They set up 140,000 visits by drug reps to tell doctors about it. They paid doctors to sign their names to articles in medical journals that claimed it was totally safe and effective. They sent reprints of Wurtman's study to thousands of doctors. Informational seminars at Holiday Inns were hosted by guys in white lab coats, who were just salesmen pretending to be doctors. Wyeth spent $52 million-[178] on marketing, mostly ads in newspapers and magazines. And *Time Magazine* put Fen-Phen on the cover as the new miracle drug."

"Purely a coincidence, I'm sure," tan suit said. "Nothing to do with all those pharma ads they bought, right?"

Gray suit chuckled. "Now you're getting it. Magazines were making a killing—pardon the pun—from the drug industry. This was the good old days before TV ads for drugs were allowed."

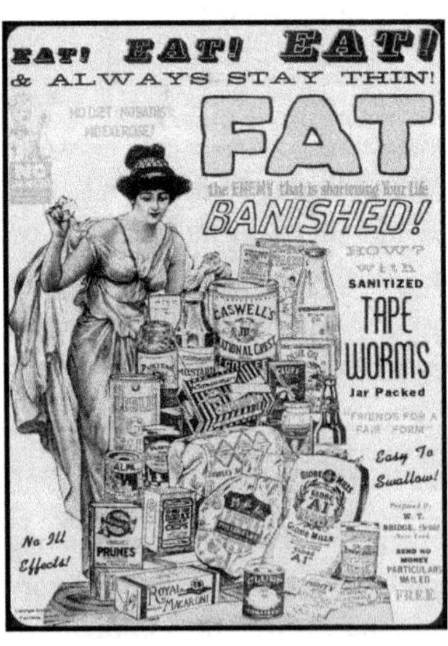

Hazardous weight-loss "miracles" are nothing new. In the early 1900s, "sanitized," "easy to swallow" tapeworms were advertised as a way to eat anything and "always stay thin" with "No ill effects." They didn't work. From the US Food and Drug Administration archives.

---

178   $78 million in 2025.

Tan suit imitated a TV announcer's voice: "Ask your doctor about FatBeGone. May cause inflammatory bowel, suicidal thoughts, brain damage and black vomit—"

"Hey, I'm trying to eat," gray suit laughed. "But you know what? They could have said all that and worse, and still millions would take it. That's how desperate people are to lose weight, especially women."

Tan suit said, "Yeah, they're easier targets. Women are never fat in TV land. Jackie Gleason? Obese. His wife? A catalog model. What's that show with the UPS driver? *King of Queens.* Fat guy, hot wife. Only on TV. Unless the fat guy is as rich as Onassis."

"Exactly. TV is the perfect platform for selling magic pills. It creates fat anxiety while it contributes to obesity with all those pizza ads aimed at couch potatoes, who sit on their sofas for six hours a night watching *Love Boat.* It's almost as if television was invented to sell miracle fat pills. And people will take anything to lose fat without exercise. One of our expert witnesses was a doctor who wrote a paper about fat-phobia. A hundred years ago people were swallowing tapeworms to lose weight without exercise. The ads said they were risk free, guaranteed harmless, no diet, no exercise. Sound familiar?"

"Ugh, I'm glad I didn't order spaghetti," tan suit said.

In the next booth, Jim pushed his salad away. Black vomit. Tapeworms. He had suddenly lost his appetite.

Gray suit said, "It just goes to show people will literally swallow anything if you tell them it will make them thin and beautiful. But I'm getting ahead of the story."

"Keep going."

"Picture this. You're a doctor and suddenly you are flooded with all these studies telling you the new miracle pill is totally safe. Your patients are demanding it, and the drug company wants to shower you with money to write prescriptions. For doctors, the Fen-Phen craze was like winning the Publisher's Clearing House Sweepstakes. We're talking 85,000 prescriptions a week nationwide. Some wrote thousands of prescriptions for Weight Watchers and Jenny Craig to hand out like candy on Halloween. AHP-Wyeth was making $20 million a month. There was even a phone number, call 1-800-4-FEN-FEN for prescriptions. They were looking at $1 billion in sales in five years. It was the biggest rollout of a drug in history—all based on a one-year study of 125 patients that claimed to show users lost 30 pounds."

"Was it that effective?"

"Is a hot brown health food? Hell no. Wyeth's own research showed only 3 percent weight loss with alarming hazards, but that was kept under wraps while the *Time Magazine* story told readers, and I quote, 'It might be worth the risk.' And USA TODAY said there was no heart damage from the diet drug. Some of the top medical schools and hospitals were giving hailing it as a wonder drug that might cure alcoholism and depression."[179]

"But it was all about the so-called obesity crisis, right?"

"Brought to you by the drug companies. They saw that Americans were spending $30 billion a year on diet books, low-calorie foods, weight-loss centers, electric vibrating fat melter gadgets, you name it. They wanted a piece of that market the way a fat man wants a piece of cake—the whole thing. So they created advocacy groups and funded research to alert everyone about the crisis of 300,000 annual deaths from obesity. Nobody asked where that number came from. The media ate it up like Hostess Twinkies and told us obesity is a disease, like diabetes. It requires lifelong treatment, which means drugs."

At the next table, Jim winced. He remembered those stories. He had even fed the obesity panic with a few columns himself.

"And they lowered the bar of the obesity definition to make more people classify as obese and overweight, right?" tan suit asked.

"Right. More fat anxiety meant more demand for a magic pill. And Wyeth came to the rescue with one they called Redux. Dr. Wurtman mixed fenfluramine with amphetamine. Now no off-label prescription was required. It was all in one pill."

"When did they notice problems?"

"The French figured it out first, like the dead canary in a coal mine. There were growing cases of primary pulmonary hypertension. Blood vessels in the lungs collapse and die. It's incurable and fatal. A nasty way to die. But Wyeth was in the final stages of FDA approval, so it was brushed aside."

---

179   Mundy, Alicia. *Dispensing with the Truth*. Macmillan + ORM, 2010.

"Didn't the FDA know?"

"They did. But FDA regulators are good to drug companies such as Wyeth because they hope Wyeth will be good to them when they join the private sector on the other side of the revolving door. I've seen FDA communications where they refer to 'our clients' as the pharmaceutical companies—not the public.[180] The FDA even hired Weintraub, the original Fen-Phen fat guru, and put him in charge of new drug approvals. It's how the game is played in DC.

"But then it got messy. When Redux came up for FDA approval, it was rejected on the first vote. And that is usually the end of it. But this time, the FDA panel did a sudden U-turn and approved it after Wyeth brought in lobbyists, including Alexander Haig."

"President Regan's secretary of state? That Haig?"[181]

"None other. He was on the board of Wurtman's drug company. When politics talks, science gets tongue-tied."

"No wonder Wyeth is getting hammered in court. If they knew it was dangerous…."

Gray suit answered, "The first cases were devastating. There was a $100 million jury settlement in Mississippi, then $23 million including punitive damages in Dallas. Wyeth saw that and offered a class-action settlement to limit their liability. Their plan was to bring all the victims into the tent for one big payday. But they made two fatal mistakes. One, they said any victims that stayed in their class action would not have to prove the cause of their injuries—"

"They admitted they were guilty!" tan suit said, surprised.

"Yes. And two, they said the plaintiffs could provide their own EKGs."

Tan suit said, "So what they intended as bait to bring victims into the class action settlement became chum for lawyers. They forfeited before the first kickoff. I would love a case like that. I could grab anyone off the street, rig a phony EKG showing heart or lung damage and settle for millions because Wyeth admitted the drug was deadly."

"That's a good summary," gray suit said.

---

180   Mundy, Alicia. *Dispensing with the Truth*. Macmillan + ORM, 2010.

181   Mundy, Alicia. *Dispensing with the Truth*. Macmillan + ORM, 2010. Haig was on the board of Interneuron, the drug company founded by MIT and Wurtman, inventor of Redux.

Jim nodded and wrote down "bait and chum—lawyers smell blood in the water."

Gray suit added, "And only 15 percent of the tests were checked for fraud. You could sail a supertanker of payouts through that loophole. Wyeth expected 35,000 claims and got 85,000. A Mayo Clinic study found heart damage in one-third of Fen-Phen users—which was alarming enough. But the lawyers somehow managed to find heart damage in about 200 percent of them."

Jim recalled the Mayo study bombshell that forced Wyeth to immediately withdraw Redux from the market. A few doctors in Fargo, North Dakota had noticed 24 women with heart damage—all of them taking Fen-Phen. One stubborn doctor would not stop asking questions, and finally, someone listened.

Tan suit said, "I heard they intentionally delayed updates to the drug warnings for years. Alarm bells were going off everywhere. Like that young woman who took pills to slim down for her wedding dress and died a few months later?"

"Mary Linnen. She was only 30. The autopsy blamed Fen-Phen."

There was a moment of silence. Then tan suit spoke. "Quite a story. The doctors got rich. The drug companies cashed in. Even people who never took the pills hit the jackpot. And then the lawyers put all of them in the weeds by exploiting the sick and dying like hyenas fighting over an elephant carcass."

"The only people who were not invited to the dance were the victims," gray suit agreed. "Like the ones in this case."

Jim thought of Willma and Herb. The federal prosecutors were demanding another $42 million from the cheating lawyers. But by the time that was paid, if ever, Willma would probably be dead. Nearly two dozen victims had already died since the lawyers handed out the first paltry settlements. And they could have gotten away with everything if they hadn't been too greedy. The whole scam fell apart when a partner of Mills noticed he was getting stiffed for his share of the spoils and blew the whistle to the Kentucky Bar.

Jim pulled out his old notebook from the trial. He had written down:

Mills takes the Fifth—of Old Crow.

Immunity for Chesley "*unusual*," says the judge.

> Cunningham and Gallion spent $57,000 of Fen-Phen money on a racehorse named Curlin that won the Preakness.
>
> Gallion spends $145,000 on a Porsche.
>
> Law clerk questions why Gallion takes attorney fees twice and is told "I am the lawyer, not you."
>
> Fen-Phen victim who was given about a tenth of what she really deserved tells the lawyers, "Thank you for being so kind."
>
> Gallion testimony: Chesley has leverage with AHP/Wyeth because he sits on a panel to approve the national class action settlement. His vote determines the how much they must pay, so they want to keep him happy. Gallion says the drug company pressured him and his partners to let Chesley in on the loot: "I got the message loud and clear that if we were going to get our cases resolved, we had to reach an agreement with Mr. Chesley."
>
> Courtroom buzzing about a stripper/exotic dancer in the gallery... Girlfriend of Gallion?
>
> Gallion on the stand: "I am <u>extremely proud</u> of what we did in this case."

It all checked out. The drug companies dangled bait for victims; lawyers smelled blood in the water; and then the Great White Sharks of litigation came to the party and they all began eating each other—a feeding frenzy, with no shark cages to protect the victims.

The following week in court, the judge looked angry enough to throw them all in prison. The jury had deliberated for nearly two days and reported that they was hopelessly deadlocked. Mistrial.

That's when Jim remembered what he had overheard at the restaurant about high-dollar courtroom consultants who could drop a gold bar on the scales of justice. So he interviewed jurors, and one said he suspected a leak in the jury room. His suspect was a juror who had nothing to say for weeks, then suddenly became a loud advocate for the accused lawyers during deliberations. "It just didn't add up," the juror said.

But the case was not over. The US Attorney's prosecutors filed new charges. Evidence in the first trial had revealed that Cunningham and Gallion had wired Fen-Phen cash to a dozen bank accounts in Florida and Kentucky. They were charged with wire fraud and both were finally convicted at a new trial in Frankfort, Kentucky. Mills, the drunk, was let off the hook—too pickled to be convicted.

Gallion was sent to prison for 25 years. Cunningham was sentenced to 20 years. They were ordered to pay $127 million in restitution. The racehorse was auctioned. The supercars and *Towne & Country* homes were sold. The stripper had to find a new sugar daddy. Then in 2024, as President Joe Biden was leaving office and staffers had control of his autopen signature, Gallion was pardoned. He would have finished his prison term in 2029. The Biden clemency left the conviction on his record but released him five years early without explanation. Jim wondered if someone in the White House profited by selling the pardon.

All of the lawyers were disbarred, including Mills and Chesley, who was separately ordered to pay $42 million in restitution. "Shocking and reprehensible," the judge said. "A cover-up of thievery."[182]

Many of the victims died waiting for restitution. Chesley litigated his own disaster with a strategy of stalling and delay, even suing some of the ailing Fen-Phen victims and their attorney.[183] He finally agreed to pay $23.5 million in 2018, a decade after the Covington federal trial, and 20 years after the first lawsuit.

The delays went all the way to the federal Sixth Circuit Court of Appeals in Cincinnati. In their decision against Chesley, the judges wrote, "Stanley Chesley appears to have been orchestrating a high-stakes shell game in an effort to escape a long-overdue multi-million dollar judgment. In the process, he has defrauded hundreds of judgment creditors, many of whom are plaintiffs here."

"Unjust enrichment," the court records said, banging a gavel to end his long and illustrious courtroom career.

But all that was still to come as Jim picked over his neglected Cobb

---

182   Searcey, Dionne, "Fen-Phen Lawyer's License at Risk," Wall Street Journal, February 4, 2011.

183   Wolfson, Andrew, "Disbarred lawyer sues former fen-phen clients," *Louisville Courier-Journal*, September 22, 2015.

Salad at Otto's and decided he would return to the office and work on a story. He put cash on the table to cover his tab, put his nearly empty ballpoint back in the inside pocket of his worn, shapeless navy blazer with the shiny elbows, and stood up. He tucked the reporter's notebooks into the back pocket of his discount-store Dockers khakis and turned to leave.

As he passed the booth next door, he met the eyes of the cop and the lawyer. Tan suit's face was blank, but gray suit smiled warmly.

"Did you get everything?" the cop asked. Not unfriendly. Not an accusation. Almost helpful.

Jim smiled awkwardly, and nodded. He made a show of patting his pockets. "Yup. Wallet. Notebooks. Pen. Everything."

The other two men nodded knowingly. The tan-suit lawyer smiled now and said, "Good. We wouldn't want you to miss anything."

Years later, Jim looked back on the case and the columns he had written about it and he had to smile at the way he had been played. The lawyer representing the Kentucky Bar had filled Jim's notebook with off-the-record details of the case against Mills, Cunningham, Gallion and Chesley. And the former cop who represented an L.A. litigant in the Fen-Phen frenzy had given him a succinct tutorial on the history of how the drug companies had rigged the system to make a killing—literally and financially—from their magic pills, while the media played sales-man like a late-night cable huckster selling "miracle" Ginsu knives.

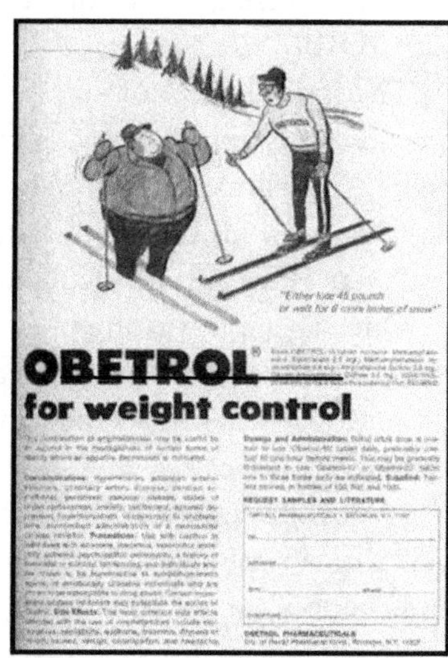

A 1970 ad for amphetamine diet pills. The cartoon caption says, "Either lose 45 pounds or wait for six more inches of snow."

He couldn't quote them. And if he did, they could honestly deny that they had ever talked to him.

There had been arguments with his editor, who wanted to make sure Stan Chesley was treated fairly, with mentions of his philanthropy and good deeds for the city. That was all true. But so was Chesley's ability to schmooze with editors and reporters, who were almost incapable of believing someone so close to their hero Bill Clinton could do any wrong.

But in the end, most of what he learned that day in Otto's was confirmed by other sources and made it into his columns.

And look at how far we have come, he thought. Now every commercial break on TV is filled with bizarre ads for obscure magic pills that work miracles. "Ask your doctor about FeelGoodium…." "See a medical professional to find out if daily shots of Euphoriax are right for you…."

Nearly the whole nation was forced or panicked into taking shots and boosters that were never properly tested or FDA approved—and the government even gave the companies immunity from lawsuits in case there were fatal or crippling side effects to "stop the spread" of COVID-19.

The spread was not stopped. The Made in China disease ran its course. And now Americans were learning, too late, that for many people, the shots were more hazardous than the disease and the "experts" were shills for the pharmaceutical companies.

It was Fen-Phen on elephant steroids.

Once again, it was the press that played phony lab-coat salesman-enforcer to make sure everyone got the jab—even toddlers and infants.

And just when it seemed the public would finally wise up about "miracle" pills….

"Ask your doctor if Ozempic is right for you."

"Wegovy mimics a hormone for long term weight loss in adults and children age 12 and older…"

"May cause nausea, diarrhea, vomiting, pancreatitis, thyroid tumors and increased heart rate… no in-person visit required…call now to order…"

Hmmm, Jim thought. *Maybe I will give it a try. What could possibly go wrong?*

Ten Places to Discover
Cincinnati History

PIONEER CEMETERY
Wilmer Avenue, Linwood

~

This is where it all began for Cincinnati and Ohio. On November 18, 1788, Revolutionary War veteran Major Benjamin Stites stepped off a boat onto the muddy bank of the northern shore of the Ohio River, followed by 26 rugged pioneers from New Jersey.

They were blissfully unaware of what they would face. Life in the early days was harsh enough to make Job a giddy optimist. The families who founded the settlement known as Columbia Station lived in constant fear of devastating floods, savage Indian attacks, bitter winters and cruel starvation.

But the life they fled in the East was bleak, cramped and hopeless. Americans needed room to grow, and they found their Promised Land here: fresh water, rich soil, abundant game and timber—room to stretch their legs and move West.

Pioneer Cemetery is probably the oldest cemetery in Ohio.[185] The first burials began in 1790, in graves that are now unmarked. The oldest headstone is 1797, for five-month-old Phebe Stites. Major Ben Stites, who died in 1804, is buried here along with most of his family. The monument to these settlers is a Corinthian pillar, taken from an 1856 Post Office. It towers over the hilltop to mark the Columbia Baptist Cemetery, which was nestled next to Columbia Baptist Church, built in 1792. It was the first Protestant church in the Northwest Territory.

At the base of the pillar, the names of Stites and 26 men and women who followed him are listed—an honor roll of Cincinnati's courageous "first families." The headstone for Stites is nearby, erected in 1922.

Their home, Columbia Station, was a stockade with blockhouses to defend against attacks by the Shawnee and Miami Tribes. During one four-year period in the early 1790s, the Indians took more than 1,500

---

184   Not including burial mounds for Adena and Woodland mound-builders that date back 3,000 years.

sons, husbands, brothers, daughters, mothers and wives, who were killed, tortured or sold to the British in Detroit.

Pioneer Cemetery is the burial ground for some of the heroic militia members and families described in *Promised Land: How the Midwest Was Won.*

Revolutionary War veterans are buried and honored here, along with veterans who fought in the Civil War. A Colonial Garden maintained by the Cincinnati Parks Department displays the type of garden planted by the settlers.

The path at Pioneer Cemetery (top) leads uphill to the site of the first Baptist Church and cemetery in Cincinnati, and the first settlement. The headstone of Maj. Benjamin Stites (left) is near the monument that lists all of the families who followed him(right).

WILLIAM HENRY HARRISON MONUMENT & CONGRESS GREEN CEMETERY
Cliff Road, North Bend

~

One of Ohio's greatest action heroes was William Henry Harrison. He was at the side of "Mad Anthony" Wayne during the long march north from Cincinnati to the Battle of Fallen Timbers near Toledo, that conquered the Indian Confederation, broke their alliance with the British and booted the British from Ohio and the Northwest Territory in 1794.

Harrison was a "child of the Revolution," son of Col. Benjamin Harrison, who signed the Declaration of Independence.

His monument overlooks the Ohio River that he traveled on to arrive in Cincinnati at the age of 18, as an ensign in the 1st Infantry Division of the first professional US Army after the Revolutionary War.

He was cited for valor by General Wayne at Fallen Timbers. Later, Harrison was present for signing of the Treaty of Greenville in 1795, that made Wayne's victory official and opened the Northwest Territory for safe settlement of Ohio, Michigan, Indiana, Illinois, Wisconsin and parts of Minnesota.

Harrison learned military tactics and discipline from Wayne and went on to fight the Shawnee Chief Tecumseh twice, including another decisive victory when the Indian confederation was allied with the British during the War of 1812. His victory at the Battle of the Thames in Canada, where Tecumseh was killed, was an echo of Wayne's victory at Fallen Timbers—he rescued the young nation from depredations by the Indians and British and opened the continent for westward expansion.

In 1795, Harrison eloped with Anna Symmes, daughter of William Cleves Symmes, one of America's first land speculators and developers. Symmes, who was a friend of Major Benjamin Stites, is buried with members of his family across the road from the Harrison monument, in Congress Green Cemetery. The Symmes Purchase was 330,000 acres between the Little Miami and Great Miami rivers, from the Ohio River north into Butler and Warren counties. Symmes was a Revolutionary War soldier who loaned the government money for the war, then was repaid with land in Ohio Territory.

Major General Harrison was the hero of the 1811 Battle of Tippecanoe near Lafayette, Indiana. He was elected governor of Indiana from 1801 to 1812, then became the nation's ninth President on March 4, 1841. He was the first president to die in office one month later—the shortest term by a president.

His grandson, Benjamin Harrison, became the 23rd President.

A little-used short hiking path behind the monument leads to a park display telling William Henry Harrison's story, from his youth in Virginia, through the military, politics and his death from pneumonia. Directly across the road, steps lead up a hillside to Congress Green Cemetery, where graverobbers in 1878 dug up the freshly buried corpse of John Scott Harrison, President William Henry Harrison's son.

The tomb of John Cleves Symmes (right) is across the road from the William Henry Harrison monument (left) in North Bend.

HERITAGE VILLAGE
Sharon Woods Park

~

What did Cincinnati look like in the 1790s? How about the early 1800s or the Civil War? Heritage Village is a time capsule of local history, a collection of original homes, offices, a schoolhouse, a church, general store, print shop, train station and a replica of the flatboats used by Cincinnati's earliest settlers.

The second home of The Rev. James Kemper is here. It's a two-story log house, luxurious for its time, where he moved his wife and 15 children after they left their cramped blockhouse that protected them from Indian Attacks in Walnut Hills—too far from Fort Washington to rely on help. Kemper courageously traveled on horseback along the Ohio River, to visit tiny stockaded settlements known as "stations," where he performed weddings, funerals and Sunday services as one of the first ordained pastors in the Northwest Territory.

After "The Battle of a Thousand Slain" in 1791, a terrible massacre of General Arthur St. Clair's expedition by the Shawnee and Miami tribes, it was Kemper who went from house to house and encouraged Cincinnati's demoralized, frightened settlers to stay and defend their "promised land" as God's destiny.

Nearby, the beautiful 1852 Greek Revival Hayner House was moved to Heritage Village from Warren County. Many of the historic buildings were dismantled and moved to Heritage Village to be rescued from demolition.

The village offers special events to demonstrate "spinning, weaving, candle-dipping, soap making, hearth cooking, carpentry work, herb lore, gardening, printing, trade and bartering, and communication."

The second home of James Kemper, founder of Walnut Hills Academy and one of
the first pastors in the Northwest Territory.

WALDSCHMIDT HOUSE
CAMP DENNISON
7567 Glendale Milford Rd., Camp Dennison

Cincinnati was still known as "The Miami Slaughterhouse" in 1794 when Revolutionary War veteran Christian Waldschmidt brought his family to the area now known as Camp Dennison. Proof of that is a large brass bell behind the house. It would be rung by women to call men from the surrounding fields if Indians were sighted.

Waldschmidt's first house was the smaller Kugler House west of the big house, built as a temporary home while the main house was being built. The Kugler House was used as a guardhouse and headquarters by the Union Army during the Civil War, when Camp Dennison was temporarily under the command of Gen. George McClellan.

Waldschmidt built a papermill on the Little Miami River, that supplied newsprint for the first newspaper in the Northwest Territory, *The Western Spy*. He also had a tavern in the house where travelers could sample "antifogmatic" from his own distillery.

The two stone houses now make a bridge in time from the earliest settlers to the Civil War. Waldschmidt House is furnished with the clothing, furniture, cooking tools and everyday items of its time, as if a family from the late 1790s still lived there.

The guardhouse is now a Civil War Museum, crowded with uniforms, weapons and artifacts found on the grounds, where more than 50,000 soldiers mustered in and were trained. In 1862, Camp Dennison added a military hospital. The camp was named for Ohio Gov. William Dennison.

Wounded soldiers rescued from the battlefield at Shiloh in Southern Tennessee were brought here by volunteers in the Hamilton County Sanitation Commission, an early version of the Red Cross. More than 300 died here, including more than a dozen Confederate soldiers.

Many of the wounded soldiers had poor dental care and were too weak to digest the tough cuts of meat served by the army, so a camp doctor began grinding the meat, then mixing it with root vegetables and gravy. His name was Dr. John Salisbury—inventor of the Salisbury Steak and the once-popular Salisbury Diet (coffee and red meat).

In 1863, Confederates attacked Camp Dennison. Gen. John Hunt Morgan's Raiders, a force of 2,500 cavalry, rode past and fought a running battle with the Union Army and nearby Loveland Militia. The skirmish followed along the Little Miami Railroad, into Miamiville.

Both buildings are available for tours, managed by the Ohio Daughters of the American Revolution.

Camp Dennison, as seen across the Little Miami Railroad, during the Civil War. The type below the drawing says it was "a permanent camp of instruction in the West" for union soldiers.

The Kugler House next to Waldschmidt House is now a Civil War museum. It was used as officers' headquarters.

5

CINCINNATI POLICE MUSEUM
308 Reading Road, Suite 201, Cincinnati

~

Think of it as the "Police Property Room" for Cincinnati and Northern Kentucky. The Greater Cincinnati Police Museum has more than 10,000 law enforcement artifacts from some of our region's most sensational crimes and unsolved cold cases.

Volunteers research and present the history of law enforcement in 160 local communities, eight counties and three states. A memorial wall in the museum is dedicated to the fallen officers who gave their lives in the line of duty to protect and preserve public safety.

The collection includes Tommy guns, blackjacks, handcuffs and uniforms dating from the earliest days of Cincinnati and battles against the Mob, as told in *Forbidden Fruit* and *Not in Our Town*), as well as police gear from the more recent past. A collection of murder weapons donated by the family of defense attorney Foss Hopkins is a popular attraction. So is a police simulator that allows visitors to test their reflexes when faced with the split-second, life-or-death decisions that must be made by police.

The volunteers who staff the museum are mostly retired cops who have many vivid stories to tell.

The "Legends in Local Law Enforcement" exhibit features some of the greatest lawmen in Cincinnati history. "Big Tom" Farragher is there—the detective in "The Black Widow and Big Tom." So is "Handsome," the police dog that was adopted by Cincinnati officers in the early 1900s and helped catch a jewelry thief in the wild and violent Bottoms in 1904.

The Cincinnati Police Museum, 308 Reading Road, Suite 201, had plans to move to a new location in 2026. Check their website at www.police-museum.org for more information before you visit.

The sergeants of Cincinnati's Fifth Police District in 1890: John H. Kiffmeyer, Louis Schmit and Edward C. "Doc" Hill. Courtesy of the Greater Cincinnati Police Museum.

THE CINCINNATI FIRE MUSEUM, 315 Court Street, Cincinnati, offers tours that tell the story of the first professional fire department in the United States, founded in Cincinnati in 1853. Children can slide down a firehouse pole, climb aboard the collection of old fire engines and sit in the driver's seat to operate lights and a siren.

The museum contains some of the oldest firefighting equipment in existence. The story of Jacob Piatt's battle to form the nation's first professional fire department is featured in *Promised Land.*

6

LEW WALLACE STUDY & MUSEUM
271 Ellston Avenue, Crawfordsville, Indiana

~

Lew Wallace is known in Indiana as a gallant Civil War general and the author of the American classic *Ben Hur*. He is the only author represented in Statuary Hall in the US Capitol.

But he was also *The Man Who Saved Cincinnati*. In 1862, an army of 10,000 Confederates marched north from Lexington to Fort Mitchell, led by General Henry Heth. Heth planned to burn, loot and hold the city for ransom. All of that could have happened if not for Gen. Wallace, who arrived just as the mayor of Cincinnati was running up the white flag of surrender.

Wallace organized the entire city under martial law. "The city will defend itself," he told the incredulous city leaders. And he made it work. In three days of hard labor, Cincinnati was united, ignoring fault lines of class, religion, race and ancestry that had torn the city apart in riots just weeks before.

Wallace built the first bridge across the Ohio River and marched thousands of volunteers across the river into Northern Kentucky, where they built rifle pits and cannon batteries across a seven-mile arc. During the Siege of Cincinnati in early September, Wallace formed the Black Brigade in which black troops were able to enlist under their own flag for the first time in the Civil War.

The siege was lifted on September 11, 1862, when Heth and his men were recalled and retreated to Lexington. Wallace was hailed by the governors of Ohio and Indiana as "The Savior of Cincinnati." Huge crowds lined rooftops to wave handkerchiefs and cheer him and the volunteers, including the Black Brigade, as they marched across the pontoon bridge back into the city.

After the war, Lew Wallace was appointed Territorial Governor of New Mexico, where he captured Billy the Kid and put down the Lincoln County Range War—the worst in US history. He was an inventor, a sculptor, a musician, a painter, a voracious reader, a military genius and the author of a book so popular it was outsold only by the Bible until the 1920s: *Ben Hur: A Tale of the Christ.*

The museum is a fascinating collection of his personal items, inventions, fiddles, paintings, sculptures, weapons and books, books, books. Every wall of the perfect cube in the avantgarde study he designed is crammed with books.

It is well worth the drive to get to know the Renaissance man who left such a huge footprint on Cincinnati and American history despite dropping out of school before he was 11. His story is told in *The Man Who Saved Cincinnati.*

This study was designed and built by Lew Wallace behind his home in Crawfordsville, Indiana, near his beloved Wabash River. The skylight mechanical vents he designed to cool the building in summertime were ahead of the times.

WHITEWATER SHAKER VILLAGE

Oxford Road, south of Howard Road, New Haven

UNION VILLAGE

OH 741 and Shaker Drive, Lebanon

~

Each Shaker Village had a name known to the Believers who lived there.

Union Village, founded in 1805, was the second biggest Shaker settlement in America in the 1840s, with 170 members of The Society of Believers in the Second Coming of Christ. It was the mother of Shaker settlements in Ohio, Kentucky, Indiana and Michigan. Meetings in the 1840s included visits from a spirit they called Mother Wisdom.

Union Village was known as "Wisdom's Paradise."

Whitewater Shaker Village, founded in 1823 near New Haven, north of Harrison, also grew to 137 residents in 1850. But it was not as prosperous or as powerful as its wealthy cousin in Lebanon.

Whitewater was known as "The Plain of Lonely Tribulation."

The Shakers believed the second coming of Christ was "Mother" Ann Lee, an English woman who emigrated to New York in 1774, bringing her visions of the spirit world that told her God wanted followers to abandon "the flesh" and be celibate. The Shakers believed she was the female incarnation of God.

Both Shaker villages, along with "Shakertowns" elsewhere, became ghost towns in the early 1900s. Celibacy meant no children to populate the future. Most of their land was sold to nearby farms.

Union Village is now part of the campus of Otterbein Senior Life. Marble Hall, once the beautiful home of the most powerful Elders, is now a museum and senior living apartments.

Whitewater Village stayed more intact, thanks to the Friends of

White Water Shaker Village. Visitors can find the milk house, stables, a barn, the segregated dorm where men and women slept in opposite wings, and the Meeting House with separate doors for the sexes, where they danced in concentric circles, stomping and "shaking like electricity," struck by trances and visions that sometimes went on for hours.

Although they seemed to live with one foot in a spirit world, they were sometimes unbalanced by infighting, power struggles, protests, abuse, banishments and attacks by their neighbors. By the late 1800s, the villages were populated only by elderly men and women. Young people who were adopted or brought to Shakertown left as soon as they were old enough.

There is something uneasy about Whitewater Shaker Village—as if spirits still linger in the stark, empty dorm rooms and cavernous Meeting Hall. It's not "Mother Wisdom." More like "The Plain of Lonely Tribulation."

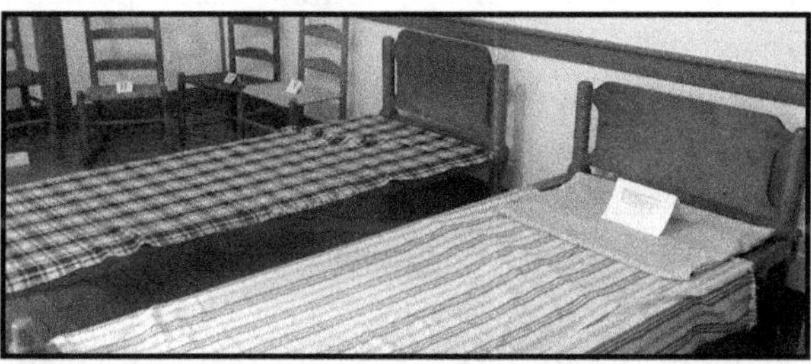

A bedroom in the segregated dorm at Whitewater Shaker Village. Life in the village was as stark and simple as their furniture.

On old photo of Marble Hall, which was the residence for elders at Union Shaker Village in Lebanon, Ohio. Courtesy of the Harmon Museum, Lebanon.

HARMON MUSEUM, BEEDLE CABIN, GOLDEN LAMB
Lebanon, Ohio

~

In 1803, Ohio was the youngest state in the union. Indian attacks were still terrorizing settlers. The 30-mile stagecoach trip from the Ohio River docks in Cincinnati north to Lebanon was filled with adventure, hazards and delays. But there was comfort in knowing that food, drink and lodging would be waiting at the Black Horse Tavern—now the Golden Lamb.

The restaurant is known as the oldest, continuously operating business in Ohio. Visitors will find the Black Horse Tavern much like it was in the early 1800s. The dining room could double as a museum of Shaker furniture. And overnight guests can stay in rooms that have been slept in by Henry Clay, Charles Dickens, Mark Twain and Neil Armstrong, among others. A dozen US Presidents have visited the Lamb, going back to John Quincy Adams.

One of the private dining rooms upstairs is named after Clement Vallandingham, a notorious Copperhead southern sympathizer and Dayton Congressman during the Civil War, who accidentally shot himself and died there while demonstrating his defense of a client on trial for murder. Vallandingham intended to argue that the murdered victim had shot himself while pulling a pistol from his cummerbund. As Vallandingham showed his friends how, his loaded gun went off.

Almost next door to the Gold Lamb is one of the Cincinnati area's great treasures, Harmon Museum at 105 S. Broadway. The museum has a collection of archeological artifacts from the Moundbuilders culture that could be second only to the Smithsonian Museum.

Just around the corner from Harmon Museum, at 141 S. Broadway in Public Square Park, is Beedle Cabin, built in 1795. In those days, southwest Ohio was terrorized by brutal Indian attacks.

It's the oldest home in Warren County, one of many log cabins that still can be found in the region. Another one is the Miller-Leuser Log House at 6550 Clough Pike in Anderson Township, built in 1796.

The Golden Lamb in Lebanon, in 1937. It is almost identical today, and dates back to 1803, the same year Ohio became a state.

Like the Beedle Cabin in Lebanon, the Miller-Leuser cabin on Clough Pike is typical of several early homes of Cincinnati pioneers. It is owned and maintained by the Anderson Township Historical Society. Tours are available.

SMALL MUSEUMS & HISTORICAL SOCIETIES

~

Say "Cincinnati history" and most people immediately think of the Cincinnati Museum Center, our premier museum of local and natural history. But there are dozens of smaller, quirky and fascinating museums with eclectic collections that are fun to explore. City and county historical societies are often located in historic homes that are furnished and filled with artifacts that show us how families lived long ago.

BEHRINGER-CRAWFORD MUSEUM
1600 Montague Road Devou Park, Covington, Kentucky

Behringer-Crawford Museum in Devou Park, Covington has a diverse collection including mammoth bones, Civil War relics and a trolley car. Courtesy of Behringer-Crawford Museum.

It all flows from the river. The first ancient Adena and Hopewell cultures built their mounds along the Ohio. The Shawnee and Miami tribes hunted along the banks. The first settlers arrived on the river, floating on flatboats. And the Ohio River made Cincinnati the Queen City of the West in the days before freeways and railroads, when rivers were the transportation arteries of the new nation.

The Rivers Gallery at the Behringer-Crawford Museum tells the story of settlement, commerce and history that grew along the banks of the Ohio and Licking Rivers.

But there is much more to see here. The museum is small but eclectic, packed with history of our region. There are exhibits on transportation, Roebling Bridge construction, airports and fossils of Ice Age mammals found at Big Bone Lick.

A small Civil War exhibit includes a musket, pistols, part of a tree with an embedded artillery ball and a replica of the Black Brigade's flag that was first flown during the Siege of Cincinnati in 1862.

ROMBACH PLACE
149 E. Locust Street, Wilmington

Another fine small museum is the former home of General James W. Denver (*Rifles at Forty Paces*), which is now home to the Clinton County History Center.

General Denver's uniforms, portraits and personal items, such as his camp desk and amazing portable tub, are displayed. The beautiful home was built in 1831. It was owned by the father of Denver's wife, Louise Rombach.

The historic General Denver Hotel at 81 W. Main Street opened in 1928. The project was led by a group of stockholders, including Denver's son, Mathew Rombach Denver.

The sun-splashed parlor of the 1863 Benninghofen House at 327 N. Second Street in Hamilton is a time capsule of life for a wealthy family more than 160 years ago. The beautiful mansion is also home to the Butler County Historical Society's excellent small museum. Courtesy of the Butler County Historical Society.

SPRING GROVE CEMETERY
4521 Spring Grove Ave., Cincinnati

~

What has a bigger population than Toledo, more distinguished names than all the politicians in Columbus, more Civil War generals than the Battle of Gettysburg—and yet remains an oasis of peace and quiet?

The population of Spring Grive Cemetery and Arboretum in August 2025 was 277,000 and steadily growing. Only half of the cemetery's 750 acres have been used. It is the second largest cemetery in the nation.

Names here include department store tycoons (McAlpin, Carew, Pogue); brewery barons (Muhlhauser, Moerlein); a chief justice of the US Supreme Court (Salmon P. Chase); Judge Jacob Burnet of the famous Burnet House hotel family (his brother David was the first president of the Republic of Texas); Cincinnati's first millionaire (Nicholas Longworth, former owner of Mt. Adams); and monuments to early pioneers such as Israel Ludlow (the man who named Dayton and surveyed Ohio) and Maj. Gen. John Gano, a leader of the militia at Fort Washington who fought in the Northwest Territory Indian War and the War of 1812.

The Civil War section is guarded by a statue of a soldier on picket duty, called "The Sentinel." More than a thousand Civil War soldiers are buried in the cemetery, along with 41 Civil War Generals, such as "Fighting Joe" Hooker, Col. Manning Ferguson Force (Medal of Honor) and Brig. Gen. Andrew Hickenlooper, the hero of the Hornet's Nest at the Battle of Shiloh.

Perhaps the biggest funeral in Cincinnati history was held in Spring Grove after Brig. Gen. William H. Lytle was killed at the Battle of Chickamauga on September 20, 1863. The Lytles were one of the most respected families in Cincinnati. William Lytle was a nationally famous poet. When he was killed in battle, Confederate soldiers posted an honor guard over his body until Union soldiers could recover it under a flag of truce.

When he was buried, his funeral procession took four hours to reach the cemetery from Christ Church Cathedral downtown. Thousands lined the streets to mourn. The procession was led by five army regiments. His impressive monument includes a bronze relief that depicts his death in battle.

Tours of the cemetery and arboretum include a self-guided walking tour. Spring Grove is Cincinnati's Valley of the Kings.

"The Sentinel" statue keeps watch over the graves of Civil War soldiers at Spring Grove Cemetery.

A bronze-relief sculpture on the impressive tomb of William H. Lytle shows his death at the Battle of Chickamauga in 1863. His funeral may still be the biggest in Cincinnati history.

WORKS CITED

Barns, George C. *Denver, the Man*. 1949.

Bauer, Cheryl, and Robert Jones Portman. *Wisdom's Paradise*, 2004.

Buress, Marjorie Byrnside. *Whitewater Ohio Village of Shakers, 1824-1916: Its History and Its People*, 1979.

Carter, Forrest. *The Rebel Outlaw, Josey Wales*. 1973.

Force, M.F., *Campaigns of the Civil War: From Fort Henry to Corinth*, 1881.

Cook, Edward Magruder. *Justified by Honor*. 1988.

"The $22 Billion Gold Rush," *Forbes Magazine*, March 24, 2006.

Frankel, Alison, *"The Fen-Phen Follies." American Lawyer*, March 1, 2005.

Geiger, Vincent Eply, and Wakeman Bryarly. *Trail to California*. Andesite Press, 1945.

Innis, James Robert, and Thomas L. Sakmyster. *The Shakers of White Water, Ohio, 1823-1916*. 2014.

MIT News, February 5, 1997.

Mundy, Alicia. *Dispensing With the Truth*. Macmillan + ORM, 2010.

Potter, David M. *The Impending Crisis*. Harper Collins, 1977

THANK-YOU NOTES

My thanks and appreciation to:

Lt. Stephen Kramer of the Greater Cincinnati Police Museum, who introduced me to Cincinnati Police detectives William Reany and Tom Farragher and helped with research. I borrowed Detective Reany to solve the mystery of the Shaker suicides. Detective Farragher plays a leading role in "Big Tom and the Black Widow." Both are local legends, bought back to life with the help of Lieutenant Kramer.

The great team at the Hamilton County Law Library helped with research on Prosecutor Dudley Outcalt and the mystery of his missing father.

My friend Ren Egbert tipped me about the amazing James W. Denver after a visit to the General Denver Hotel in Wilmington.

My longtime friend Dr. Jay Logeman helped with research and explanations of the possible causes of the "cherry-red" skin of suicide victim Ida May Dill.

Marge Henn helped by digging through her archives of reference materials on the Shakers. Her knowledge of Shaker history at Whitewater Village and Union Village is outstanding, and she generously gave me a tour of the museum in Marble House at Union Village, which is now at part of Otterbein Senior Life in Lebanon.

Jennifer Bournemann of the Friends of White Water Shaker Village helped with research on the Whitewater Shakers.

Andrew Outcalt of Avon Lake, Ohio, the unnofficial historian of the Outcalt family, provided pictures and background of Dudley Miller Outcalt, the prosecutor in the Anna Marie Hahn trial..

Jack Greiner, one of Cincinnati's top experts on media law, did a legal review of "Feeding Frenzy."

And thank you to all the readers who have sent me great ideas for books and short stories, and who have encouraged me to keep writing about our rich and fascinating local history.

ALSO BY PETER BRONSON

The surprising story of the 40-year empire of organized crime that ruled Northern Kentucky and made Newport nationally known as "Sin City." The Mob's control was broken in 1960 by the famous George Ratterman frame-up, but the presence lingered and haunted the Beverly Hills Supper Club fire in 1977 that killed more than 165 people. Evidence from the people who were there and the FBI's vault of once-secret documents shows the fire was no accident.

The story of Cincinnati's quiet war on the Mob to keep organized crime from creeping into the Queen City. Men such as Cincinnati Police Detective "Machinegun Bob" Meldon and Prosecutor Simon Leis fought the mafia on the streets and in courtrooms. As organized crime moved from bootleg booze, illegal casinos and hookers to pornography in the 1970s, Cincinnati drew national attention for its battle against mobbed-up porn king Larry Flynt and his Hustler Club.

The life and accomplishments of Lew Wallace would defy fiction, but they are all true. He fought valiantly at the Battle of Shilo as the youngest Union general in the Civil War, saved Cincinnati from a Confederate attack in 1862, created the first Black Brigade in the Civil War, captured Billy the Kid as territorial governor of New Mexico, put down America's worst range war, fought Geronimo, and wrote an American Classic, *Ben-Hur: A Tale of the Christ*. If he had not rescued Cincinnati, the Union might have lost the war and America would be two nations, not one.

The exciting story of the Revolutionary War veterans who settled "The Miami Slaughterhouse" when Cincinnati was a wilderness terrorized by Shawnee and Miami Indian warriors. What we now call the Midwest was once the West, a "promised land" for American expansion. After repeated defeats and massacres, the Northwest Territory was finally saved by "Mad Anthony" Wayne at the Battle of Fallen Timbers. *Promised Land* tells the story of the mysterious Moundbuilders, how Cincinnati saved Texas and the national conspiracy known as The Knights of the Golden Circle.

Signed books available at www.ChilidogPress.com

Chilidog Press LLC